STAT SHEET

Name: Cadence St. John

Title: Duke of Raleigh

Age: 33

Country: Korosol

Current occupation: Acting Korosol Ambassador to the United States

Eye color: Dark blue

Hair: Black

Height: 6'1"

Personal history: A former army commander, he is a duke in title only. Cade joined the army to earn a living after his father gambled away his inheritance. As an outcast from the world in which he was raised, he follows no rules but his own.

Current mission: CLASSIFIED

EYES ONLY

Dear Harlequin Intrigue Reader,

The summer is here and we've got plenty of scorching suspense and smoldering romance for your reading pleasure. Starting with a couple of your favorite Harlequin Intrigue veterans...

Patricia Rosemoor winds up the reprisal of THE McKENNA LEGACY with *Cowboy Protector*. Yet another of Moira McKenna's kin feels the force of what real love can do if you're open to it. And not to be outdone, Rebecca York celebrates a silver anniversary with the twenty-fifth title in her popular 43 LIGHT STREET series. *From the Shadows* is one more fabulous mystery coupled with a steamy romance. Prepare yourself for a super surprise ending with this one!

THE CARRADIGNES come to Harlequin Intrigue this month. *The Duke's Covert Mission* by Julie Miller is a souped-up Cinderella story that will leave you breathless for sure. This brawny duke doesn't pull up in a horse-drawn carriage. He relies on a nondescript sedan with unmarked plates instead. But I assure you he's got all the breeding of the most regal royalty when it counts.

Finally, Charlotte Douglas brings you *Montana Secrets*, an emotional secret-baby story set in the Big Sky state. I dare you not to fall head over heels in love with this hidden-identity hero.

So grab the sunblock and stuff all four titles into your beach bag.

Happy reading!

Sincerely,

Denise O'Sullivan
Associate Senior Editor
Harlequin Intrigue

THE DUKE'S COVERT MISSION

JULIE MILLER

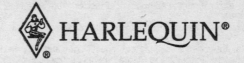

HARLEQUIN®

TORONTO • NEW YORK • LONDON
AMSTERDAM • PARIS • SYDNEY • HAMBURG
STOCKHOLM • ATHENS • TOKYO • MILAN • MADRID
PRAGUE • WARSAW • BUDAPEST • AUCKLAND

Special thanks and acknowledgment are given
to Julie Miller for her contribution to
THE CARRADIGNES: A ROYAL MYSTERY.

ISBN 0-373-22666-7

THE DUKE'S COVERT MISSION

ABOUT THE AUTHOR

Julie Miller attributed her passion for writing romance to all those fairy tales she read growing up, and to shyness. Encouragement from her family to write down all those feelings she couldn't express became a love for the written word. She gets continued support from her fellow members of the Prairieland Romance Writers, where she serves as the resident "grammar goddess." This award-winning author and teacher had published several paranormal romances. Inspired by the likes of Agatha Christie and Encyclopedia Brown, Ms. Miller believes the only thing better than a good mystery is a good romance.

Born and raised in Missouri, she now lives in Nebraska with her husband, son and smiling guard dog, Maxie. Write to Julie at P.O. Box 5162, Grand Island, NE 68802-5162.

Books by Julie Miller

HARLEQUIN INTRIGUE
588—ONE GOOD MAN*
619—SUDDEN ENGAGEMENT*
642—SECRET AGENT HEIRESS
651—IN THE BLINK OF AN EYE*
666—THE DUKE'S COVERT MISSION

*The Taylor Clan

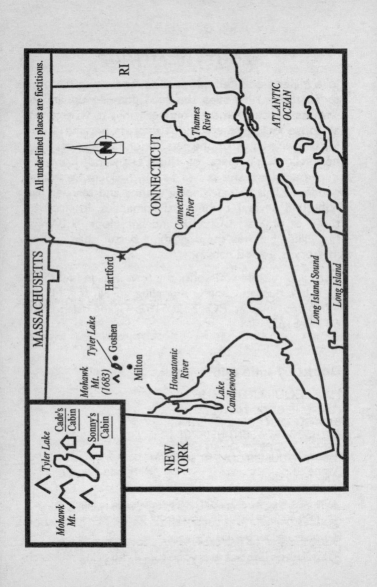

All underlined places are fictitious.

MASSACHUSETTS

RI

CONNECTICUT

NEW YORK

ATLANTIC OCEAN

Long Island Sound

Long Island

Thames River

Connecticut River

Hartford

Housatonic River

Lake Candlewood

Tyler Lake

Goshen

Mohawk Mt. (1683)

Milton

N

Tyler Lake

Mohawk Mt.

Cade's Cabin

Sonny's Cabin

CAST OF CHARACTERS

Cadence St. John, Duke of Raleigh—A royal in name only. Once one of the finest covert operatives in the Korosolan Army. He's never had any qualms about breaking the rules to get the job done—including kidnapping a princess.

Eleanor Standish—Plain and proper secretary to King Easton of Korosol. All this Cinderella ever wanted was one night as a princess. Now she has to see the masquerade through to its end, and choose whether to betray her country—or her heart—in order to survive.

Jerome Smython—He liked his money, his women and his smokes—and there'd be hell to pay for anyone who got in his way.

Leonard Gratfield—A thug for hire? Or a man with a hidden agenda?

Paulo Giovanni—The chauffeur was in the wrong place at the wrong time.

Winston Rademacher—A professional power broker. Who is he working for this time?

Tony Costa—He said he'd gone to Connecticut to fish.

Remy Sandoval—Leader of the Korosolan Democratic Front. Has he really given up his opposition to the monarchy?

Bretford St. John—He left nothing for his son but a legacy of shame—and a list of business associates who want to collect the debt owed them, one way or another.

Princess Lucia Carradigne Montcalm—Ellie's fairy godmother. She was supposed to be on her honeymoon.

King Easton of Korosol—Ellie adored him like a grandfather. But not everyone loved the aging monarch.

For the valiant soldiers, firefighters,
police officers and citizens who do what needs
to be done to take care of this country every day.
Thank you.

Prologue

"I am Princess Lucia Carradigne of Korosol."

Liar. Eleanor Standish shook her head at the reflection in the compact mirror she held in her left hand. She didn't feel particularly princesslike at the moment.

A head-to-toe makeover, courtesy of her new friends—CeCe, Amelia and Lucia Carradigne, the American granddaughters of Ellie's employer, King Easton of Korosol—had done nothing to change the woman inside.

CeCe's hairdresser had added highlights to Ellie's mousy brown curls and swept them up into an elegant French roll. Amelia had hired the staff from a trendy New York spa to paint her fingernails and toenails, and massage and loofah body parts in between. Lucia, the youngest Carradigne sister, had lent Ellie a smashing gown of beaded red silk so that Ellie could attend the Inferno Charity Ball in her place. Meanwhile, Lucia planned to be whisked out of town on her honeymoon with her brand-new husband.

Princess for a night. A dream come true.

Ellie huffed a sigh through her clenched teeth and tugged at the low-cut bodice of her gown. "Some Cinderella I turned out to be."

She might look like a princess on the outside, but inside Ellie still felt like that shy secretary who'd grown up on a sheep ranch in the western mountains of Korosol. That quiet country girl who fantasized about life's grand adventures while balancing accounts and chasing lambs in from the pasture. The dutiful daughter who had put her dreams on hold to keep her family together after her older brother ran away to save the world all by himself.

Her three fairy godmothers might have transformed her outward appearance with stylists and a gown, but no one had waved a magic wand over her self-confidence.

Ellie looked into the compact mirror and repeated her message, wondering if she'd believe it any more the second time around. "I am Princess Lucia Carradigne of Korosol."

"Miss?"

Startled by the intrusion into her conflicting world of self-talk and self-doubt, Ellie jumped. The compact snapped together and clattered to the sidewalk at her feet. She lifted her fingers to adjust the rims of her glasses and nearly poked herself in the eye.

"Drat." She'd forgotten. There were no glasses tonight. No pink metal rims weighed down by thick lenses to hide behind. No fuzzy world mere inches beyond the end of her nose. Tonight she wore contact lenses and could see without her glasses.

Tonight the world could see her.

She pushed her way past the billowing skirt of scarlet taffeta and knelt to retrieve the mirror. But the man in the black chauffeur's uniform beat her to it.

"Sorry, miss. Didn't mean to startle you." Ellie froze, bent over, eye to eye with the sandy-haired, middle-aged man. He looked pleasant enough, a tad stout, and his uniform smelled of cigarette smoke. But he possessed the drawl of a native New Yorker. He smiled as his black-gloved fingers brushed against hers. "Here you go."

Was this the prince she'd fantasized about meeting tonight? One of those rough, rugged Americans she'd seen in movies? An independent scoundrel who owned a fast car and a heart of gold? True, he wasn't handing her a glass slipper, only the silver compact that had belonged to her godmother, the late Queen Cassandra, wife and royal consort to King Easton.

But he *was* being polite. He *had* noticed her when he could have just as well ignored her.

Her heart beat a bit faster at the possibility of her fantasy coming to life. He might really be a prince in disguise. He might whisk her off in his long black limo and serve her champagne or that milk-frothed coffee that Americans seemed to thrive on. He'd twirl her onto the dance floor and they'd waltz, a courtly dance that reflected the elegance of her borrowed gown, and set the romantic stage for a man and woman falling in love.

"Thank you." Small talk had never been her forte, but at least she'd managed to speak.

"Allow me." The chauffeur extended his hand and Ellie took it, wrapping her fingers around his and balancing herself as she stood. Maybe this was the sweeping-her-off-her-feet part.

Or not.

Somehow reality never lived up to fantasy.

The man's dark gaze focused at a point well below her eyes. She snatched her hand away in a rush of dignified self-defense as she realized his fascination centered on the two rounded swells above her plunging neckline, not herself.

So much for Prince Charming.

Ellie flipped the matching silk stole across her chest and shoulder, hiding everything from her neck to her cleavage from his view. She tilted her chin at a regal angle and ignored the clicking sound of disappointment he made with his tongue.

"Where's Paulo?" she asked. Paulo was the Carradignes' regular driver, a young and unassuming man who tended to mind his own business. How unpleasant that he'd been replaced with this leering fellow.

"I'm just the substitute, miss, called in from the driving service for the night." He walked to the rear door of the limousine and opened it for her. "Can't tell you why the regular guy didn't show."

"And you know the way to the Inferno Ball?" She clutched her silver beaded purse, which contained the invitation to the gala.

He smiled again. She found the effect less charming this time. "Yes, Your Highness. I have my instructions."

Ellie climbed in and slid to the center of the black leather seat, pulling her skirts along behind her before he could reach down and tuck the hem of her gown inside the car.

Your Highness.

Would anyone besides this cad really believe she was a princess?

After he got behind the wheel and pulled the limo into traffic, Ellie opened the silver compact and looked into the mirror once more.

Staring back at her with eyes a mite too big to be pretty was that country girl who knew more about breeding the sheep that produced her native country's fine wool than she did about high fashion. She could balance numbers, take dictation and jury-rig a computer program better than she could carry on a casual conversation. She understood the intricacies of government duty better than she understood a man's flirtation.

And though her heart longed for adventure—while *she*

longed to be a woman who lived adventures—she was content to mind her place in the world.

Except for tonight.

In a few weeks she and the king and his entourage would return to Korosol, a tiny seaside country nestled between France and Spain. She'd don her glasses and put on her sensible suit. She'd fade into the woodwork and do her job with impeccable reliability and the satisfaction of knowing she worked for a kindhearted, generous man.

She had to play Cinderella now—or never.

Ellie squared her chin and picked up a champagne flute from the console in the side wall of the limo. She didn't fill it. She didn't want any alcohol to impair her memories of this special night.

The Carradignes had given her so much. She couldn't let them down by surrendering to shyness and self-doubt.

She lifted the glass and toasted her alter ego for the night. "I am Princess Lucia Carradigne of Korosol."

She let her silk stole fall down around her elbows. A princess would carry herself with precise posture. She fingered the choker of diamonds and rubies that matched the teardrop earrings hanging from her earlobes, marveling at how the facets caught and reflected in the limo's back window.

Ellie frowned and moved her face closer to the smoked glass and peered outside at the buildings towering above her on either side of the street. She hiked her skirt and petticoats up to her knees, climbed over to the opposite seat and knocked on the see-through partition. "Driver?" The partition opened halfway. "Are you sure you know the way to the ball? I have a pretty good sense of direction. We should be heading east, but we're going north."

He muttered something under his breath before smiling at her reflection in the rearview mirror. "I have to take the long way around, miss, because of construction. Don't worry. I'll get you where you need to be."

A detour hadn't been part of her Cinderella fantasy. "Are you sure? I don't want to be late."

"We're almost there."

The partition closed before she could ask the name of the street they were on. She raised her fist to knock again, but then pulled it back down to her lap. A princess wouldn't crawl around the back of a limo, hounding the hired help.

A vague sense of unease that had nothing to do with her shyness rippled down her spine.

She put the champagne glass back in its slot and returned to her seat in the back. The endless city lights, which had beckoned to her small-town heart like stars in the sky, now seemed to be flashing some kind of warning.

Ellie pushed at the boning that pinched her ribs and pulled up the draped neckline to cover more of her chest. She realized she was squirming and forced herself to sit still. A princess would be comfortable with her figure, even if it wasn't as willowy thin as the woman the dress had been made for.

"I am Princess Lucia—"

The limousine pulled to a stop. Ellie reached for her glasses before remembering they weren't there. She caught the mistake and moved her fingers to touch the diamond at her ear.

"All I want is one dance."

One dance. One waltz.

Ellie's face relaxed into a smile.

"One dance, Cinderella," she promised herself.

Her confidence swelled with the less-daunting task.

Even if she had to grab one of the waiters, she would have her dance.

Then she could run home to Korosol before she turned into a pumpkin and embarrassed herself any further.

"Princess Lucia?"

The door beside her opened and the driver reached in to help her out.

Ellie softened her lips into a serene smile.

She stepped outside and her smile vanished.

Where was the red carpet? Where were the photographers? Where was the doorman with the white gloves to announce her arrival?

What was that gas pump doing in the middle of the parking lot?

Ellie rubbed at her temple. Why was she standing in the middle of an empty parking lot?

"Driver?" Ellie turned, but he had disappeared around the front of the car. She followed him, her uneasiness swelling to outright suspicion. "Did we need to stop for gas?"

When she rounded the front fender, Ellie screamed. A huge, hulking mountain of a man materialized from the shadows. With her hand at her throat she backed away. "Driver!"

The giant wore black from head to toe, including the stocking mask that covered his face. Black-gloved hands the size of bear traps reached for her.

"Stay away from me!" Ellie screamed, then spun around to run, but smacked into the belly of a second man. "No!"

Stocky, and more than a foot shorter than the giant, this one wore the same faceless outfit. He grabbed her by the shoulders and shoved her back. "Load her up," he ordered.

She slammed into the wall of the giant. His arms closed around her like a vise, trapping her hands at her sides. The short man stuffed a pungent cloth into her mouth, muffling her cry for help. The big man slapped his hand over the gag and picked her up. Ellie gasped for air, but the sting of chemicals burned her sinuses and brought tears to her eyes. The short man jogged ahead of them to a black car hidden in the shadows beside the gas station.

Actions drilled into her long ago by an overprotective big brother kicked in. She twisted and jerked and jabbed the heel of her silver sandal into her attacker's shin.

He cursed and her small victory thrilled her, giving her a rush of adrenaline and the strength to pry herself from his grasp. Ellie landed hard on her knees on the concrete. But as the pain jolted through her bones all the way to her skull, she pulled the gag from her mouth and screamed.

"Stop her!"

Ellie tried to crawl, and her legs and petticoats tangled with the giant's feet and he tripped. He crashed to the ground and she dodged to the side.

She didn't get far. Her head was swimming. It was too dark. It was happening too fast.

Raw with fear, Ellie slapped at the hands that lifted her. The words were vile, the touches rough. A third man got out of the car and opened the trunk.

Ellie twisted, fought, struggled for air and begged for her life before they dumped her in. She landed beside a bundle of black laundry. She clawed at it to right herself, but succeeded only in rolling the bundle over and revealing a cold, colorless face with blank, staring eyes.

Ellie screamed.

But Paulo Giovanni, the Carradignes' chauffeur, never heard her.

"Shut her up!"

She didn't understand. Crazy observations floated through her blurring vision. Ski masks in June. Big man. Little man. Dead man.

Something sharp pricked her shoulder, and she yelped

between sobs. A numbing sensation turned her limbs to jelly and her brain to mush.

By the time the trunk lid closed above her and she slumped into the inescapable darkness, she could think of only one thing.

She'd never gotten her dance.

Chapter One

The cold woke her.

Ellie stirred on her hard bed and pushed her eyes open to a squint. But her eyelids felt like leaded curtains clinging to her dried-out contacts. She rolled onto her side, and something gritty scratched her cheek.

She turned away from the discomfort and shivered. Her head throbbed at that slightest of movement, and a carpet of goose bumps prickled the skin on her bare arms. Instinctively she wrapped her arms around herself, huddling for warmth in the dank, musty air. Her fingertips rasped against the nubby cloth she was wrapped in.

Her red dress. Cinderella. Three men in masks.

Paulo's dead eyes.

Each image blipped into her clouded brain and brought her to a new level of awareness.

"Oh, God."

She'd been kidnapped.

A silent scream rasped through her lungs.

She placed her palms on the cold, concrete floor beneath her and shoved herself up to a sitting position. She shut her eyes against the pinball effect of marbles bouncing off the inside of her skull. Once the marbles stopped rolling and the pain eased into the dull throb of a mere headache, she opened her eyes and scanned her surroundings.

She was in a basement. A rusted furnace sat in the far corner, a flight of open-backed wooden stairs disappeared into the exposed ceiling joists above her, and a pair of small windows were set high on the cinder-block walls that entombed her.

She'd figured out the where and the what. What she didn't understand was the *why.*

Ellie Standish didn't get kidnapped.

She followed the rules and minded her manners and took care of other people. She didn't make enemies.

Why?

She was a plain, unremarkable woman.

Woman.

For one hideous, horrible second she thought… She ran her hands down her body. She'd been unconscious. Had they…?

She brought a hand to her chest and forced herself to exhale.

Bruised and sore. Scared out of her mind. But not violated.

Ellie sat where she was and simply breathed for several minutes, muting the urge to panic.

When she could think halfway rationally again, her shy-woman's mind took over. It had always been her way to take stock of a situation before speaking or acting. If she had a plan, if she knew her way around a place or people, she was less likely to freeze up, more likely to act on her natural human instincts.

So much for her night on the town. Morning had come, or maybe it was afternoon, she couldn't pinpoint an exact time from the sunlight filtering through the greasy window-panes.

Her Cinderella dress had been transformed into rags during the night. The skirt was torn at the waist seam, and a palm-size smudge dirtied one hip. A two-foot length of lace trim dangled like a tail from her petticoats. One of the shoulder straps had been ripped from the bodice, leaving it up to the gown's stiff boning and tight fit to keep her decently covered. She tugged at the dipping neckline and let her arm rest there, in a gesture of self-defense rather than an attempt to find any real warmth. As her fingers drifted up to her neck, she clutched at the bare skin there.

The ruby choker.

Gone.

She touched her bare earlobes. The diamond drop earrings.

Gone.

She plowed her fingers into the messy upsweep of her hair. Lucia's tiara.

Gone.

Along with the beaded purse in which she'd carried her own silver watch in.

"Oh, no." Ellie rubbed her hands up and down her arms, oblivious to the ache of bruises that dotted her skin.

They'd robbed her. They'd stolen Lucia's self-designed jewelry and Ellie's own, less-valuable trinkets.

She blinked back the tears stinging her eyes. It didn't make sense. Yes, she'd worn diamonds and rubies—works of art. But there would have been hundreds of other guests at the ball with far more expensive jewelry and purses and wallets to steal.

Something more than a simple theft was going on here. This felt personal.

Drugging her. Murdering Paulo. Abandoning her here—wherever here was—didn't make sense.

Abandonment.

That was when the silence registered.

That was when the panic gathered strength.

"Hello?" Her voice echoed off the walls and got swallowed up by the damp air. "Hello?"

New York City was a constant hum of traffic and people, machinery and music.

The silence here pounded in her ears, mocked her attempt at bravery.

This wasn't New York City.

She scrambled to her feet. "Hello!"

She'd been abandoned in the middle of nowhere. Abandoned! Her teeth chattered from fear as much as from cold. Left behind. Unnoticed. Forgotten. Never missed. Alone.

"Help me!" Her native European accent thickened as an age-old fear seized the opportunity to resurrect itself.

She dashed for the stairs but was jerked to a sudden halt that toppled her off her feet. The hard landing jarred her hands and triggered a jolting reminder of her battered knees. But the pain didn't frighten her half as much as the ominous clank of metal scraping against metal behind her. Ellie rolled over onto her bottom and yanked up the hem of her skirt.

"No." She tapped her fingers at her temple, nervously pushing at her nonexistent glasses. "No!"

A steel band had been cuffed around her left ankle. And a shiny new chain of stainless steel had been padlocked to the cuff. She traced the path of interlocking links, each the size of a golf ball, to a steel O-bolt anchored into the center of the concrete floor.

Chained to the floor like one of the elephants she'd seen at the Korosol Royal Circus last year.

Ellie climbed to her feet and, like that sorry animal, paced as far as the chain allowed.

Whoever had put her here had measured the trap carefully. Even at its fullest length, with her leg stretched out behind and her body tilted forward as far as she could go, she was still a good two feet from the bottom of the stairs. The windows hovered above the reach of her outstretched hand. The only thing within her grasp was the broken-down furnace and a knee-high wooden stool.

"All the comforts of home," she whispered. *If one was a condemned prisoner on death row.*

Ellie sank down onto the stool and hugged herself, refusing to surrender to futile tears.

"You'll think of a way out of this, Ellie." She tried another pep talk, but the echo of her voice did little to encourage her. She'd made it all the way from her mountain home to the capital city of Korosol la Vella. She'd made it across the ocean to America. She'd made the harrowing journey through crosstown traffic into the heart of New York City.

"I'll make it out of here, too."

The question was—how?

Her jewelry was gone, along with her purse and her stole. And her shoes.

Anything that might be used as a weapon had been taken from her. The tiny canister of pepper spray in her bag. The house key attached to it. The heels of her shoes.

Ellie sat up a little straighter as she latched on to one hopeful thought.

If they'd disarmed her, that meant her kidnappers were coming back. They hadn't abandoned her. Yet. They'd prepped her for their return.

As if the thought of her abductors had the power to summon, she heard a key turn in the lock at the top of the stairs. Ellie shot to her feet and moved behind the stool, putting the one available obstacle between her and her visitor.

The door opened and a single, bare lightbulb switched on over the bottom of the stairs, bathing her in an austere circle of light and creating a translucent wall of dust motes in the heavy air. The tread of footsteps on the stairs told her it was a man, one who was balanced and sure on his feet, despite his bulky silhouette.

Ellie squinted to see who had come to visit her in her prison cell, but the lightbulb created shadows that hid the man's face. He moved through the curtain of dust and she could see that better illumination wouldn't help her identify him. He wore a black knit stocking cap that covered everything but his eyes.

Just like the men last night.

Ellie shivered as he walked toward her. He seemed to grow larger and suck up more of the breathable air with each step. She jumped back, needing space, needing room to run. "Don't come any closer."

He stopped. Though she couldn't see his eyes in the play of light and shadow, she felt his stare. Her skin crawled as if his hands and not his assessing gaze were touching her.

"What do you want with me?" Her voice sounded as shaky as her backbone.

No answer.

His hefty shape had been deceptive, as well. She curled her toes into the cold concrete as he set a blanket, a canteen and a handful of silvery foil envelopes on the floor in front of her.

"What are those?" she asked, looking at the items that had been piled like an altar offering before her.

In answer, he picked up one of the silver packages, straightened and tossed it to her. Ellie caught it out of pure reflex. "That wasn't a difficult question, was it?"

The man said nothing.

Like one of the questionable souvenirs from her brother

Nicky's mercenary days, she recognized the markings on the bag as a military field ration. Applesauce.

"I suppose you want me to eat this?"

He nodded.

Damn, the man's silence was unnerving. It distracted her from thinking. She could only react.

"Is this how you killed Paulo?" The man's head jerked up. "Did you poison him?"

The only sound she could hear was her heart pounding.

Just when she thought she might scream from the tension in the air pulling at her, the man took the packet from her hands and tore it open. He stuck his finger inside, scooped out a dollop of beige paste and lifted his mask high enough so she could see him eat it.

She caught a flash of inky black beard stubble, but nothing more. Even before the image registered, he'd covered his chin and handed her the packet.

She'd barely touched her dinner the night before because of nervous anticipation of the ball and had slept through any other meal since. Food might help her headache. And she'd need sustenance of some kind to keep up her strength and keep herself mentally sharp.

Her companion's watchful stillness made her think she'd need every ounce of strength and intelligence she could muster in order to survive this…this…

"Why have I been kidnapped?" she demanded, tilting her chin up with an authority she didn't really feel.

His shoulders lifted with a cocky bit of "don't care," but he gave no answer.

"Why won't you say anything?"

She dipped her finger into the packet and scooped out a bit of the dry paste. Tentatively she carried it to her mouth and tested it with her tongue. If she used her imagination, she could taste something that reminded her of apples and sawdust. But it was hard to imagine anything with her keeper standing so utterly still just a few feet away.

The goose bumps that had assailed her earlier pricked her skin again at his eerie silence. "You know, it's very rude not to talk."

And nerve-racking and frightening and out-and-out intimidating.

Ellie had never been one to complain. She'd been raised to make the best of things. To solve her own problems. To endure.

But the words came tumbling out now. "I don't know what you want from me. I don't have much money. The jewels you took don't even belong to me." The man was made of stone. "I can't help you if I don't know why I'm here!"

Her little outburst left her feeling flushed and useless. And, damn it all, she had always found a way to make herself feel useful. She so desperately hated feeling helpless and unnecessary.

Expendable.

"Are you going to kill me, too?"

For a moment she thought he might actually speak. She heard a sound from behind his mask, a quick intake of breath. Ellie caught her own breath and held it, waiting for his answer. But...

Nothing.

Her breath whooshed out, along with her defiance.

Like the good, dutiful girl she'd been raised to be for the twenty-six years of her life, Ellie opened the bag and squeezed out another bite. She allowed the dry applesauce to sit on her tongue a moment, letting her saliva add enough moisture to make it palatable.

Now that she had done what he asked, the man began to circle her. While she ate, Ellie followed him with her eyes, noting any details that a man dressed in black from head to toe might reveal.

He wore black cargo pants, with a shadowy camo print and lots of pockets. They were tucked into a pair of calf-high military boots. A knife handle protruded from the top of a nylon sheath attached to the right boot. Ellie turned her head, quietly chewing, keeping him in her sight.

She recognized him as the driver of the second car last night. The one with the dead body in the trunk. She didn't know much about the ways to kill a man, but she'd seen Paulo's bulging eyes and protruding tongue and knew the young man's death hadn't been an easy one.

This man could have killed Paulo. Just by looking at him, Ellie had no doubt that this man had killed before.

His black knit shirt hugged broad shoulders and expanded over the swell of his chest. Then it clung farther down, revealing a flat stomach and narrow waist. He stood as tall as her brother—an inch or two over six feet—and was all sinew and muscle, as lethal-looking as the sleek steel sidearm riding in a black leather holster at his hip.

When he disappeared from the corner of her vision, Ellie spun to her right and watched him walk around the other side. She'd never studied a man so boldly before. And while his silence unnerved her, there was something oddly mesmerizing about the pantherlike precision of his movements. Ellie's heart stuttered, then beat again. Her breasts expanded against the stiff confines of her gown. Her perusal of the mysterious visitor bordered on fascination.

And she was ashamed that survival might not be the only reason she kept staring at him.

"Who *are* you?" Her fingers slipped to her temple, nervously searching for her absent glasses. She curled the flailing fingers into a fist and pulled it down to her chest. "Why won't you talk to me?"

Fascination or no, this man was her captor, she his prisoner. His chained, secluded prisoner, who'd been left in the dark in both the literal and figurative sense.

"What do you want with me?" She breathed in deeply, but her cool bravado was quickly failing her. "Who are you?"

He ended his circle where he'd begun, standing in front of her, barely an arm's length away.

Was he toying with her? Mocking her? Trying to scare the very heartbeat out of her?

He was succeeding more than he could possibly imagine.

"Talk to me." Her demand sounded dangerously close to begging. "Show your face, you coward!"

She had finally pushed him too far.

He closed the distance between them, swooping in like a hawk, moving so swiftly that she shielded herself with her arms and backed away. The chain at her ankle rattled. A frightened sob shook her, but she caught the gasp between clenched teeth.

Ellie was transfixed. Caught in a deadly snare of unknown intent. He never touched her, but she trembled all the same. She could smell him now. He was heat and soap and exotic spice.

And from the middle of that black mask he marked her with eyes of such an intense dark blue they seemed unreal. He held her in place with those eyes. Beautiful eyes. Demon eyes.

"I'm sorry." Ellie dropped her gaze, unable to withstand the power of his. She struggled to breathe. "Don't hurt me. Please."

And then the man tormented her in the most unexpected way. With her chin tucked to her chest, her gaze firmly fixed on the floor, he lifted his hand. She could see now, in her peripheral vision, that his hands were the only visible part of his body. Five fingers of streamlined power, scarred and callused, reached for her. Ellie curled into herself, bracing for a grab or slap or... The hand closed in on her face, and she could see a fine dusting of black hair along the dark tan of his skin. She squeezed her eyes shut, blocking out the moment when his fingers would touch her. But she couldn't block out the heat from his skin. It seemed to scorch her cheek.

"Please." Her body convulsed on a frightened sob.

"Sinjun!"

The heat at her cheek evaporated at the shout from above. Ellie's eyes popped open, and she saw the man in black tuck his hands into his pockets and cross to the base of the stairs.

"Is she awake?" The short, stocky creep who had given the orders and injected her with a knockout drug last night tromped down the stairs, commanding the room with his blustery voice.

Then the walls themselves seemed to shake as the giant from last night followed a few paces behind. Like the silent man, they were both dressed in black—from ski mask to military boots to the guns strapped at their sides.

Ellie's chest expanded with the first deep breath she'd taken since the man who'd brought her food and water had first begun to circle her. Recognition of her three kidnappers brought with it a healthy amount of fear and caution, but she seized on the anger that their reappearance triggered in her. She threw her shoulders back and tipped up her chin. "I demand to know why you've done this to me."

The small man laughed. "She *demands.*"

The big man responded with a hitch and lift of his shoulders, in what she supposed passed for a laugh at her expense. Her gaze flitted beyond them to the silent man. No movement. No laughter. Nothing.

And then Ellie realized she couldn't let her attention wander. The short man had walked right up to her, close enough that she could smell the cigarette smoke that permeated his clothes. She knew that smell.

Her silly fantasies about Prince Charming had been destroyed by the man who smelled like that. "You're the substitute chauffeur from last night."

"Bingo." He sounded almost pleased that he'd made an impression on her. "How's our princess doing this afternoon?"

Princess?

He plopped a plastic pail down on the stool and sniffled loudly beneath his mask. "How do you like the fancy accommodations, Your Highness?"

Highness.

A light of understanding flashed on in Ellie's head.

Oh, my God. Of course! They thought… "I'm not—"

Fortunately he interrupted her protest, giving Ellie time to see the wisdom in keeping her identity a secret. "We furnished all the comforts of home, sugar. Even a bucket for you to do your necessary business."

Shock sailed through Ellie, clearing the path for the helpless fear that followed. These men thought they'd kidnapped a princess. The short man's taunting sarcasm aside, they wouldn't be pleased to learn that they'd nabbed a lowly secretary by mistake.

If they found out they'd abducted the hired help… Paulo's dead staring eyes leaped to mind.

Think, Ellie, she coached herself. A jumble of ideas vied for consideration. How did she play this game? It had taken every bit of her nerve to try just to look like a princess last night. How could she act a part she was so unsuited for? And more importantly, how did she get out of this mess? Alive and safe?

What would a real princess do?

"How did you...find me?"

"Pick up the princess at the Carradigne penthouse. Red dress. Inferno Ball. That's all my contact said I needed to know." The short man sidled right up to her and fingered the broken strap that had fallen down her back. He draped the frayed silk across her shoulder and pulled the length of it between his index and middle finger. Ellie sucked in her breath and flinched away from the purposeful caress. "Sorry about the dress."

He paused with the back of his knuckles resting atop her breast where it pillowed above the neckline of the gown. She held his lustful gaze, imagined him smiling or slobbering or some other foul thing beneath his mask. Knowing she watched him, he pressed his palm to her bare skin and squeezed.

Ellie smacked him away. "Don't touch me!"

She jerked back and slammed into the wall of the big man's chest. Her instinctive struggle was quickly subdued by the large hands that pinned her arms—and the long knife pressed against her throat.

For his burly size, the short man had moved with surprising speed. "Now let's review the facts, Princess." He stroked the blade along her collarbone and slipped it beneath the remaining strap of her gown. "I have all the power, and you—" with a flick of his wrist, he severed the strap and the bodice dropped to an indecent level "—have none."

Ellie withered in the big man's hands.

I am Princess Lucia Carradigne of Korosol. The chant she'd used to build her self-confidence the night before now played like a death knell inside her head.

She had no idea where she was. No idea who these men were or what they wanted. Did they have a grudge against

Lucia or her new husband, Harrison Montcalm, a retired general and outgoing royal advisor to King Easton? Did these men or their contact want something from King Easton himself? Power? Money? Korosol was a small, but wealthy country. The king had his own fortune at his disposal. He had the power to sway Parliament. Was their motivation political? Economical? Vengeful?

Or did they simply enjoy torturing her with her own inadequacies?

"What do you want from me?" Her docile voice and downcast eyes seemed to have a calming effect on the short man.

He laughed again as he propped his foot up on the stool and put his knife away in his boot. "We just want you to be a good girl and mind your manners. Sinjun here has fixed the place up real nice for you. And we'll be right upstairs if you need anything."

What sort of name was Sinjun? She glanced across the room to the silent man. She wasn't foolish enough to believe he'd be her ally, yet he had been kind enough to bring her food. To insist she eat.

"It's almost time for the call, Jerome." The big man's deep voice resonated in the air behind her, though he was surprisingly soft-spoken.

He finally released her, and Ellie turned her attention back to what little she *could* do to protect herself. She tugged up the bodice of her dress to better cover her exposed skin, then crossed her arms in front of her.

Jerome seemed amused by her attempts at modesty. "Sugar, you do exactly what we tell you and you won't get hurt."

"How do I know that? How do I know I won't end up dead in your trunk?"

A dangerous glint replaced the amusement in his dark

eyes. "You don't. You might be used to calling the shots back home at the castle..." The notion registered that he didn't know Lucia had never lived in a castle. But then, these men didn't know Lucia at all, or they wouldn't have mistaken the plain brown mouse that she was for the vibrant, *blond* Lucia. "...but around here, I'm in charge."

"The call?" the big man prompted, already striding toward the stairs.

"I'm on it, Lenny."

Lenny. The big man was named Lenny. Jerome was the short and smelly jerk with the all-too-friendly hands. The silent one was Sinjun. She didn't know how the information could help her, but she filed it away, anyhow.

"Don't worry, sugar. I'll be back to keep you company. I have a phone call to make. I'll bet there's somebody wondering where you are."

Jerome and Lenny climbed the stairs and disappeared without another word. Sinjun spared her one final look, then headed up after them.

"Wait."

At the last moment Ellie acted on the desperate need to escape. Dragging her chain behind her, she scuttled to the bottom of the stairs in time to see the door close and hear the dead bolt slide into place.

Exhausted, confused and more frightened than she had ever been in her life, Ellie sank to the floor and let the tears she'd fought finally overtake her.

Jerome was a mean little man. Lenny was an immovable force. Both were dangerous. Of that she had no doubt. She'd had firsthand experience with their easy violence. And yet neither one of them spooked her the way Sinjun, the silent panther of a man, and his intense blue eyes had.

I'll bet there's somebody wondering where you are.

True. Several people would wonder where Princess Lucia had disappeared to if she'd vanished. Her new husband. Her sisters. Her mother. King Easton himself, Lucia's grandfather.

But Eleanor Standish?

She'd been easy to overlook her entire life.

Would anyone be missing *her?*

Chapter Two

Cade St. John locked the basement door behind him and pulled off his ski mask. He wiped his sleeve across his sweaty brow and combed his fingers through his hair, settling it into neat waves across his crown. Whenever it got beyond the crewcut stage, it had a tendency to curl and fan above his forehead, giving him a deceptively youthful look that belied his thirty-three years—and masked a life experience that on some days qualified him for retirement.

Days like this one.

Are you going to kill me, too?

The woman's voice and those sad, accusing eyes had struck a nerve.

Dammit, that wasn't supposed to have happened—taking out the chauffeur like that. No one was supposed to get hurt. This job was already unraveling from the original plan. Cade wasn't naive. That meant he'd been too damn arrogant to think he could control this gig with a loose cannon like Jerome Smython calling the shots.

Jerome was just a middleman with delusions of grandeur. Whoever had hired the three of them had been stupid enough or callous enough to give Jerome free rein with his temper. Maybe if Cade knew who the boss really was, he could argue his case.

Problem was, Cade didn't know who had hired him.

Big problem.

He tossed the mask onto the countertop extension that served as a kitchen table and headed straight for the half-size refrigerator. If he was in charge of this operation, he'd be wearing a ball cap and dark glasses. But then, he wasn't in charge. He did have a few useful connections, though. He knew his way around guns and explosives, and could drive an untraceable getaway car from Manhattan to the Connecticut countryside in record time.

"Sinjun. Hand me a beer."

Cade shrugged off his instinctive response to a man like Jerome Smython telling him what to do.

Two weeks ago Jerome had come into Cade's office at the Korosolan Embassy in New York with one very interesting proposition.

Let's kidnap a princess.

Cade might possess a royal title himself, but it was no secret that his family was bankrupt. That his late father had gambled away his inheritance. That the lands they had once owned had been auctioned off to make an inroad into Bretford St. John's accumulated debt. That Cade's mother had found herself a wealthy Texas oilman to keep her in jewels and furs, and written off Korosol—and her son—in the process.

So Cadence St. John, Duke of Raleigh, former army officer, acting Korosolan ambassador to the United States, accepted the lure of a one-million-dollar payoff for services rendered and signed on to Jerome's "proposition."

Cade pulled out three beers, twisted off the caps and carried them into the living room, where Smython and Lenny Gratfield had made themselves comfortable on two mismatched couches. He crossed to the scarred window that overlooked the woods surrounding the abandoned house where they were hiding, and pretended an interest in the gray-green surface of the lake beyond the trees.

But with just a shift of his eyes, he could keep an eye on the other two men by watching their reflections in the window. He took a long swig of beer to cool his throat and quietly studied them. He'd already run a background check on his two compatriots—a basic rule of survival meant knowing who you were dealing with. They were mercenaries who'd received some of the best training on the planet as former members of the Korosolan Army. He'd gone through the same training himself when he was twenty-one. But it was an old habit of his—always watching. He'd gotten himself out of sticky situations, kept himself alive more times than he could count, by simply keeping an eye on everything going on around him.

Jerome lit one of his imported European cigarettes and kicked his feet up on the frayed ottoman that doubled as a coffee table.

Lenny peeled the stocking cap from his shaved head and pulled out a thin black notepad. He jotted something down. Was the big guy keeping a journal? Writing a friend? Recording expenses? Cade had noticed a zenlike calm about him, a quiet sense of purpose that bore up well under Jerome's hot-tempered actions. Fire and ice, Cade had dubbed them.

But while Jerome's interest in kidnapping Princess Lucia seemed to be rooted in nothing more complicated than old-fashioned greed, he couldn't say the same for Lenny. The big guy didn't share Jerome's interest in fast cars and big yachts and the women they attracted. He hadn't figured Lenny out yet. And until he did, Cade would keep an especially close eye on the man.

Cade checked his watch. As the big hand hit the twelve, Jerome's cell phone rang. Right on cue. He swallowed another drink of the cold, bitter brew and turned, showing a mild interest in the expected call, but wishing he had an extension to eavesdrop on.

Mr. Fire of the hot temper and smoky stench waited for the second ring before picking up. "Three o'clock," he said. "I like punctuality." His thick chest shook as he laughed at his own clever greeting, and Cade wondered if the caller found Jerome as amusing as Jerome did. "Yes, sir. The package is safe and secure. Not too much trouble. I'll make the call as soon as we're finished here." He pulled a long drag on his cigarette and sat up straight. As he exhaled the sweetly pungent smoke, his puttylike features mirrored his displeasure with whatever was being said. "I don't like being left out of the loop."

Jerome hopped to his feet and paced the length of the room. "Three days?" He eyed Lenny and Cade over his shoulder, his expression changing back to its good-ol'-boy facade as the caller placated him. He nodded. "We can manage three days. As long as we get paid what we're due."

Another moment passed and then he pulled the phone from his ear and punched the off button.

Lenny tucked his notebook back into his pocket. "Three days?"

"Yeah." Jerome tossed the phone onto the empty couch and finished off his cigarette. "We're to hold the princess here while he takes care of the ransom."

A faint twinge of alarm made Cade step forward. Maybe it was the instinctive danger he felt at having to alter their original plan. Maybe it was his conscience kicking in. "Her family hasn't been contacted yet?"

Jerome shrugged and reached for another cigarette. "He says it'll take that long to negotiate the deal."

"What deal? Don't we get paid cash? And who's *he?*"

Fire-man grinned. He took the time to cup his hands around his mouth and light his cigarette before answering. The bum knew all about power, but nothing about team leadership. "You'll find out when I do. All I needed was that hundred-grand retainer fee to get this project started. Nab the woman in the red dress. Bring her here. Wait for the call. I can take orders for the kind of money we're making on this deal. So can you. If he says to turn the little lady over in three days, that's what we'll do."

Cade challenged him on the impracticality of blind faith in a man he'd never met. "You ever wonder what makes a man willing to commit treason and risk a lifelong prison term by kidnapping a member of the royal family?"

"I don't know. You're one of those royals. You could have the world eating out of your hand, if you wanted." Jerome blew out a cloud of smoke and flashed his teeth in a smug grin. "But for the right price I finally turned you. For the right price, a man'll do anything."

Cade resisted the urge to cross the room and ram the cigarette down Jerome's throat. "So we just sit here for three days and trust this guy to show up?"

Lenny rose, consuming a good portion of the room with his mammoth size. He, too, was clearly interested in Jerome's answer.

"He's coming here tonight to check out the merchandise. You can voice your concerns then." Jerome spread his arms wide and shrugged. "Frankly, I don't care why the man wants to do it this way—I'm just the hired help. As long as the money's there, he has my loyalty.

"But I guarantee you, by Monday night, if I don't get my million, her highness is dead. And so is he. And then his motive won't make a damn bit of difference, now will it?"

Jerome left the room with a cloud of that sickening

smoke trailing behind him. Lenny sat back on the couch and pulled out his notepad again. Cade strode into the kitchen, grabbed a bag of pretzels and sat at the breakfast bar. As he munched, he let his gaze stray to the bolted basement door.

The light snack gummed up his throat as he thought of the year-old C rations he'd given their prisoner. At least she'd been smart enough to take the food, though cautious enough not to trust him. She'd seemed so young. So frightened.

So innocent.

She was nothing like the world-savvy women he'd known over the years. Ling in Hong Kong. Rosa in Brazil. Elise in London and Jeanne back home in Korosol. He'd always sought out women who knew the score. Women who enjoyed a night of great sex when he was in town, but who never expected more than a few days of clubbing and dining and bedtime fun.

The woman in the basement looked as if she still believed in heroes and happy endings. She had the wide-eyed wonder and indignant shock of someone who expected to find good in people. She seemed more suited to pen pals and puppy love than that damned two-sizes-too-small red gown she'd poured herself into.

When was the last time he'd seen such a wide-eyed look? Big, beautiful blue eyes the same clear shade as the mountain lakes of his boyhood home.

Cade took a swallow of beer. Then another. And another, angrily reminding himself he had no business reminiscing about childhood memories or guileless blue eyes.

He had a job to do. And despite all the transgressions he'd committed in his life, he'd always taken pride in being very, very good at his job.

He pitched the empty bottle across the room into the box

of trash and considered all that was about to happen to her, all that she had already endured. He made no excuses for being a part of that dangerous destiny, but he did make her a silent promise.

He hated men like Jerome Smython. Men who used others to fulfill their own avarice, men who bartered with people's lives and fed on their fears to get that intoxicating rush of power over others.

Cade had done a lot of things in the name of getting the job done that weren't exactly in line with the law. In fact, he was damn good at circumventing the authorities when he needed to. But breaking the rules and breaking someone's spirit were two different things.

And that woman in the basement, though she was chained and frightened and clueless about the events unfolding around her, definitely had spirit. She'd stood to face him when she could just as easily have cowered in the corner. She'd made demands and called him rude when he refused to answer. He'd seen her spirit in the determined tilt of her chin.

It had nearly killed him when she finally bowed her head and surrendered to her fear of him. He'd had to be tough with her, he reasoned. He had a job to do. But he'd felt an alien urge to comfort her. He'd almost touched her, almost offered some lame platitude about bucking-up and hanging-in-there.

And then Jerome and Lenny had arrived on the scene. And just like that her spirit reasserted itself. She'd tilted that regal chin and faced the new attack, just as she had faced him.

A woman like that, innocent to the games and cruelty and power plays of a man like Jerome, would expect this all to turn out right. Despite coming face-to-face with the chauffeur's dead body, she'd expect to stay safe.

Cade found himself making a rare, foolish promise.

He'd do that for her. He could do nothing to stop the chain of events her kidnapping had already set into motion—he didn't *want* to. He wanted to find out who was paying them for the job.

But he could keep her safe.

It was his responsibility, after all.

Because Cade knew something Jerome and Lenny didn't. They'd kidnapped the woman in the red dress, all right. But the wrong woman was wearing that dress.

He'd met Lucia Carradigne Montcalm at her sister CeCe's wedding a couple of months ago. It had been a big affair, a princess marrying an American millionaire. Lucia had made a bit of a spectacle of herself at the reception.

The woman chained in the basement had a lot of class, but she wasn't any princess. She wasn't even a Carradigne. She seemed familiar to him, but he couldn't place her. Maybe he'd met her at an embassy function. Or back in Korosol.

Cade eased his conscience with the promise of keeping her identity a secret. She might not understand or appreciate the importance of that favor—but he did.

Because if Jerome and Lenny and the man on the phone even suspected she wasn't Princess Lucia, they wouldn't just break her spirit.

They'd kill her.

"HE SAYS THEY'LL kill her."

His Royal Highness, King Easton of Korosol, hung up the phone and sank wearily back into the ornate mahogany chair, feeling every one of his seventy-eight years.

He'd sent men into war, weathered the lean years of a budget crisis with his people and worked tirelessly to ensure his country's future by selecting the best possible suc-

cessor to the throne. He'd buried a wife he loved and ne-
glected his family in America in order to carry out his
responsibilities to the citizens of Korosol.

But nothing had drained him the way that phone call had.

Maybe it was his age. Or the rare blood disease that was
slowly sucking the life out of him.

Maybe it was the guilt of asking a trusted friend to make
a sacrifice for Easton's beloved homeland.

If Ellie was here, she'd know the right thing to say or
do to cheer him up. The girl spoiled him silly, and like an
old fool, he let her. Eleanor Standish had proved a much
more valuable resource than just a sensible, reliable secretary. She read his moods, saw to his comfort, quietly went
about working her miracles and taking care of him so that
he could take care of his country.

And now... He didn't even want to think about what the
poor girl must be going through.

Easton sat up straight in the chair and surveyed the select
group of men he'd summoned to the study of the Carradignes' Manhattan penthouse. He pulled off his glasses and
set them on the desk before him.

"I was afraid of something like this when I came to
America. Afraid of putting my family in jeopardy. But Ellie's all right for now. I've been given until midnight Monday to answer the ransom demand."

His closest friend and advisor, retired general Harrison
Montcalm, crossed his arms and assumed a pose that reflected his military background. "Any idea who's behind
this?"

"The man's voice was altered with a mechanical device.
He sounded like a robot." He'd have to be a heartless robot
to endanger Ellie's life.

A steely voice cut across the room. "What's the ransom?
Whatever it is, we'll pay it, right? How much?"

Easton looked up at the blond man marching toward him, a man fired up with a thirst for action. Nicholas Standish couldn't be blamed. Hell. If Easton was forty years younger, he'd charge after Ellie himself.

But Harrison offered them both a sobering reminder. "We don't negotiate with terrorists."

"What do they want?" Nick asked.

"My throne." There was a curse, a gasp of shock, even a condolence, before a deathly pall settled on the room. Easton listened to the forced, steady breathing of the other men. He placed his hand on his chest to subdue the pounding of his own heart. He had prayed the transition of power from one ruler to the next would never come to a crisis like this. "Whoever *they* are, they want me to step down from the throne. And, of course, they made mention of several million dollars."

The fourth man in the room, Devon Montcalm, a younger, taller version of his father and captain of the Royal Guard, stepped forward. "Do you think it's the Korosolan Democratic Front? My sources tell me their funds are nearly depleted."

"Possibly."

Nick braced his fists atop the desk and leaned forward. "I thought they'd agreed to use peaceful means to resolve their differences with the monarchy."

Easton shook his head. "It wouldn't be the first time a political faction has used violence to speed along the process."

As usual, Harrison offered a prudent course of action. "You want me to get ahold of Remy Sandoval?"

Easton pulled out his handkerchief to clean his glasses while he considered the offer. He had a suspicion as to who was behind this kidnapping. But until he had absolute proof, he didn't want to leave any stone unturned. After several tense, uninterrupted moments he stood and put on his glasses, preparing himself to do business both mentally and physically. "Yes. Sandoval's still their party's spokesman. I'd like to know if everyone in the KDF is cooperating with the truce, or if there's someone from the old guard he can't control."

Easton reached out and laid a comforting hand on Harrison's shoulder. "I know this is difficult for you. I appreciate you stepping in and filling the role you always have for me. I know you were looking forward to your honeymoon."

Harrison's grim look matched his own. "Well, considering it's my wife who was their intended target..." A riot of fiercely protective emotions surfaced before his rigid mask of propriety returned. "I've put Lucia in a safe place, and Devon's posted twenty-four-hour security."

"I've put a guard on everyone in the immediate royal family," added Devon.

Father and son exchanged a look of purpose and promise before Harrison turned back to the king. "I'll go make those phone calls."

As Harrison left to make contact with the Korosolan Democratic Front, Nick jumped to his feet. "Isn't it a little late to beef up security? The damage has already been done. I know I've been out of the country for several years, but is this how you handle a crisis? Make some phone calls? Bide your time? My sister could be dead already. What were your granddaughters thinking, dressing Ellie up and sending her out—"

"Standish," Devon warned.

"She knows nothing about these kinds of men. She never left the ranch. All she knows are her books and her dreams."

Easton absorbed the tirade, placing the blame for Ellie's

kidnapping squarely on his own shoulders. "She's not a child anymore, Nick. Ellie hasn't seen much of the world, I know. But she's smart. Resourceful." Around a conference table or behind the scenes of the royal court, he amended silently. Easton did worry that his shy guardian angel might be way out of her league in this crisis. But he reassured them both. "She'll be all right."

And then he did what he did best. He took charge.

"Devon. Put your best men on alert. I may need your help."

"Already done, sir."

Nick turned and headed for the door. "I'm going after her."

"No." Easton said the bold, bleak word with all the rank and authority of a royal pronouncement. Certainly, as a former mercenary, Nick Standish had the qualifications to make an incisive strike into an enemy stronghold to rescue his sister. But Easton would play this game *his* way. He would not be swayed by terrorists or fear or even a brother's love.

While he could not reveal all that had transpired over the phone, he could do a little to lessen Nick's concern.

"I already have someone on the job."

He just hoped it was someone he could trust.

ELLIE'S EYES WERE on fire. She'd been wearing her contact lenses for more than twenty-four hours, and her eyelids felt dry and gritty. The bout of crying hadn't helped. Her sinuses were plugged, and the salty tears had only aggravated her condition.

Her condition. Ha!

She was chained to the floor of a damp, dusty basement, wearing dirty, uncomfortable clothes, eating unappetizing food, and having little else to do besides imagine the potentially gruesome outcome of her kidnapping.

And the indignity of doing her business in a bucket made an outhouse seem like a luxury!

If she was a woman who cursed, she'd have damned her captors over and over. But Ellie was a woman of thought, not reaction. Her quiet personality gave her plenty of time to consider her choices before making a decision. There was a security in that planning, a sense of control over her own destiny.

She'd already considered the option of popping out the lenses and easing the irritation in her eyes. But that would put her at an even greater disadvantage.

She'd been a bookworm by the age of five, worn glasses since the end of second grade. Before she was twelve, she'd devoured the entire Nancy Drew mystery series. As she got older, her tastes turned to the classics—*Jane Eyre, Eight Cousins* and *Rose in Bloom*. As an adult, travelogues and romantic-suspense novels gave her a vicarious thrill of adventure.

All those books might in some small way have prepared her for dealing with criminals and difficult men, but they had also taken their toll on her eyesight. Combined with all the years she did the accounting for her parents' ranch and the computer work she did for King Easton, Ellie's vision was a myopic disaster. Even in good light, without her glasses or contacts, her vision was limited to mere inches. In dim light she was virtually blind.

Physical discomfort and tearing eyes were a small price to pay for at least having the opportunity to see danger when it headed her way.

The click of a key in the lock at the top of the stairs put her on instant alert. She rose from the stool and pulled the blanket more firmly around her naked shoulders. The tread on the stairs was too light to be Lenny's, too deliberate to be Jerome's. That meant...

"Sinjun."

She had hoped to catch him off guard by calling him by his name. But he acted as if she hadn't even spoken. Her masked visitor dropped two bundles at her feet and glanced back over his shoulder at the stairs.

He knelt beside her, made quick work of a few knots, then flung open a sleeping bag. He picked up what she could now see was a knapsack. Ellie shuffled to the right to avoid being pushed aside when he stood.

She took a deep breath and steeled her nerves to try again. "Excuse me. I—"

"Act like you're asleep."

"What?" The sound of his voice startled her as much as the odd request.

"Move it *now*, lady." The crisp command in the hushed velvet voice fluttered along her skin.

Ellie hugged the blanket more tightly around her, conquering the urge to bolt to the end of her chain. She rolled her neck, pulled up her chin and remembered she was supposed to be a princess. "So. He deigns to speak to me."

He ignored her attempt at sarcasm and pulled out a battery-powered lantern. He set it on the stool and turned it on, flooding the basement with a warm glow that softened the harsh glare from the bare bulb over the stairs. He dug into the knapsack for something else, sending another darting look behind him, apparently oblivious to her presence only a foot away.

She tried to scoot around his shoulder and at least talk to the eye holes in his stocking cap. "I want my glasses. Keep whatever else is in my purse, but I need to remove my contacts."

He turned on her then, nailed her with that dark-blue

gaze that at once frightened and compelled. "Is that what's wrong with your eyes?"

He'd noticed her eyes?

Her fingers flew to her temple self-consciously. Now that she had his full attention, an attack of shyness squeezed her throat, and she was unable to push any words past it.

Men didn't notice details about her. Men didn't notice her, period.

Precious seconds swept by in silence as their gazes locked. His, questioning, searching. Hers, hoping for understanding, wishing she hadn't been cursed with an inordinate self-awareness that made her analyze every look, every word, before responding.

"I—"

But the opportunity to plead her case had been lost.

"Lie down," he ordered.

The words were like shock therapy to her frozen systems. "I beg your pardon?"

"Lie down." He climbed halfway up the steps, lifted the knapsack above his head and wrapped it around the light-bulb where it dangled at the end of its wire. The perimeter of the basement was plunged into darkness, and the circle of lantern light, now the only source of illumination, seemed to shrink.

Sinjun swung the bag against the wall. The bulb shattered inside. Ellie sank to her knees, seeing his actions as a demonstration of what those strong hands could do to her if she didn't cooperate. He rolled up the bag with the broken glass and tossed it beneath the stairs. "If you want to stay alive, you'll do exactly as I tell you."

In a perverse trick of psychology, fear sent fire through her veins and unlocked her ability to talk. "You have no right to speak to a princess that way."

Suddenly he was on his knees in front of her. He

snatched her by the upper arms when she tried to scramble away, lifted her inches off the floor. He held her like that, suspended by his incredible strength, and dragged her right up to his chest.

Ellie put her hands out to protect herself. The heat of him seared her palms through his shirt. But it was like shoving against a brick wall. He pulled her so close she could feel his hot breath through the knit mask. "I don't know who the hell you are, but you're *not* Lucia Carradigne."

Time froze for an instant. Ellie just hung there, supported by Sinjun's hands and the link to those hypnotic blue eyes.

The shock wore off a heartbeat later and Ellie pounded her fists against him. "No! Let go of me."

They wanted a princess. If they knew the truth—no one paid ransom for royal impostors—she was as good as dead.

He shook her once, pulled her impossibly closer. Now the heat of the man singed her from chest to thigh. He dipped his mouth to her ear and stilled her struggles with words, instead of strength. "Right now, that's just our little secret. But if you don't do exactly what I tell you, *when* I tell you…"

His voice trailed off with a brush of wool against the shell of her ear. A chill rippled down her spine, leaving a path of goose bumps in its wake.

"How did you know?" She could barely hear her own whisper. "I suppose you want something from me now. I don't have much money. The gown and jewelry were borrowed."

"Shh." He set her down and Ellie collapsed onto her folded-up legs. "We'll talk later. Company's upstairs."

He moved his hands to her hair and began pulling out pins, freeing what was left of her upswept style and fluffing the tendrils to fall around her face and shoulders. Her breathing came in shallow gasps at the feel of strong fingers sifting through her hair and dancing across her scalp in what felt like a caress. In the aftermath of his controlled show of strength, his quick, gentle touches made her tremble with inexplicable emotion.

She was smart enough to know these were not tender reassurances. The purposeful stroke of his hands wasn't intended to soothe.

Yet she did feel comforted by his touch, reassured by his gentleness. It might be a naive, horrible trap to fall into, but Sinjun's touch gave her strength.

Enough strength to realize that, no matter his motive for keeping her identity a secret, she needed to play along in order to survive the next few minutes of her life.

She made no protest when he guided her down to the sleeping bag.

"Act like you're asleep." He brushed her hair down so it hid her face, then covered her with the blanket. "Keep your face to the wall and don't move. In this light, I don't think anyone will question your identity."

"Why are you doing this?"

For the first time she could hear voices at the top of the stairs. Lenny's deep one. Jerome's nasty laugh. And a third man—someone soft-spoken and deliberate with his words. Ellie huddled in the shadows, staring at the rusted-out furnace. At first she didn't think Sinjun would answer her.

But then she heard his velvety voice, blending in with the darkness around them. "We all have our own agendas."

The door opened and Ellie closed her eyes.

What was Sinjun's agenda?

And had she just been transferred from one untenable situation to another now that she was completely at his mercy?

Chapter Three

That had gone better than he'd planned.

Jerome's contact had arrived at 9:00 p.m. on the dot. He'd been content to observe the fake princess's sleeping form from the distance of the basement stairs, despite Jerome's offer to wake the little lady. Their guest, in fact, seemed eager to leave the damp, musty basement, though Cade suspected it had more to do with an abhorrence for his surroundings than pity for the girl's trauma-induced exhaustion.

Cade hung back in the archway that connected the living room to the kitchen, while Lenny sat on the floral-print sofa. Jerome paced the width of the room, lighting up one of his foul cigarettes. He darted back and forth with the speed and repetition of a revolving arcade target, giving Cade the urge to pull out his sidearm and shoot him. That would put Jerome out of his manic misery and ease the tension building in the room.

But Cade had a much more pressing issue to deal with than his team leader's agitation. He focused his powers of observation on the man in the brown Armani suit who had joined them for this late-night meeting. Winston Rademacher pulled a pristine white handkerchief from the pocket of his jacket and dusted the arm of the gold plaid sofa before perching there.

Interesting. The man didn't like to dirty his hands either literally or figuratively.

Jerome blew out a cloud of smoke, then turned and walked right through it. "All I'm saying is, we ought to pawn the jewels we took off the girl and make this deal as profitable as we can."

"The necklace is a handmade work of art that bears the royal coat-of-arms of Korosol. Pawning it would lead the authorities directly to us." Rademacher's thin lips barely moved when he spoke. "It will be returned with the princess."

Jerome turned again. "You're the one who lengthened the time frame on this job. You need to compensate us."

What happened to the loyalty the hundred-grand retainer fee had purchased? Cade thought.

Since the conversation was mostly Jerome's efforts to finagle more money for the contracted job, Cade tuned him out.

Rademacher was an old acquaintance of sorts. Cade had met him on more than one occasion, though they'd never had a conversation beyond introductory pleasantries. The man was a professional power broker. A favored guest among royals and high society the world over. His dark hair and high cheekbones hinted at his Middle-Eastern ancestry, but Cade couldn't remember where the man actually hailed from.

He wished he had his computer with him or at least access to some of his information contacts. He hated not knowing more about a man he had to work with than what he'd read in the papers. While Jerome complained and Winston looked bored, Cade ran through what he did know about their employer.

In recent years Rademacher had served as a personal advisor to Prince Markus of Korosol. Markus was the only child of King Easton's eldest son, Byrum. Since Byrum and his wife had died in a tragic accident while on African safari over a year ago, Markus was next in line to become king. But King Easton, declaring the right of royal privilege, had decided to travel to America and meet his extended family there before officially naming his heir. Cade wondered if Rademacher was working for Markus, if this kidnapping could somehow be used as leverage to ensure Easton named Markus as his successor.

"Hell. We don't even have decent plumbing here." Jerome's whine interrupted Cade's thoughts. "What kind of house puts a pump in the kitchen and makes you shower outside?"

"Mr. Smython, is there a point to all this?"

Rademacher also had ties with a political group in Korosol that wanted to end the monarchy system altogether and establish an independent republic. His one-time business partner, Remy Sandoval, was the self-proclaimed leader of the Korosolan Democratic Front. For the right price, as Jerome claimed every man had, would Rademacher sell out king and country?

Or was Winston Rademacher's motive something more personal? Perhaps kidnapping Princess Lucia and demanding a ransom was simply a new type of profit-making business deal the man had put together.

"I don't care how you dispose of the body, so long as it isn't found. I thought I'd made it clear that my client didn't want any casualties."

Client? Cade tuned back in to the conversation.

"The kid put up a fight." That was the extent of Jerome's defense for murdering the chauffeur. "I should have given him a bigger dose of the serum."

"Yes, indeed." Rademacher stood, rebuttoned his jacket and smoothed his lapels.

One thing was certain. The man revealed no hint of motive or emotion in the perpetual squint of his dark-brown eyes. He was cold. Clever. Unreadable.

The faintly accented tone of his voice revealed nothing more than irritation with Jerome's incessant banter. "I have a backup plan in place should you choose to deviate from my instructions again."

Cade's self-preservation radar kicked in at the matter-of-fact warning. "Whoa. What do you mean, backup? What else aren't you telling us?"

Winston looked at Cade and blinked, as if he'd forgotten his presence in the room. Fat chance. Cade didn't buy the eyebrow arched in aristocratic surprise for one instant.

"I've told you everything you need to know...Your Grace."

Cade had borne the brunt of enough condescending gossip from snobs like Rademacher to let the smirk in his voice bounce off his toughened hide. He'd suffered far worse than mock pity and survived. He walked right up to Winston and used his slight height advantage to look down on the man. "You've told us everything except this new backup plan. And who we're doing this baby-sitting job for."

Rademacher folded his handkerchief and tucked it into his jacket before responding. He laughed. It was a controlled, low-pitched sound that held no trace of humor. "You're as persistent a dog as your father was, aren't you."

Other than the fist he buried inside his pocket, Cade held himself perfectly still. He let the angry resentment slam through him, then trapped it in the spot where his soul used to be. "I don't make the same mistakes my father did."

Winston acknowledged the assertion with a slight nod. "I hope not. Bretford died owing me money. I consider your cooperation on this job as payment in trade. Your services in exchange for your father's debt." He splayed his manicured fingers in the air like a magician casting a spell. "It all seems so karmalike, don't you think?"

"Hey, we were talking about *my* money." Jerome waved his pudgy paw at Cade and Winston, intruding on the duel of unbending wills.

Rademacher's eyelids moved an infinitesimal distance and shut. He took a deep breath and his nostrils flared, as if an annoying gnat had buzzed into his ear. With the stand-off broken, Cade stalked to the far end of the room, silently cursing himself for letting wounded pride and old hurts get in the way of finding out what he needed to know.

"I grow tired of this, Smython." Winston moved only his eyes to look at Jerome.

Cade closed his ears to the conversation and watched their employer make short work of Fire-man. He'd never play cards with a control freak like Rademacher. But his father had.

Cade leaned against the archway, uncomfortable with thoughts of his father even now. Bretford St. John had lost nearly as much money at the tables as he had making bad investments. His addiction to gambling had cost him the family fortune, his son's respect and ultimately his life.

Their guest wasn't directly responsible for Bretford St. John's suicide, of course. His father had been the only one at the house to pull the trigger that night.

But Rademacher's trade-off burned like salt in an open wound. Cade had yet to meet a man who mourned his father's death. As a grieving young man, he'd turned to what he thought were family friends and business associates, looking for comfort and understanding. Instead, he'd been greeted with invoices and IOU's, and branded as the heir to his family's scandalous past.

"If you're not satisfied with the arrangements I've made, you can easily be replaced on this project." Winston's warning was clear, even to Jerome.

Maybe. Jerome tossed his cigarette butt into the stone fireplace that heated the house in the winter. "Is that a threat?"

Winston wasn't impressed with the flash of anger. "Do I need to make a threat?" He silenced Jerome by refusing to hear any more. He turned his attention to Lenny. "Mr. Gratfield."

The big man unfolded himself from the couch, rising as if he'd been summoned by a superior officer. "Yes, sir?"

"Get the jewelry and put the items in my attaché case. I'll use them as a token of the princess's well-being." He inclined his head toward the leather briefcase at his feet. "I'll meet you at the car."

Lenny took the case and slipped out. As Winston moved to follow him, Cade stepped out and blocked his path. He wasn't done pressing for answers yet.

"Why the hush-hush about your client?" He crossed his arms in front of his chest and demanded a response.

"This may be too complex for you to understand, Sinjun." Like Jerome and Lenny, Winston slurred Cade's last name with a trace of their native accent, giving *St. John* an almost British pronunciation. "I'm a man who makes things happen. I connect the right people so that they can become something greater than themselves. Understandably my client doesn't wish to be linked to a kidnapping—or the likes of you and your comrades."

Winston never so much as blinked. He hadn't even revealed if his client was a he or a she.

"And while you're making these *connections,* what do

you expect us to do with Princess Lucia? I signed on for a kidnapping, not a double murder.''

Winston laughed. It was an imperious sound, and the smile on his lips never reached the squint in his eyes. ''Careful, Sinjun. It almost sounds like you've developed a fondness for this girl. You wouldn't want me to think you're changing loyalties, would you?''

''I'm loyal to myself. Period.'' He shrugged, pretending his mounting frustration over Rademacher's evasion of his questions was no big deal. ''I was just curious as to where your loyalties lay. Mentioning a backup plan makes me think you'd leave us hanging if something went wrong.''

''My loyalties are to the project. I intend it to be a success. Lucia is a means to an end. Surely you can handle a twenty-six-year-old girl so that nothing goes wrong.''

Cade's fingertips suddenly itched with the memory of handling that twenty-six-year-old girl's hair. It had been long and wavy, soft in color and touch. Cade curled his fingers into fists, damning himself for getting distracted from his purpose.

''The girl's not who I'm worried about,'' he lied. ''How do we know we can trust the man you're working for?''

''You don't.'' Winston adjusted the already impeccable knot on his French-silk tie. ''You don't even have to trust me. Just do your job and have that girl prepped for her return Monday night.''

A rheumy laugh reminded Cade there was another person in the room. Jerome sauntered up to them and asked, ''Do we have to bring the princess back in the same condition we found her?''

Winston's expression never changed. ''Smython, you disgust me.''

Jerome cursed in French and Spanish, intimating he wasn't the only one who had considered getting to know their prisoner *better*. "I'm headin' outside." He waved off both Winston and Cade, and stormed out of the house.

Lenny returned, giving Jerome's huffy exit a curious glance before handing the briefcase to Winston. "I'll walk you to your car," he offered.

Winston nodded a curt acceptance. He butted his shoulder against Cade's as he passed. Then he stopped and turned, daring him to challenge his authority. Cade nailed him with a glance that acknowledged the conflict between them.

But wisdom prevailed over male posturing. Cade stepped aside and let Winston pass. He had too much at stake to risk alienating his employer now.

When the screen door had slammed behind them, Cade raked all ten fingers through his hair, venting his frustration and fanning his bangs into a spiky mess.

This whole setup felt wrong, from the unplanned murder of the Carradignes' chauffeur to the mystery employer to the wrong victim. He'd been on enough missions as a soldier and on his own to trust his instincts about the failure or success of a plan. His gut was screaming at him now, warning him this one was going to go very, very wrong before it was over.

Cool, clever and unreadable. Rademacher hadn't revealed a damn thing.

Cade noted that he'd never said no to Jerome's last request, either.

SOMETHING WAS WRONG.

Cade dropped the keys into his front right pocket and closed the basement door behind him. He pulled the scratchy stocking cap down over his face and scanned the shadows as he descended the stairs and tried to pinpoint what felt out of place.

The soft glow from the lantern made this damp hellhole look almost hospitable. A chain rattled, reminding him that his hospitality left a lot to be desired.

"Is that you, Sinjun?"

God, he hated that nickname. That slurring together of syllables as if his own name wasn't important enough to pronounce correctly. But under the circumstances, he could hardly correct her.

He stepped into the circle of light and let her identify him by body shape. The woman on the sleeping bag sat up, pushing a long fall of toffee-colored hair off her face. She adjusted her shoulders beneath the blanket and clutched it securely around her as she stood.

"Did I pass the test with your boss?"

Her big blue eyes blinked rapidly as he walked closer. Her eyes looked raw with suffering. Guilt warred with pity inside him, but both were ultimately defeated by admiration for her courage and perseverance. Finally he answered her expectant look with a nod and she smiled.

Barely. The flash of teeth and curve of her wide mouth lasted only a split second before she dropped her gaze to the floor. But the image stayed with him. The woman was really rather pretty when she smiled, he thought. But he got the impression she didn't smile very often, and that observation got him to wondering why.

"Good," she continued while he removed the bucket and replaced her canteen with a fresh one. "I don't know why you're helping me, or if you're really helping me at all. But since I'm still alive, I figured that's a good thing, right? I've never been kidnapped before, and I don't know the proper etiquette. But my goal should be to stay alive, and I should be grateful to you for helping me, and it shouldn't matter why you're doing it."

The talking. That was different. She hadn't put so many

words together at one time in the entire twenty-four hours she'd been here. But he wasn't psychic. He couldn't have foretold her nervous rambling from the top of the steps. Something else had to be out of place to keep nagging at his subconscious mind.

The meeting with Winston Rademacher had made him edgy, that was all. He didn't quite buy that excuse, but he was already busy making other observations.

She backed away when he knelt in front of her to pick up her discarded ration packets, and the movement gave him a glimpse of her torn gown and petticoats. Maybe that was why he hadn't really noticed her looks before. Other than the size of her eyes, her features had seemed unremarkable. But the fire-engine red of that gown was so overwhelming it would make all but the most striking of women look drab in comparison.

Cade imagined this woman would look pretty in softer colors. Soft like her. Yeah. He allowed himself a smile beneath his mask. If her hair was any indication, this woman was soft. Really, really…

Wham!

He didn't see it coming until the claw was right on him. The force of the blow rang through his skull and knocked him off his feet. The sharp metal hook that she'd anchored in her fist snagged in the knit of his cap and plowed through the top layer of skin on his cheek as she ripped the mask right off his head.

In the moments it took him to recover—to shake his head and clear the dizziness from his vision—he felt her hand at his waist. Butting against his hipbone. Diving into his pocket. Moving dangerously close to…

He heard the jingle of keys and knew her intention.

Adrenaline cleared his head with a soldier's clarity of instinct and purpose.

He clamped his hand around her wrist and knew that *she* knew this sneak attack had failed.

Her split second of hesitation gave him an advantage he didn't intend to surrender again. She jerked back with a grunt, but Cade held fast, using her momentum to pull himself to his knees. He felt her shift, saw the metal hook flying toward his face again. He snagged that wrist, too, and rolled his shoulder into her thighs, toppling her onto her back.

He dodged the knee that rose to strike him and dropped his body weight onto hers, pinning her to the sleeping bag beneath him. For an instant she went still and Cade damned himself, thinking she'd hit her head on the concrete floor.

Instead, she'd paused to stare.

"Cade St. John?" She squeezed his name out in a mix of accusation and shock. "The Duke of Raleigh?"

The recognition caught him off guard. She'd seemed familiar, but he still hadn't placed her. "How do you know me?" he demanded, pushing himself up onto his elbows at either side of her, giving her room to breathe without completely freeing her.

Her teeth bared with determined fury. "You traitor!" She pried a hand loose and slapped his face. She twisted her hips, shimmying along the floor beneath him. "King Easton invited you to be part of his American entourage. How could you betray that kind—" Cade thrust his arm beyond her rolling shoulder "—sweet—" he bent his elbow, twisting her flying arm to the floor "—man?"

Her cry of pain was more of a strangled moan. But whether her inspiration came from patriotism or her own personal fear, she still writhed beneath him. Kicking at his calves and shins. Pushing the hook toward his face with fury-charged strength. She was wild. Out of control.

Cade mentally stripped himself of any kid gloves, any guilt. He had to defend himself and keep her from hurting herself. He wound his left leg around both of hers and stilled her kicking. He pulled his hips over hers, damning propriety and letting his weight crush her diaphragm, robbing her of the ability to breathe deeply.

And then he tackled the damn hook. He stretched her right hand up over her head and shifted his grip around her wrist. It wasn't a matter of overpowering her so much as finding that particular bundle of nerves near the base of her palm. He pressed the spot with his thumb and her fingers popped open. He shook the hand once. Twice. The curved piece of metal flew out and clanged against the concrete floor. It was the handle from the lantern. Somehow she'd managed to pry it off and arm herself with a weapon.

The muted wince of pain he heard in her throat was her final protest. For several moments all was silent, all was still, except for the sounds of heavy breathing. His, measured and deep. Hers, quick and shallow.

Cade refused to ease his grip on her. The little spitfire had surprised him. Unmasked him. Drawn his blood.

Now that she'd recognized him, judged him to be a traitor to her beloved king, he suspected she'd do it again, given the chance.

And that was when Cade became aware of something else altogether.

Somewhere in their struggle, that gown with the broken straps—the gown that didn't quite fit—had ripped down the front. And there, pressing against his chest, teasing him again and again with each fevered breath she took, was a naked breast.

He raised himself ever so slightly. Seeking oxygen, her chest heaved for a deep breath. Cade watched in shameless fascination as the breast pillowed between the shreds of torn silk and came free of the black lace bra that couldn't contain its bounty. The chilled basement air—or maybe his own heated wish—coaxed the peachy circle at its tip to pucker and the nipple to strain to attention.

Cade became aware of other things, too. The cradle of her hips flaring with generous proportions beneath his. The gentle nip of her waist. The rounded, full, glorious splendor of her unintended display. His own body's immediate, healthy male response to such unexpected feminine treasures.

And the frightened, doe-eyed wonder of those big blue eyes desperately seeking to make contact with him.

"Who are you?" he whispered on a curiously husky plea.

She stared at him, one arm pinned above her head, one pinned at her side, completely vulnerable to him. Somehow she found the strength to answer.

"Ellie." She swallowed hard and Cade followed the movement down the length of her throat. "I'm called Ellie."

"Ellie." He tested the word on his tongue. The name suited her. Soft. Quietly elegant. Not an exotic, sophisticated concoction like Lucia Carradigne.

Because he wore scandal like a second skin, he let his gaze linger on the peach and porcelain wonder of her breast, and wished its mate had popped free, as well. But because his stint in the Royal Korosolan Army had taught him a few things about honor, he lifted his gaze to hers and tried not to look like the ogre she probably thought him to be.

He'd release her slowly, he decided, still remembering the need to protect himself from her surprise attacks. Very slowly.

He freed her arm and pulled his hand down along her body. Her eyes widened to panicked pools and she snatched at his wrist. Okay, so maybe he'd hovered a bit too long above that tempting mound. But he wouldn't touch her that way without her permission. Cade had never forced a woman to do anything she didn't want to.

Even the one he'd kidnapped.

He let her hold him off and looked into her eyes until he saw a glimmer of trust there. Only then did he move again. He reached for the end of the blanket that lay beneath them and pulled it up, covering her exposed breast. He nearly smiled at the gratitude that flooded her eyes. The transformation from fear to thanks washed her pale features in a warm, pretty color, and Cade was suddenly supremely glad that he wasn't a complete jerk. A man like Jerome Smython would never get to witness such a beautiful, shy smile.

He propped himself up a little further on his elbows and let her use both arms to tuck the blanket in a demure shield around her neck. Her unadorned lips parted in a silent thank-you.

An unfamiliar emotion, somewhere between curiosity and lust, made him want to kiss her. He wondered if she'd freak if he just touched his lips to hers. She'd had the temerity to attack him even though he was stronger, bigger and free to move around. She'd had the guts to damn him to his face and hadn't surrendered to anything more than her own modesty.

Maybe just one kiss. Something gentle. An apology of sorts for ruining the damn dress. "I'm sorry if I hurt you," he whispered. "But you didn't leave me much choice." He moved closer by degrees, watching her lips tremble, her eyes blanch, her lips again as they came together in acceptance, if not invitation. "You're really something, aren't you."

He was close enough to feel her breath mingling with his. She was so sweet. So tempting. So—

"Ellie?"

Cade froze. Recognition kicked in a moment too soon to sample her softness. Absolute, stunned surprise swept the fog of desire clear of his brain.

"Ellie Standish? King Easton's private secretary?"

She nodded.

He scrambled off her, his body protesting the speed of his movements as he pushed to his feet and stalked to the farthest corner of the basement. He raked his fingers through his hair and swore at his stupid luck. He spun around and looked at her again, not believing with his eyes and body what his mind was trying to tell him.

She had rolled up to a sitting position and was trying, with awkward success, to stand up while holding the gaping front of her dress closed in one hand and the blanket tight around her neck with the other. Her billowing skirt and ankle chain didn't help her coordination.

He didn't move to assist her. "What the hell are you doing here?"

She slid him a glare of pure hatred. Dumb question. He deserved that one.

"I thought you looked familiar, but I couldn't..." He couldn't equate the image of the Eleanor Standish who'd accompanied King Easton on embassy visits and private and political functions with this soft, voluptuous beauty. Even dressed up for CeCe Carradigne's wedding, she'd blended in with the furniture.

She'd been quiet and unassuming. Hidden those unique eyes behind thick glasses and a downturned face. Frumpy, colorless clothes had masked that curvy figure like baggy camouflage.

"You're Ellie Standish."

She tilted her chin. "You can stop repeating yourself now." She tossed her head, trying to shake a lock of hair out of her eyes, but the golden-brown curl wouldn't co-operate. She turned her back to him, released her grip on something and tucked the hair behind her ear before re-cinching her wool-and-silk armor and facing him again. "I don't suppose knowing my name will get me out of this prison any faster?"

She already knew the answer so Cade didn't respond.

Disgusted with himself for having a passing interest—no, for being way too interested—in kissing her, Cade sought out and found both his stocking cap and the handle to the lantern. He stuck the latter into a pocket and pulled the cap back onto his head. He didn't roll it down over his face yet. He wanted her to see his expression, to understand the seriousness of what he was about to say.

"I'm sorry you got mixed up in all this. But I can't—" He broke off. How could he explain everything he had to deal with right now? How could he warn her away or prom-ise to keep her safe when he didn't even know who had wanted to use Princess Lucia in the first place? "I don't want you to get hurt. But you have to understand I have a job to do."

"How much money do they get for princesses nowa-days?" The vulnerable edge to her sarcasm made him feel about two feet tall.

But then, he was Bretford St. John's boy. He was used to feeling shame.

"You have to keep your identity a secret from the others. These are dangerous men I'm working with. They're inter-ested in money and themselves. And not necessarily in that order. They won't think twice about killing someone who's deceived them, even if it's their mistake."

"I'll bet Paulo Giovanni didn't deceive anyone. What excuse did they use for killing him?"

None.

He let that guilty wound fester a bit before answering. "They don't need an excuse. That's the point."

Instead of crying or cowering or begging for help, she walked toward him. The ominous dragging of the chain behind her gave him a morbid flashback to an old Christmas story and ghosts from his past coming back to haunt him.

Dammit. Didn't she have the sense to get scared?

He stood a good six or seven inches taller than Ellie, but the way she tilted her chin and walked right up to him made him think she had the advantage over him, not vice versa.

Cade braced himself, refusing to be swayed by her righteous plea. "What are they paying you for selling out King Easton? He's a good man. A fair ruler and a generous human being. He loves his granddaughters. I can't imagine what he'd do to anyone who tried to hurt them."

Cade could imagine. A man whose loved ones had been threatened, especially a man with Easton's financial power and political influence, would make a dangerous opponent. It wasn't a risk he'd want to face.

"What about you?" Instead of defending himself, Cade turned the question back on her. "Easton must know we don't have his real granddaughter. Do you think he'll pull out all the stops to get his secretary back?"

"I don't know." Her pious defense of Easton weakened and she bowed her head. "Are you worried about not getting your money?"

"I'm worried—" Cade clamped his mouth shut, feeling an unfamiliar stirring in his chest. It had nothing to do with business. Nothing to do with the beautiful breast that had given him such lusty thoughts. He wanted to comfort her. He wanted her to hold her head up and flash that timid smile that transformed the inconspicuous secretary into a regal beauty.

But he didn't know how to make that happen. Short of setting her free. And he couldn't do that. Not yet.

Instead of freedom, instead of comfort, he offered her some practical advice. "You're not going to try to escape again, are you?"

"I won't make any guarantees."

Hardly the dutiful no he'd expected to hear. "Ellie, listen—"

"Hey, Sinjun! What's taking so long?" The door at the top of the stairs swung open, and the stench of cigarette smoke preceded Jerome down the stairs. "I said see to her needs, not take care of your own."

Cade covered his face and moved away from Ellie before Jerome reached the basement and ground out his cigarette on the floor. "The princess was concerned about her safety," he explained.

"Relax, Your Highness. We'll keep you safe." Jerome went over to Ellie. "I'll personally guard your body, if you want me to."

He stroked Ellie's cheek with the back of his grubby fingers. She smacked his hand away, marched over to the stool and sat, saving Cade from acting on the impulse to pry Jerome's touchy-feely hands from the end of his arm.

He'd promised himself to keep Ellie safe, but he couldn't cross the line and betray his own goals on this job.

Fortunately Jerome laughed off the rejection and headed for the stairs. "It's gonna be an awful long three days if you don't start acting friendly with the peons, princess."

"Three days?"

"Now, now, sugar. Nothing's going to happen to you. As long as you keep our identities a secret and can't put a name and a face together, you'll be free to go. That's a personal promise." Ellie turned away at his use of "personal," and huddled inside the blanket. Jerome's mask stretched as he yawned. Apparently he was too tired to pursue his offer of protection right now. He switched his focus to Cade. "You'll keep first watch, then? Wake Lenny at 0700 hours to relieve you."

"Got it."

After Jerome left, Cade stayed where he was. Maybe he should say something about that almost-kiss. Tell her why he'd wanted to. Tell her why he hadn't. Ask her how a quiet plain Jane could get him so worked up so fast.

But he didn't say anything. He stared at her back for a minute or more, then decided he should leave the whole topic well enough alone. He couldn't worry about her feelings right now. Hell, if she was a woman who'd had some experience with men, they could both chalk it up to just base animal attraction. They could acknowledge it was there and move on.

But Cade had a feeling Ellie Standish knew very little about adult physical interaction. Her next words reaffirmed his hunch about her naiveté.

"Three days to pretend I'm a princess." Her heavy sigh rippled all the way down the blanket to the floor. "And you know what's most frustrating about all this? I got dressed up to play the part, but I never got a chance to dance at the ball."

Cade didn't believe in fairy tales the way she did. But his guilt—and admiration for her brave, hopeful spirit— made him reach into the pocket on the side of his right pant leg and cross the room to join her. "It's no glass slipper. But here."

She stood and put some distance between them before accepting his gift. Her glasses. "Lose the contacts and give your eyes a rest. You'll need your sleep."

She clung to them as if he'd handed her her freedom. "Thank you, Cade."

He took little pride in her pleasure. "Don't confuse me with Prince Charming, Ellie. By midnight Monday, you won't be thanking me."

Her bright blue gaze shot up to his. After Jerome's threat, he knew exactly what she was thinking.

She'd seen his face and knew his name.

Cadence St. John, Duke of Raleigh.

Princess or not, come midnight Monday, he'd be expected to kill her.

Chapter Four

"Today, Princess?"

Ellie ignored Lenny's prompt from the other side of the wooden door and tied the ankle drawstring of the tan army pants she'd changed into.

Never in a million years would she have expected she'd have the desire to linger in an outhouse. But despite the bottomless pit of stinky mystery stuff behind her, she was making the most of the opportunity to enjoy some privacy without worrying about one of her captors paying her a visit.

Pretending to be someone else turned out to be a surprisingly wearing occupation. Always thinking about how she should look and act. Working up the nerve to speak her mind and make demands when the real Ellie would have sat back and evaluated all her options before saying or doing anything. Trying to figure out what anyone would want in exchange for her. Fearing what Cade had told her—that she'd be a dead woman if Lenny and Jerome found out she wasn't Lucia.

She sank onto the wooden bench beside the hole, feeling light-headed and helpless. She leaned forward and rested her head between her knees, fighting the sensations of a world spinning beyond her control.

How could she *not* be a dead woman? Cade St. John knew who she really was. While she didn't think King Easton would sacrifice her intentionally, mightn't he or the people who worked with him let it slip that Lucia Carradigne was safely tucked away in a private bungalow somewhere on her honeymoon, and that the woman they were negotiating for was an impostor?

Ellie braced her hands on her knees and pushed herself into an upright position.

She had to find a way out of this. On her own. Now.

Her escape attempt last night had been born out of fear and desperation. She'd been foolish to think she could overpower any of these men. This morning, she was smarter. She knew more about her situation and could make some reasonable decisions. She could better plan her chance at survival.

She reached for the canvas camo shirt that hung from a peg and continued dressing. The men were already showing more trust in her by freeing her to come outside to use the facilities this morning. Maybe it was nothing more than an act of pity, but they'd also given her a set of clean men's clothes and told her to throw the ruined red dress on the fire where Jerome was heating water for a shave.

The morning sun had hurt her eyes at first, but in the shade of the giant white oaks surrounding the house, the air was cool. A clean cool, not like the moist, heavy air of the basement. It was the kind of clear spring day that reminded her of her home in Korosol.

Thoughts of home inspired her creativity. Strengthened her resolve to be free again.

And made her wonder why fellow Korosolan native Cade St. John, who had flown to America in the very same plane as she and King Easton had, would commit such a heinous crime.

His small acts of kindness—bringing her fresh water, returning her glasses, covering her exposed body—didn't fit with her image of a traitor. Of course, she'd never known a man who'd sold out his king for personal profit before. She hadn't known many men, period.

And perhaps that was the thing that disturbed her the most. Not fear for her life, though the threat to it was real and omnipresent. Not her quest for adventure that had turned into a nightmare, instead of a dream come true.

It was her fascination with Cade St. John. The tall, dark, sexy man was her jailor. A conspirator against her beloved king. Her enemy. Yet she was drawn to him like Eve to the forbidden fruit. Confused, yet captivated by the things he made her think and feel. That was what truly frightened her.

Her fingers slowed as she fastened the buttons over her strapless bra and remembered the way he had looked at her naked breast. She'd been afraid at first, embarrassed that she lay there so completely vulnerable to him. But she'd seen something in his eyes that moved her past her fears. Hunger. An intense, intimate awareness that matched her own curious need. His indigo irises had darkened to midnight and she'd felt an answering tingle in the tip of her breast. A sparkling of tiny stars reaching out toward the night sky of his eyes.

A sharp, unexpected pressure pooled between her legs even now just thinking about that prickly feeling—one that had opened every pore in her skin as an overwhelming heat had sought a way to escape her body. She'd never been so close to a man before, never known the synchronous wonder of male angles fitting against female curves. She'd never known how her skin could burn with want for a simple touch.

Ellie squeezed her eyes shut and fought to regain control

of her body's treacherous responses—the shallow breaths, the achy heaviness, the quickening pulse.

"Now who's the traitor?" She chided herself in a whisper, wishing her stern mother or overprotective father or brother were here to shake a finger at her for being so foolish. But there was no one to tell her what to do, no set of rules she could follow when it came to getting a dangerously wrong man out of her system.

With a sigh of shame and longing, Ellie braided her hair and finished dressing. Like the pants, the shirt was sized for a man, but she rolled the sleeves and pulled the collar up around her chin.

"Oh, no," she muttered.

It smelled like *him.*

These were Cade's clothes.

She dipped her nose to the canvas neckline and inhaled the tantalizing combination of soap and spice.

God help her. She needed to get out of here before she developed some sort of psychological disorder and became completely enamored with a man who was willing to barter with her life.

"I'll give you two minutes to come out, Princess. Then I'm coming in." Lenny's warning spurred her into quicker, focused action.

As she tied the borrowed size-ten running shoes onto her feet, she formulated her best two-minute plan.

In her stroll from the house to the outdoor facility, she'd made several observations. Only one man guarded her at any time. They rotated shifts, one resting, one patrolling the house and grounds, one staying with her.

She had no map, but she'd studied the direction of the house and the position of the sun. The gravel road in front of the house ran north-south. That meant civilization or a crossroads would lie in one of those directions. Beyond the immediate area cleared to accommodate the house, she was in the middle of a forest of oak, pine and maple trees. Away from the road, the growth was too thick to drive a vehicle through. Anyone following her would have to pursue her on foot.

She could lose them in the woods, follow a path parallel to the road and end up...somewhere. Anywhere but here.

The trick was, of course, breaking away from one of the men and getting enough of a head start to make it into the woods in the first place.

Ellie stood. She took a deep, steadying breath and smoothed her sweaty palms down her hips.

She'd wanted an adventure. *No time like the present.*

Stretching up on tiptoe, she peeked through the moon-shaped opening. Lenny stood about two feet from the door, his head bent over his hands as he wrote something in a little black notebook. Jerome sat by the fire, his suspenders hanging around his hips. He held a mirror and was shaving around one of those perennial cigarettes between his lips. Cade was still inside. Asleep, she hoped.

Ellie closed her eyes and said a silent prayer. When she opened them, she grabbed the cross-piece on the wooden door, put all 130 of her pounds behind it and shoved.

She didn't look back to see the results of the thump and the curse behind her.

"She's running!"

Ellie was into the trees before she heard the menacing gallop of heavy feet behind her. There were shouts and curses. A crashing sound. A door slammed. More shouts.

She tuned out the words and used the sounds only to gauge the distance between her and her pursuers. From the position of the sun, she judged her direction to be roughly southwest. She tore through branches that grabbed at her clothes and bit into her forearms.

Lenny hadn't allowed her a belt, saying it was a potential weapon, so her pants sagged and caught on her hips, bunching between her thighs and forcing her to shorten her stride. She had to pick her knees up high as she ran so she didn't trip over the toes of her big shoes. The contorted stride pulled at unused muscles and made her lungs burn.

This was too hard. She wasn't built for this. She couldn't make it.

"Princess!" That was Jerome's voice, wheezing a warning from a different direction.

She had to make it.

Fifty yards. She counted off the steps with every slap of her shoes on the carpet of moss and grass. Fifty yards into the woods and then she'd turn due south.

Ellie had taken up running with her school chum Jillian for a whole semester in an effort to lose weight and streamline her body. She'd hated running back then. It hurt her shins. It hurt her hips. And she hadn't lost a single pound.

"Thirty-two." She gasped the number, sternly reminding herself that she had no choice. She had to run.

She heard a blast of shattering wood some twenty paces behind her. A pungent stream of vile curses rang through the trees, every one of them directed at her.

Forty-one. The trunks of the trees seemed to grow smaller. They'd been as wide as a barrel by the house. These were the size of her waist. The numbers of trees thinned and still she ran.

Forty-six. The trees were the size of her thigh.

"No!" She could barely squeeze the word past her tight, aching throat.

She didn't have fifty yards.

Ellie slowed her pace as a blue-gray mirror peeked its way through the trees. She scraped her hand on the deep-grooved bark of a maple and jerked herself to a stop above a five-foot drop, kicking a shower of pebbles and dirt over the edge.

A lake. She'd run forty-nine paces straight to the edge of a lake.

Her jaw dropped as she sucked in reviving air. Her chest bobbed up and down in time with the ripples she'd created across the surface of the water. She looked to the left. Looked to the right. Looked to the distant shore and trees the size of toys that told her it was too far to swim across.

She tried to hear above the pulse pounding in her ears. The shouts had stopped, but she could still hear the smash of branches and thunder of footsteps. Ellie dared a glance behind her. But she was already backing to the south, twisting the surplus waistband into a knot to free up her legs when she heard the sound.

A motor.

She scanned the silvery water closer to the shoreline and saw what she had missed before. A boat! A fisherman was pulling into a cove just beyond the next rise. Hidden by the trees, she would have missed the dock altogether if she hadn't known to look for it.

"Help!" She left the shoreline and charged straight up the hill. When she crested the top, she waved both arms and called to the fisherman again. "Help me!"

Was the old man deaf?

"Hel—!"

She slipped on an exposed mossy rock and landed on her rump. The muddy earth jarred the rhythm of her breathing and she doubled over in a fit of coughing.

But with the forced stop, she realized she'd made a huge mistake.

She'd given away her position.

She could hear what sounded like only one of them now, booted feet slapping the ground, tracking her down like a dog on the hunt. Change the placid woods to a tropical jungle and she'd put herself smack in the middle of that scary dinosaur movie where the raptors closed in on her, unseen, from every direction.

"No." The protest was a growly rumble in her parched throat. "Help me." She kept breathlessly articulating the same two words, over and over, pushing herself to her feet and stumbling forward.

She was close to a clearing now, where a little fishing cabin sat back from the lake's edge. The fisherman had climbed onto the dock and was tying down his boat as Ellie cleared the last tree. A cramp twisted her right calf into punishing knots, nearly crippling her. But she lurched forward, toward the old man, limping her way toward freedom.

"Sir?" She stopped on the path leading down to the dock and channeled her remaining strength to her lungs and her vocal cords. "Sir?"

The fisherman raised his head and turned around. As he stood, Ellie could see he wasn't terribly old at all. Maybe late fifties, sixty tops. His stark white hair had fooled her. Ellie tumbled forward, barely catching herself. He could help her. He had to help her.

"Please." She wiped the sweat and tears from beneath her glasses and pushed them up on the bridge of her nose. "I need your help." It was so hard to breathe and talk at the same time. "I was kidnapped." She reached out to him, willing him to walk up the path to meet her. "I need a phone. We have to call the police."

She tripped again, but her legs had turned to mush and she collapsed onto the ground. The white-haired man swam in circles before her eyes.

"Please help me," she begged, feeling the last of her will draining away. "Please."

CADE RACED THROUGH the trees, heading straight for the sound of Ellie's voice. He pumped his fists harder, compensating for the booby-trapped terrain of slick moss and exposed roots by shortening his stride and running at a faster pace. He'd left Jerome and Lenny far behind. He'd jump-started his body from his catnap on the couch the moment he'd heard Lenny's shout and hadn't slowed since glimpsing Ellie's caramel-colored hair flying out behind her shoulders through the trees ahead of him.

He didn't know what the girl was running on, but even he was panting from the exertion of their cross-country dash. When he heard her moving along the shoreline, he adjusted his course to cut her off.

Cade crested the low-rising slope and swore as the dappled shade gave way to clear sunshine. She'd reached another cabin. That willful, little— "Son of a bitch."

He backpedaled to a stop, skimming his feet across the tops of the slippery rocks exposed by erosion on the lee side of the hill. He caught himself with his hand and straightened in time to see Ellie collapse in a heap on the gravel path below him.

Giving himself a moment to catch his breath, he wiped the sweat off his upper lip with the back of his hand. He walked slowly, purposefully down the hill, watching Ellie refuse to surrender to the weakness of her spent body. She jerked herself onto her hands and knees and crawled toward the water.

"Ellie." He called to her, warning her to stop, begging her not to push her body beyond its limits. She didn't hear him.

Knowing his compatriots in crime might be within hearing distance, he covered her identity before shouting. "Princess!"

Cade felt the other man's eyes the instant the word left

his mouth. His soldier's instincts buzzed an internal alarm, clearing his head, priming his body to face the unidentified threat.

Hidden by the growth of infant saplings that followed the shoreline, the man stood on an old wooden dock, not more than six feet from Ellie.

Cade hurried his pace, but didn't run. No sense frightening the man until he had him figured out. He looked like an ordinary fisherman. Rust-splotched green boat with an outboard motor. Jeans damp to the ankles above muddy rubber boots. Plaid shirt. Green vest with fishing lures pinned in the nylon mesh.

But something about him didn't *feel* ordinary. Like his not rushing forward to help a woman who had fallen. Like his not backing away from a six-one, lean, mean, armed-and-dangerous machine of a man stalking out of the woods toward him.

"Please."

His guilty conscience almost tripped him up at the quavering rasp in Ellie's voice as she reached out to the man. But instead of giving in to the pulling need to run to her side to see whether she was truly hurt or just winded by her long run, Cade fixed a smile on his face and slipped into a more laid-back role.

"Morning." The man watched him with a curious gaze as Cade nodded a friendly greeting.

Cade walked right up to Ellie. He bent his knees far enough so he could slip his hands around her shoulders. She shrugged and tried to shift out of his grasp. But it was a token gesture, really. He could feel the gelatinlike tremble of muscles that had been pushed too hard and were refusing to cooperate.

He kneaded the weary muscles, giving the appearance of tender care to their one-man audience. He had to get her on her feet. He had to get her out of there and back to the house before Lenny and Jerome arrived on the scene and spooked the fisherman enough to call the authorities. Or worse, they might just bypass the intimidation stage and kill the innocent neighbor.

Ellie reached up and with boneless fingers tried to pry Cade's hands from her arm. "Don't."

"It's all right, honey. I've got you." The endearment slipped out without conscious thought. But he heard it when he said it. Ellie's big blue eyes rounded behind her glasses, indicating she'd heard it, too. For a moment Cade wondered whether his undercover training was so thorough that it had popped out naturally, or his subconscious mind was thinking things that were sure to get him into trouble somewhere down the road.

So the lady was hurting. So he was partly responsible for her suffering. So what? The job came first. He gave himself the stern mental reminder. Ellie Standish was a necessary means to an end, nothing more. If he wanted to reach out with a little compassion, then that was just part of doing his job. He was protecting his interests, not being taken in by the pain and pretty eyes of this determined Cinderella.

Cade squeezed harder and pulled Ellie to her feet. She swayed and seemed to favor her right leg, so he kept his hands on her shoulders. Just to steady her. Just to protect his interests.

Now, to get her out of here before the white-haired man tried something chivalrous.

"How's the fishing?" Cade asked, hooking an arm around Ellie's waist and moving a step closer to the other man while aligning himself with her.

"It's all right, I s'pose." Cade watched the gears shift in the man's dark eyes. He was having second thoughts about minding his own business. "I' she okay?"

For a moment Cade didn't answer. Not because he didn't have a lie on hand, but because of the man's voice. The humming modulation, almost running his words together, sounded familiar. Not enough to trigger an alarm, but enough to make him cautious. Had he heard that voice on TV? The radio? Maybe the guy was some famous actor trying to get away from the spotlight. That could explain his reluctance to help Ellie.

Cade zipped through the catalogue of observations and acquaintances stored inside his head but came up empty. The man's face, complete with perfectly-tanned skin and a scar, instead of crow's feet, beside his left eye, didn't seem familiar. Surely that shock of snowy-white hair would be impossible to forget.

He wasn't done with this yet, not until he knew where that sense of recognition came from. But Cade had to nip the man's concern in the bud before he acted on it. He had a starlet of his own he wanted to hide from the public eye.

Cade spread his fingers over the swell of Ellie's hip and tucked her to his side. It was a subtle move to angle her out of the man's direct line of sight and position himself between them. Her exhaustion was evident in the fact she didn't struggle to get away from his possessive touch.

"I'm working as a bodyguard for the lady," Cade offered in explanation. "We had a bit of a scare back there. Thanks—for helping out, Mr...."

It was a lame gambit to try to connect a name to the voice, but it worked. "Costa. Tony Costa."

Cade scanned his memory. No bells of recognition. Nothing. He'd come back to it later.

"Thanks, Mr. Costa. Good luck."

"He's not..." Ellie began to protest. Cade felt her palm flatten against his chest. But she barely pressed hard enough to stand herself up, much less push him away. She seemed to realize her weakness at the same time. Her chest expanded in a hard, shuddering breath. "Mr. Costa, why won't you help me?"

"I've got everything under control now, hon." Cade turned into her, brushing his fingertips across her cheek and feathering them into her hair. It would have been the most natural thing to pull her cheek against him and hold her, to let her absorb the warmth and strength of his body until she reclaimed enough of her own fire to give him hell again.

But despite the way his body seemed to wake up to the feel of her curves against his chest and hip, Cade knew they had to leave. This was all about the job, he reminded himself, ignoring the bothersome nick on his conscience. The job, and not the woman, was the most important thing. "We'd better leave Mr. Costa alone now."

Cade nodded to the fisherman, who responded with a simple, "Ma'am. Stay safe."

Ellie's hand fisted in the front of Cade's shirt. But she made no other protest when he circled around her to steer her off the path and up into the woods. They walked two steps before her right leg collapsed beneath her like a limp noodle. Stumbling off balance with her, Cade righted himself and scooped her up into his arms.

It wasn't exactly the way he'd envisioned hauling the prisoner back to camp, but at least he had her secured. He'd get her out of sight, hide his face beneath the mask once more, then lock her in the basement where she couldn't cause him—or herself—any more trouble.

He started up the slope, felt his foot slide across an exposed rock and knew this return trip was going to be tricky. He climbed a few more careful steps before glancing over his shoulder to see Costa kneeling on the dock beside his boat, his meeting with the neighboring princess and her "bodyguard" apparently forgotten in favor of the local trout.

Ellie's weight felt good in his arms. He felt inexplicably relieved knowing she was this close. But in order to keep an eye on Costa, support Ellie's injured leg and catch Jerome and Lenny before they stumbled onto Costa's clearing, he needed to get himself centered again—both physically and mentally.

"Can you put your arms around my neck?" he asked.

He focused on her downturned face, waiting until she lifted her gaze to meet his before saying anything more. When their eyes met, he could see a tiny bit of rebellion in the pursed pout on her lips. Good. Her body might have given out on her, but her spirit was still alive and kicking.

Enough sunshine filtered through the locked doors inside him that Cade thought he might remember what having a soul felt like. He almost laughed at the invisible daggers the little firebrand was spitting his way. Almost. He summoned a rusty smile, instead. "Please? You can lecture me on impropriety later, but I don't intend to waste any more time getting you back to the house. And if I fall down, we'd both get hurt."

She never answered him with words, but she lifted her arms. Her fingertips brushed against his chest. His skin shivered at the unexpected caress, but he held himself still. She touched his shoulders and the sides of his neck, as if checking to see where she might find the surest grip. By the time she finally hooked her fingers together behind his neck, Cade was startled to realize that he'd stood there, unmoving, for nearly a minute. Even more startling was the cautious admission that he was willing to stand there even longer, waiting until she was ready to move on.

Ellie wasn't like any of the women he'd spent time with. She didn't know all the right moves to make around a man.

There was no practiced seduction about her, no playing a man to get what she wanted. She was out of her comfort zone with his practical request. He had expected that her hesitation to throw her arms around his neck would make him uncomfortable or impatient. Instead, he found himself calmly anticipating what she might do next. Silently hoping there'd be a reward of some sort, like a smile or another touch, or maybe even a kiss.

This was Ellie Standish, after all. Gentle-natured and pure of heart, a tempting antidote to his dark, godforsaken world. But not weak. Never weak. He'd served with soldiers who had less strength and courage than this woman. Given time to figure out her options, she'd do what needed to be done. She'd find a way to accomplish her goal.

Trouble was, if these tentative, unintended caresses distracted him so, what would a purposeful touch do to his concentration?

"Tighter," he coached her. He'd always been a big one for getting into trouble. "I won't break."

Cade hiked her up in his arms and she held on more tightly. Her body relaxed until several of those curvy inches of hers dissolved into his chest, letting her weight become part of his balance. Settled at last, Cade bent his mouth to the silky curls above her forehead, teasing them and his own resolve with his lips. "Here we go. Trust me?"

"Never." She whispered the defiant word in a taut little exhalation of breath against his neck.

Cade threw his head back and laughed. This was his reward. Her spirit had been bowed, but not broken. A glimmer of that unshaken hope wound its way inside him, casting a little light into a heart that had long ago given up on finding goodness in people. He cinched his arms securely around her and carried his prize back to the house.

Chapter Five

"Put me down."

It took Ellie a few minutes to regain her strength, her senses and her will to survive. Now all three had returned in full force and she was painstakingly aware of how hopeless her attempt to run away had been in the first place.

The tight band of Cade's arms surrounded her back and thighs and pinned her against his chest, trapping her as surely as that steel chain in the basement had. She had no idea how far she'd run when she reached the fisherman's dock and a chance at freedom. Maybe a mile, not more than two. But the trip back to her prison, shackled against Cade's hard body, seemed to take forever.

Just as he'd subdued her in the basement when she'd foolishly tried to use physical force against him, he'd run her down like a doe in the woods. Even with a head start, she'd been no match for his predatory skills. He'd tracked her, claimed her from the fisherman as if he'd staked his territory against a rival male. And now he carried her back to his lair with long, steady strides that showed no signs of tiring.

In another time and place, the sensation of being swept off her weary feet into such strength would have been a fantasy come true. She could imagine Cade St. John sheltering the woman he loved with the fierce protective instincts of a knight from long ago. She could see him atop a coal-black charger, clothed in armor, with a long broadsword, instead of that steel gun strapped to his side.

She'd grown light-headed from a lack of oxygen on her run. Her heart had threatened to beat right out of her chest. But she could think clearly now and tuck her storybook fantasies away inside her wishful heart.

Only, now she had to combat a very different, very modern type of fantasy.

She'd never been picked up by a man before, not since she was a little girl, not since her father had been the hero who'd saved her from skinned knees and broken bikes. Carried aloft in her father's arms she'd found comfort.

Riding in Cade's arms made her feel something entirely different.

Dizzy. Afraid. Warm. Alive.

All the places Cade touched her, however impersonally, tingled with a strange, exciting heat. Her arms, her thighs—the left side of her body from breast to knee—all seemed to quiver with anticipation.

Cade's hard body was all planes and angles. He was a variety of sensual textures, from the sandpapery beard stubble that clung to his neck and jaw to the silky fringe of hair that kissed the nape of his neck. The man was all coiled energy and pantherlike grace. He was haunting indigo eyes that spoke a language all their own. He was tall and tough and impossibly broad.

Too much man. Too close.

A soldier of fortune. A law unto himself.

And he had awakened her. Of all the eligible males in the world—true knights and simple, good men—he was the one to tempt her from her cocoon where daydreams had been enough to sustain her adventurous heart. Now that she'd left her safety net of anonymity behind her, she wanted to learn more about the differences between men and women firsthand.

She wanted Cade St. John to teach her.

Some dormant instinct that overrode logic and common sense told her he was a man who was more than what he appeared. A man who was better than circumstances allowed him to be.

But Ellie had never been one to trust her instincts. As much as she'd longed for excitement and romance, she thrived on security. She was a creature of loyalty and duty, while Cade's only loyalty seemed to be to his latest "job."

And though even his simplest touches and intense looks thrilled her with unknown desires, she had enough gumption to recognize that Cade knew more about women than she knew about herself. He would never need or want a thing from a nearsighted wallflower like her.

She was nothing more than a means to an end. A property for him to ransom. And she wasn't even the real bargaining chip he'd wanted in the first place.

That sobering thought put her budding hormones on simmer and reminded her that Cade wasn't a gallant knight rescuing the princess. His title aside, he was the enemy of her king. The enemy of her own resolve. She needed a knight to save herself—from him.

Only there was no knight for her out here by the oaks and pines and water in the middle of who knew where.

There had never been a knight for Ellie.

She had to save herself.

"I said put me down." She felt his eyes snap in her direction, as if he was unsure whether the haughty clip in her voice stemmed from arrogance or panic.

"Don't be ridiculous. Your leg—"

She kicked out with her feet and wriggled out of his

grasp, ignoring his protest. When she shoved at his chest, he let her drop, instead of stumbling over the top of her as she pulled him off balance. Ellie would have landed on her rump if Cade hadn't gripped her elbow and steadied her as he easily righted himself.

She jerked her arm from his grasp. She was too smart to try to run again, but she didn't have to be so close to Cade that her mind got all muddied up in the curious sensations of her fanciful heart and traitorous body. She squared her shoulders and set out ahead of him. But when she put her weight on her right leg, a flash of pain shot through her calf. Ellie grit her teeth to stifle a groan and kept walking.

"Ellie." She ignored his pitying voice and took another tender step. "Enough."

He closed his hands around her shoulders. She squeezed her eyes shut and fought the urge to lean into his strength and let him help her. But ultimately, practicality won out over pride, and she braced herself on his arm and lowered herself beside the trunk of a nearby tree.

With her back resting against the bleached bark of the towering white oak, she breathed in deeply and willed the pain to subside. Cade followed her down, kneeling at her side. He untied the hem of her borrowed pants, wrapped his hands around her right ankle and squeezed. Then he ran his hands up her leg, pressing, searching, stirring up all kinds of curious sensations. She grew achingly aware that these were his clothes she wore. Achingly aware of the casual intimacy of his touch. His scent. His…

Ellie batted his hands away. "I'm all right."

"No, you're not." He lifted her leg and gently bent it at the knee and ankle, testing each joint. "You couldn't walk back at the lake, and now you're favoring this leg. Let me check it."

He slipped his hand higher, and Ellie's breath hissed

through her teeth at the feel of his hand on her inner thigh. Cade looked up, judging her reaction to his probing touch. Locked in the darkness of that indigo gaze, Ellie couldn't move. He squeezed once, and her thigh muscles clenched. The fever spread straight up to that tender spot between her legs.

She swallowed hard, alarmed that she wasn't protesting against his familiar touch. Instead, she pressed her lips together and wondered if it always felt this hot, this edgy, this quick when a man touched a woman. Maybe she was some sort of spinsterish freak who got off on his clinical, perfunctory contact because she had nothing else to compare it to.

Oh, God, she felt like an idiot, drowning in a sea of confusing thoughts and sensations. Why couldn't she think clearly? She'd always been so sensible. She'd always found a way to make a tricky situation bearable. But not with Cade. Not with this.

Ellie salvaged what dignity she could by thrusting her chin out and pushing his forearm back to her knee. "It's farther down."

Cade studied her for one intense moment, conveying a message she didn't understand—shouldn't understand—before looking away and freeing her from those magic eyes of his. He skimmed his hand along her leg, almost stroking her. Though there was a machinelike economy in his movements, the touches were gentle. And that truly confused her. How could a man so hard, so deadly, show her such inexplicable kindness? "You could just sling me over your shoulder and haul me back to the house. Why are you helping me?"

"Because you need help. It's okay to stand back and let somebody else be strong for a change."

Ellie puffed out a frustrated sigh. "Not you. I don't need you to take care of me or touch me or— Ow!"

Every muscle in her body jumped when he pushed against the sore bundle of nerves in her calf.

"That's the spot, huh?" He reached beneath her leg and kneaded the muscle spasm. His touch was a new experience in torture as pain radiated from her calf.

Tears stung her eyes and she grabbed his wrist. "Stop."

He easily overpowered the protective grasp of her hands. "I know it hurts. And I know you don't want my help. But I'm giving it to you, anyway. Just try to relax."

Relax? With Cade the predator kneeling so close she could smell his spicy scent? With Cade the protector massaging her injured leg? With Cade the champion of her feverish fantasies touching her as if he had every right to? Each healing stroke was a mind-blowing mixture of soothing tenderness and jabbing pain. She clenched her teeth together and refused to cry out.

His shoulder blocked his ministrations from view. Behind the relative safety of his back, she dared to study him more carefully, using the distraction to steer her thoughts away from the sharp ache in her leg.

The soft knit of his shirt tugged and stretched over a sleek set of muscles each time he moved. As broad as he was through the shoulders, his rib cage tapered down to a narrow waist. Below his belt, his buttocks flared in a graceful arc. She traced the shape of man and muscle with her eyes, boldly following the powerful line downward until it was interrupted by a thin black notebook that protruded from his rear pocket.

Ellie's curiosity drew her deep into thought and away from her pain. Lenny had carried a little black notebook just like it. Was it the same one? The big man could have easily lost it when she'd knocked him to the ground and taken off. Maybe Cade had picked it up when he ran out-side after her.

But why stop to do a favor for a friend when their meal ticket—and incriminating witness—was running away? Had Cade stolen it? He was already a kidnapper and killer. Petty theft would mean nothing to him. But why?

Ellie lifted her fingers, wondering in a moment of mad-ness if she could pick Cade's pocket and satisfy her curi-osity.

"You hanging in there?" He glanced over his shoulder and Ellie snatched her fingers away. She reached up and adjusted her glasses instead, leaving her hand there to hide herself from the probing question in Cade's gaze.

"I'm fine."

And then the knot suddenly released itself as if a trap had been sprung. Ellie's breath came out on a sigh, and she sagged against the tree. Sexy men and curious notebooks were momentarily forgotten as that raw, grabbing pain in her calf finally vanished. "Thank you."

He did a double take, as if he hadn't expected her thanks. He adjusted her pant leg and retied it at the ankle. "You're welcome. It'll be tender for a while, but you should be able to walk on it."

Cade rolled to his feet, then took her hand to help her stand. Ellie pulled the oversize shirt down over her hips and clutched at the hem. She breathed in deeply, gingerly testing her ability to support herself on her own two legs.

But just as she began to walk, his wide chest blocked her way. Ellie stopped, changed directions, but he moved again, blocking her path.

"What's wrong?" she asked, a vague apprehension put-ting her on alert. She pressed her spine against the tree, leaning as far away from him as possible before risking a glance up into his eyes. Big mistake. Once she met his downturned gaze she was trapped.

He braced one hand on the tree above her head and leaned in. Ellie's breath rushed out in a strangled gasp as he moved close enough for her to feel the heat from his body at the tips of her breasts and chin. He brushed a lock of hair off her face and tucked it behind her ear. When his hand lingered, she dropped her gaze to the front of his shirt, confounded by this mock show of tenderness.

"Do you have any idea how much trouble you are, Ellie Standish?" His voice was a soft caress to her ear. She heard no threat. Instead, she detected a trace of that same laughter that had rumbled through his chest when she'd said she would never trust him.

"You mean Princess Lucia."

"I mean Ellie Standish." Had he drifted a centimeter closer, or was that her imagination? Or had she leaned toward him?

Drat. If only she had two wits of experience with men, she could tell if this was flirting. Or a taunt. Or something she really needed to fear.

She decided to interpret the question literally. At least she couldn't make a fool of herself with an honest answer. She opened her eyes and talked to his chest, avoiding the dark snare of his eyes. "I've never caused anyone any trouble in my entire life."

"Never?"

"No." She looked up.

Oh, God. He was there. Right there. Close enough to see in clear focus over the tops of her glasses. Close enough to feel his warm breath dance along her cheek. She swallowed hard and his gaze darted to the movement of her throat. She swallowed again, feeling those eyes like the brush of a fingertip.

Then his gaze moved lower, to the erratic rise and fall of her breasts as she tried to quell her nerves. Like that first night when he'd wrestled her to the floor, the intensity of Cade's gaze made her feel tingly and off-kilter. It made her want things that a woman in her position shouldn't want.

This was a new kind of torture, one that frightened her more than chains and knives and guns. One that got beneath her skin and attacked her where she was most vulnerable. She tried to fight back. "Why are you doing this to me?"

His articulate stare grazed her lips before meeting her beseeching eyes. "What am I doing?"

She answered in a strangled croak. "I don't know." In her fairy-tale books, the heroes and the villains were always clear. But Cade St. John remained a mystery. He'd kidnapped her. He'd brought her her glasses and decent clothes. He tended to her injury but refused to let her go free. He sheltered her one minute, threatened her the next. And now? "I think you're playing some kind of game with me. I'm sorry, but I don't know the rules."

Cade trailed a finger across her cheek and tapped the end of her nose. His bottom lip arced in a wry smile and he pulled away. "No, I don't suppose a woman like you would."

A woman like her? Shy? Plain? Afraid to take a risk because failure might mean disappointing the people who depended on her?

Ellie was free to move, but she still clung to the tree for support. She dug her fingers into the rough bark behind her and watched him walk away. There was purpose in his stride. What had been his purpose a moment ago? What would a more experienced woman understand that she hadn't been able to?

Something stirred in the untapped resource of feminine intuition inside her. She couldn't quite decipher the message. "If I was a real princess, would you have kissed me just now?"

That stopped him. His shoulders rose and fell with a massive sigh before he turned back to face her. He still wore that irksome smile. "Did you want me to kiss you?"

"I…" What had she wanted? Shamed by her bold curiosity, Ellie seized on the anger it caused and gathered strength to push herself from the tree. She adjusted her glasses and found the nerve to look him in the eye. "No. Of course not."

She tipped her chin to a regal angle and marched past him, berating herself for knowing so little about men. For being plain. For being foolish. For being so damn lonesome in her quiet little world that she had practically dared her enemy to kiss her.

Cade grabbed her wrist as she walked past and jerked her to a halt. She swung around with her fist, but it deflected uselessly off his shoulder. "Let me—"

Before she could utter a proper protest, he'd snatched her chin, angled her mouth beneath his and kissed her. Ellie screamed in her throat, but she only succeeded in making her ears ring. Her lips flattened against her teeth beneath the force of his mouth. Her twisting hips and pounding fist did no good. He simply backed her into the tree, trapping her between the equally solid trunks of man and white oak. Ellie gasped for air. Grasped at sanity.

Marveled at the suddenly gentle fingers that spanned the width of her jaw. Her body relaxed its protest and the pressure on her mouth eased. He ran the tip of his tongue along the curve of her bottom lip in something of a silent apology. Ellie nearly smiled. The caress reminded her of the ticklish lick of a cat. A big, black panther cat.

She heard the laughter in Cade's throat as she made something very like a purring sound in response. A sudden heat flooded her face, but the callused tips of Cade's fingers scudded across her cheeks and feathered into her hair, calming her, reassuring her. His fingers tunneled farther and cradled her skull, gently tipping her head back.

Though his thighs still pressed against hers, stoking the heat that burned low in her belly, he was giving her the chance to voice her protest, an opportunity to slap his face.

But she did none of those things. Her eyelids fluttered open and she found herself bathed in a fire of pure indigo.

"There's not much that stops me if I want something." His husky voice grazed her ears like a caress.

So kissing her meant what? That he wanted her? He continued to hold her gaze, never blinking, waiting for her to absorb his meaning.

A hot thrill of expectation coiled inside her, making her catch her breath. For the barest fraction of an instant, Cade's gaze dropped to the quick thrust of her breasts as she inhaled. As if he couldn't help himself. He *did* want her.

Ellie curled her fingers into the front of his shirt, eliciting a small gasp as she caught a hair on his chest. Drat! She just didn't know how… "I'm sorry."

"I'm not." He flattened one hand over hers, pressing her palm against his heat and corded strength, stilling her frantic clutch of withdrawal.

He caught her with his bewitching eyes once more. They loomed large above her as he pressed his thumb to the seam of her lips. She opened them for him. Maybe Cade claimed her, maybe she surrendered.

His beard had been rough on her mouth before, but now his touch was exquisitely gentle. He slipped his hands behind her shoulders, dragged his palms down her back, cupped the flare of her hips and pulled her away from the tree and into his heat. He taught her the intimate secrets of that sensitive skin just inside her lower lip, the tugging sensation she felt deep in her feminine core when he pulled the tip of her tongue between his lips. Cade instructed her mouth in just the right way to tremble with passion and ache with need. And she was his willing pupil.

But while her lips were quick learners, her hands darted across his chest in ignorance. She didn't know where to put them. But Ellie was nothing if not observant.

He had said to put her hands around his neck when he carried her. He'd wanted her close, to maintain his balance. Now she wanted to be close. She slid her hands up his chest and curled them behind his neck. As she lifted herself into his kiss, her breasts rubbed his chest. The hard resistance teased the aching tips into rapt attention. He moaned against her mouth and ground his hips against hers. She moaned in response as something warm like honey ruptured inside her and spilled into her veins.

"Cade?" she breathed, panicked by her body's urgent reaction to his. He shifted his hold on her, slipping his hands up beneath her shirt, searing her back with needy caresses that were more arousing than rough. He pulled her body flush against his, encouraging her to discover and enjoy the aching rapture of two bodies embraced like one.

"Open for me."

Ellie obliged. Cade's tongue thrust in, stamping her with male possession, clueing her in to her female power over him.

Self-consciousness vanished, leaving her to absorb her body's glorious new discoveries of desire.

She'd been kissed before—once by Robert Porter in the seventh grade. It had been her first, a perfunctory smack on the lips. Then there was the time she'd gone home on holiday from university and run into one of the ranch hands in the shearing barn. Hap Worth had been his name. Worthless was more like it. He was drunk; she was female. His leery, wet-mouthed sucking of her face had sent her running into the house for a hot shower.

But she'd never been...kissed.

Cade's sweet seduction of her mouth—the worshipful praise of each corner and curve of her lips—*this* was a kiss. More thrilling than any fairy tale. More erotic than any romance novel she'd read. More intoxicating than any starry-eyed fantasy she could devise.

And just when she thought she might explode at the next touch, the next sweep of his tongue, Cade lifted his mouth. He let her back down to earth slowly and gently, pulling his hands from her bare skin. He straightened the shirttail over her hips, then wrapped his arms loosely around her waist.

Ellie settled back onto her heels and wedged her elbows between them, forcing enough space to allow the morning breeze to cool her hot skin.

"There's more, Ellie. There's so much more." He sifted a lock of her hair between his fingers, studying it for a moment before tucking it behind her ear. If she couldn't hear the regret tainting the dark fog of his voice, she could feel it in the subtle withdrawal of his body from hers. She swallowed hard and braced herself for whatever cold thing he was about to say. "But the last thing in the world I want is to see an innocent like you get hurt."

She frowned at the apology in his words. He had kissed her, not at all like the villain she thought him to be, but the way she imagined a hero would. Before she could convince herself that she didn't really have anything much to compare the embrace to, she seized onto that heroic image. "Then let me go. Cade, you're a better man than this."

"A better man?" He shook his head. "Ellie, I just assaulted you."

"No. I wanted you to kiss me." She admitted her frustrated curiosity with self-deprecating honesty. "I just didn't know how to ask, and then I didn't think you wanted to, and—" She clamped her mouth shut, sensing she was starting to babble like a schoolgirl. She steadied herself with a cleansing breath and tried to sound like the twenty-six-year-old woman she was. "Now I'm glad you did."

"You shouldn't always tell the truth, Ellie. Revealing all your secrets puts you at a disadvantage."

He released her and turned away, plowing his fingers through his hair, spiking up the thick black waves into a surprisingly vulnerable-looking mess. Ellie crossed her arms in front of her and rubbed at the sudden chill that prickled the skin beneath her sleeves. She knew a foolish urge to straighten that hair for him, to offer some kind of comfort to offset the look in his eyes as he stared into the distance. Was that why Cade was so secretive? So he wouldn't put himself at a disadvantage?

His mouth curled down in a grim frown. "You shouldn't get involved with a man like me."

"A man like what?" She circled around him and tugged at the front of his shirt "Part of you doesn't want to kill me, or you wouldn't waste time massaging cramps and seeing to my comfort. You wouldn't have kissed me just now." She tugged again, forcing those indigo eyes to meet hers. "You know you have the wrong woman. You wouldn't have to tell the others. You could say I got away from you. That the fisherman helped me."

"*You* got away from *me?*"

His incredulity bordered on insult. But Ellie was beyond feeling its sting. She'd beg if that was what it took to survive. "You know I'm not worth whatever you're asking for. Let me go. I'm sure King Easton would take into consideration how you've protected me. I'd put in a good word for you. Even if you killed Paulo, I'm sure there's some sort of leniency or plea bargain—"

"I didn't kill anyone." He pried her fingers from his shirt. "But, princess or not, I can't let you go."

Just like that, the kiss that had transformed her from a meek bookworm into a woman who finally understood words like *passion* and *sexy* and *self-confidence* was set aside.

He put on his mask and unfastened his holster, slipping back into his role as her captor. He pulled out his gun and pointed it at her ribs, signaling her to walk in front of him. "Your Highness."

Resigned, Ellie gave up her attempt to reason with the remnants of the good man who resided inside this tall, dark and heartless killing machine. But she wasn't quite ready to surrender her womanly curiosity. She might never understand men, but she wanted to understand herself. She needed to know if she had misread his participation in what had just happened between them, or if the sexual attraction that still hummed like a forbidden memory through her veins had touched him at all.

She picked her way through the trees at a slow but steady pace, keeping herself a few inches ahead of the gun barrel trained at her back. "Why did you kiss me, Cade?"

"Because I wanted to." The matter-of-fact intonation in his pitched voice gave her no reason to celebrate. "And that's the same reason why I'm taking you back."

"Tempers are getting pretty hot here."

Easton Carradigne paced to the far end of the study and pressed the cell phone closer to his ear. Though the line was secure, he knew his staff and advisors were waiting just outside the door. "Are you any closer to finding out who's behind this?"

"I've got a couple of leads, but I haven't had a chance to follow up on them yet. We had a bit of an incident here. Smython twisted his ankle pretty badly."

Incident. Easton suspected his man was prone to understatement. But if the situation had unraveled completely beyond his control, he'd have reported it.

"When do you think you'll know something?"

"Soon."

"Our time is running out."

"I know."

Easton rubbed at his forehead, wishing Ellie was here to bring him an aspirin. Wishing she was here, period. "Can you keep her safe?"

The pause at the other end of the line worried him. "I'll bring her home, sir. When it's time."

Easton shook his fist in the air, giving vent to the normal human frustrations he rarely showed as king. "Dammit! I want to know who is using the people I care about to hurt me."

"I'll keep working on things from my end."

Marshaling his composure, Easton nodded. "As will I."

A quiet knock interrupted the terse conversation. The king turned as Harrison Montcalm opened the door. "Your Highness. You have company. It's not…"

Easton acknowledged him and returned to the phone. "I have to go. I'll be expecting your call."

"Understood."

He folded the phone, disconnecting the caller. He crossed to the mahogany desk and set the phone on the blotter.

"Did I interrupt something important?"

The breath whooshed out of Easton's lungs at the sound of that falsely chipper voice. There was enough pomposity in the rich European accent to identify him as his grandson, Prince Markus, before ever turning around.

"Sorry, sir." Harrison apologized, then left the room at Easton's dismissive wave. There was no easy way to deal with his grandson, but he'd never backed away from a task because it was difficult.

"Markus." Easton extended his hand in greeting, following protocol, if not his heart, at the moment. "This is a surprise."

Not necessarily a pleasant one. As king, he waited for the prince to approach him, though the younger man hesitated, as if he expected to be met halfway. The delay allowed Easton to note how the cut of his double-breasted jacket emphasized Markus's growing gut. His self-indulgent paunch reminded Easton of a spoiled child—not an attractive characteristic for a thirty-five-year-old man.

Markus shook hands and then added the flourish of an Old World greeting by kissing him once on each cheek. Too much style and not enough substance for Easton's tastes. A primary reason for not naming Markus as his successor. The boy drank too much to be reliable and was too self-absorbed to take care of his country.

Right now, Easton wasn't in the mood to humor Markus and his latest whim. "I have business to attend to. This isn't the best time for a social visit."

"Grandfather, you wound me." Markus pressed both hands over his heart in melodramatic fashion. "I just heard about Cousin Lucia."

The news of the kidnapping had been kept strictly hush-hush, but Easton's face revealed nothing of his surprise. "What have you heard about Lucia?"

"That she turned you down." Markus laughed. "That she's chosen that soldier fellow over your offer to make her queen."

A subtle cough from the doorway punctuated the announcement, turning their attention to the solid, six foot tall "soldier fellow" who had been honored as knight, royal advisor and friend to king and kingdom. Easton silently applauded the deadly look Harrison sent Markus.

"Remy Sandoval has arrived, sir. He's downstairs."

"Thank you."

Harrison nodded, drilled Markus with a warning gaze, then left to usher in their guest.

Markus unbuttoned his jacket and sat in one of the guest chairs at the desk, ignoring etiquette and making himself at home. "Well, that was embarrassing, wasn't it?"

Easton circled behind him, wondering if the boy might not really be Byrum's child, or if there was some other way to excuse his misplaced senses of humor and duty. "Why are you here, Markus?"

"I can't pay my grandfather a visit?"

"I'm a busy man. I have a country to run."

Markus spun in the chair to face him. Without his charming veneer, there was something almost sinister in his smile. And though Easton searched, he could find no spark of caring or conscience in his watery blue eyes.

"I'm concerned about that country, too. Have you finished playing this game of meeting all the American cousins and leaving Korosol untended?"

That accusation could not go unchallenged. "No one loves Korosol more than I."

Markus rose, his face flushed with emotion. "Then name your successor. It's my rightful place to be the next king!"

If he'd stamped his foot, the tantrum would have been complete. Easton grabbed the back of the chair and leaned on it for support. He didn't know if age or illness or disappointment made him suddenly feel so weak.

Would Markus be willing to do more than yell and whine to get what he wanted? Easton feared the sad truth might be yes.

And it made his resolve to protect his country even stronger. He straightened with the kingly bearing that had rested on his shoulders for more than five decades.

"Don't ever raise your voice to me. I'll name my heir when I am ready. Now, if you'll excuse me, as I said, I have business to attend to." He crossed to the door and opened it himself.

Harrison and their guest were waiting outside. Markus took his time buttoning his jacket and following the king. He dropped his head in a curt bow. "Grandfather."

"Good day, Markus."

Remy Sandoval was a tall, lean man with dark eyes and thinning hair. He looked distinctly uncomfortable in the suit and tie he wore, and he surveyed the elegantly appointed study warily before following Easton to the desk. After formal greetings, he sat in the chair Markus had vacated.

The former rebel leader and newly elected member of the Korosolan Parliament was as anxious to get down to business as the king. "I'm not used to being summoned in the middle of the night and flown across the ocean for a meeting. What's going on?"

Easton had weighed the decision of how much to share with Sandoval. Though they had differing political views, Easton did admire the man's blunt nature. He'd decided the direct approach would serve best.

He pulled a long, flat jewelry box from the desk drawer and set it on the blotter. Then he opened it.

"Pretty baubles," said Remy, revealing little interest.

"Diamonds and rubies. As you can see, the silver filigree work on the necklace bears our country's coat-of-arms."

"You brought me here to show me the crown jewels?"

Easton closed the box. "Actually, my granddaughter Lucia designed it herself. She's quite an artist."

"A national treasure, I'm sure."

''She was wearing the necklace two nights ago when she was kidnapped.''

To the man's credit, Sandoval's face registered genuine shock. ''I'm sorry. Your family must be quite upset.''

Easton savored the condolence for a moment. But only a moment. ''Her kidnappers are asking for five million dollars and a written statement saying I will abdicate the throne by year's end. Since you represent the antimonarchists...well, you can see why I might want to talk to you.''

''*Are* you abdicating?''

Spoken like a true reformer. Though Easton needed information, he had no plans for making any concessions to the man. ''Not until I name my successor. The monarchy will stand.''

Remy inhaled deeply and reached for the top button of his shirt. ''May I?'' Easton nodded and Remy loosened his collar and tie. The king remembered that same habit from when they'd negotiated a political settlement a year and a half ago. It was a sign of pending cooperation. ''So you're asking me to confirm or deny whether any of my people are behind this plot to unseat you?''

''I'm asking you—in the good faith I showed when I signed the KDF Development Accord—to give me straight answers.''

''This is the first I've heard of the kidnapping. I'll ask around. Some of the extremist party members are more loyal to the cause than to me.''

It was all Easton wanted to hear. He stood and reached across the desk. ''Thank you.''

Sandoval stood and took his hand. ''Your Highness?'' He followed Easton to the door where Harrison waited. ''Admittedly my first training was as a soldier, not a politician. Talking and waiting don't come naturally to me. But I can see that you are making a legitimate effort to include my party's views in your policy-making decisions. I don't want to jeopardize the progress we've made. I'll vouch for my party's innocence in this matter. But if an individual has taken your granddaughter in the Democratic Front's name, I'll find out about it.''

Easton squeezed his shoulder in a gesture that was at once a promise and a warning. ''If it is one of your people, tell them I want her back safe and unharmed. Or all the progress we've made *together* will be undone.''

Remy nodded his understanding. He clicked his heels and bowed before leaving.

Harrison shut the door and turned to Easton. ''Do you think he's telling the truth? That his party has nothing to do with this?''

''In a way, I hope he is lying.''

''Your Highness!''

Easton shook off his worry. ''I haven't gone mad. It's just that there aren't that many people who would benefit from my stepping down. If it's not someone who wants to overthrow the entire monarchy, then it's someone who wants the throne for himself.''

''The prince?''

''There's something wrong with that boy.'' His suspicions saddened him, made him weary to the bone. ''But I don't have any proof that he's behind this—any more than I can prove Sandoval and his people are. Without proof, my hands are tied by the laws of succession. I want answers.''

Harrison took him by the elbow and walked with him down the hall toward the guest suite. ''You need your rest, sir.''

''I need those answers more.''

Chapter Six

Cade lay on his belly in the grass. His black hair and infrared field glasses were the only things that extended above the rise at the edge of the clearing, rendering him nearly invisible to anyone in the cabin below.

The swirling cloud cover played peek-a-boo with the full moon, creating plenty of shadows in the trees to hide among. But he'd be open game once he cleared the tall grass and rocks at the foot of the hill. Looking through the glasses at the eerie glow-in-the-dark world of infrared, he scanned the path one more time to verify that the place was deserted. Temporarily, at least. There was no vehicle in the driveway, but the boat was still anchored at the dock, and the boat's trailer was parked in the grass nearby.

Cade shoved the field glasses into a side pocket and pulled on his mask. He'd allowed himself twenty minutes for this neighborly visit. If he hadn't satisfied his curiosity about the unexpected proximity of their guest by then, he'd head back. No sense getting Jerome's nose any further out of joint than it already was. A better boss might have praised Cade's initiative. Jerome, however, in real physical agony after turning his ankle on an exposed tree root in their pursuit of Ellie, would only whine that Cade was neglecting his assignment and leaving more work for him and Lenny.

Cade slipped silently down the slope and, in a crouching run, made his way across to the wooden dock. Something about their white-haired neighbor, this Tony Costa, had bugged him ever since he heard the man speak. Cade still hadn't placed the voice, but he trusted his gut instinct that told him once he did make the connection, he wouldn't like it.

Besides, Winston Rademacher had supposedly chosen this particular tract of woods in northwest Connecticut specifically because it was remote. The summer-rental cabins and roadside motels had been abandoned after a new state-of-the art lodge and camping facility had drawn the tourists closer to Mohawk Mountain on the far side of the lake.

And Rademacher was no fool. The man not only had a plan for this kidnapping, but according to their conversation last night, he also had a backup plan. And despite how closemouthed the Armani-suited snob had been about his employer, he wasn't the kind of man who'd make a mistake like this.

Cade had watched his back long enough to know something was up. The coincidence of two of the old cabins being occupied wasn't impossible. That the two cabins being occupied were neighbors was too much coincidence for Cade to ignore.

His booted feet made no sound on the dock, and the gentle sound of water lapping against the stony shore was enough to cover the creak of the old, dry wood as he climbed down into the boat.

Besides needing answers, he needed some time alone. Time to figure out just where he'd made the mistake of taking a personal interest in Ellie Standish. The woman was trouble, just as he'd told her. Not because she'd chosen the wrong night to play dress-up and pretend she was a princess. Not because she had more backbone than any quiet mouse of a woman should.

She was trouble because she looked at him with those big blue eyes and made him wish he was something more than Bretford St. John's son. She was trouble because she'd never been touched by a man. She was sweet and pure and trusting, and she'd gotten the damn-fool notion in her head that he was the one who could teach her about passion.

Sure, he could teach her a thing or two. But not much. The woman was a natural. In her innocence, she'd held nothing back. And the delicious, body-hugging sensation of Eleanor Standish clinging to him as if she never wanted to let go had punched him right in the gut.

Or maybe it was the groin. He tried to excuse his little tenderhearted obsession before it got out of hand. Ellie was an enigma, that was all. The women he'd known had always been experienced. Every one had her own angle to play, whether her relationship with him had been business or pleasure. He'd played his angle, too. The work always came first. *Commitment* and *long-term* weren't in his vocabulary.

And Ellie? Hell, it seemed Ellie still believed in that kind of stuff. That should give him more than plenty of reason to run from wide-eyed comments like *You're a better man than this.*

Whatever the explanation, his fake princess was a distraction he couldn't afford. This job had gone sour long before he realized they had the wrong woman. If he wanted to survive this deal, he had best forget about her surprisingly sharp tongue and unexpectedly soft curves and concentrate on figuring out the puzzles surrounding this kidnapping, instead of the ones surrounding Ellie Standish.

Cade St. John didn't fail. And he wasn't about to let

hidden motivations or mysterious neighbors or virginal secretaries keep him from success.

So with nightfall and Ellie safely tucked into her basement sleeping bag, he'd slipped past Lenny's snoring form on the flowered couch and run through the woods for a quick inspection of Tony Costa's cabin.

He checked the boat from bow to stern. Nothing fancy. Probably a rental from one of the locals. The forty-horsepower outboard engine had seen better days, but appeared to be in good working order. He found a first-aid kit and flare gun in the cubby beneath the steering wheel. He pulled the tackle box from under one of the seats and opened it.

Plastic worms. Dozens of them. Either Costa knew a secret about the lake trout that the other fishermen would love to steal, or the guy knew beans about fishing. Cade picked up the lone box of hooks between gloved fingers. It had never been opened.

He replaced the box and inspected the fishing rod lying in the bottom of the boat. No hook on the line.

How did the man expect to catch anything?

Cade stowed everything where he had found it and turned his eye to the storm brewing in the sky above him. Static lightning flashed in the clouds to the west, matching the turbulence growing inside him. What self-respecting angler left his gear out in the elements?

Cade's misgivings blazed into outright suspicion.

Within the next two minutes he had circled the perimeter of the house and found a way in. This place was in better shape than the cabin they occupied, though the decor had a terminal case of 1970s avocado green. The refrigerator was well stocked, the indoor bathroom rust-stained but clean. The sofa bed's flocked upholstery was dated, but the sheets inside were fresh.

Nothing to give him a clue to the man's identity. No telephone numbers, no photographs, no ID. Not a damn thing.

Maybe the guy really was some celebrity just trying to escape the limelight. But Cade wasn't ready to buy that idea. He propped his hands on his hips and surveyed the studio-style cabin one more time.

A drumbeat of thunder rumbled overhead. When the first drops of rain hit the corrugated tin of the porch's roof, Cade found his answer. Enough of one, at least, to prick open every pore in his body and put his reflexes on wary alert.

It was the glint of metal peeking from inside the tissue box on the fake mantel above the space heater. Cade crossed the room and plucked the cylindrical steel tube from its hiding place. He rolled the small projectile between his fingers.

Like the others hidden inside the box, it was a high-powered rifle cartridge—7.5 mm. About the right size to fit an FR-F2 bolt-action rifle. A sniper's gun. Not uncommon in the Korosolan military.

Cade curled his fist around the deadly round of ammunition and swore. ''Don't tell me you're here to shoot the fish,'' he queried aloud in a whisper that got lost in the pounding staccato of the rain on the roof. Just what kind of prey did their white-haired neighbor have in mind?

He knew damn well that the only type of killing this size of firepower was used for was assassination.

Just like the mayor of Montavi two years ago. The loyal monarchist leader of southwestern Korosol's largest city had been taken out by a sniper's bullet like this one. Cade's gut tightened a painful notch as he remembered working behind the scenes on that mess. They'd traced the shooting back to the Korosolan Democratic Front. It was their last

act of rebellion before King Easton had negotiated a settlement and returned peace to his kingdom.

The KDF had turned over the shooter as part of the
agreement.

Or had they turned over a martyr, instead?

Who the hell was Tony Costa?

I' she okay? Cade replayed the man's voice in his head,
trying to connect that distinctly slurred, resonant tone with
a tangible memory. Tony Costa. The name just didn't gel.

Cade squeezed his eyes shut and tuned his hearing in-
ward to the memories of missions past. *Ge' me outta here.
Now.*

The knot in his gut twisted a bit tighter.

A voice on the radio. A routine retrieval job for his covert ops unit in Central America. Five men in. Six men out.
Only there'd been no one at the rendezvous site. Certainly
no snowy-haired man. Nothing.

Nothing but a few spent shells that indicated their pickup
had shot his own way out of trouble and left them stranded
in unfriendly territory. A gun for hire who'd mumbled his
words and disappeared without a trace. The wild-goose
chase had twisted his stomach into knots then. But he'd
gotten his men out. Not all in one piece, perhaps, but he'd
gotten them out.

His gut screamed at him now.

"Sonny."

The recognition hit him with all the finesse of a sledge-
hammer, but Cade was already at the door, about a mile
and a half away from where he needed to be. Now. Yesterday. Before a professional sharpshooter with the code
name Sonny found their house. And Ellie.

Or rather, Princess Lucia. What other target of any value
was camped out in the backwoods of northwest Connecticut?

Pocketing the rifle cartridge, Cade dashed out of the cabin into the night. The cool rain pelting his face couldn't erase the crawling sense of dread that warned him the white-haired fisherman armed to the teeth was all part of Winston Rademacher's self-proclaimed backup plan.

And that innocent Ellie Standish was about to pay the price for her kidnappers' mistakes.

THE PERVASIVE SOUND of the spring thunderstorm outside muffled the scrape of the bolt sliding out of the lock at the top of the stairs. But when the rectangle of light from above hit the wall in front of her, Ellie knew she had company. She quickly left the broken-down furnace where she'd worked her fingers raw trying to pry loose the old nameplate, and slipped down inside the sleeping bag. With her eyes open, she waited for her visitor to announce himself.

But whoever it was, he had stopped at the top of the stairs. He hovered like a ghost in the doorway, standing too far away for her to recognize his silhouette. She was a lump in the shadows, soundless herself unless she moved the chain. A chill crept along her skin, leaving goose bumps in its wake. Was somebody watching her?

"Hello?" she whispered, when the creepy, watchful silence had finally stretched her nerves to the limit. "Who's there?"

The ghost's smell reached her nose the instant before he spoke. Stale smoke and spilled beer.

"Hi, sugar. It's me." Something hard like a gavel clunked against the top step, and Ellie jumped in her skin. Jerome reeled into view, balancing himself on the walking stick he had carved from a sturdy tree branch and hopping down one step at a time in an awkward descent.

Oh, God. This wasn't good. Not good at all. Ellie's breath gathered in her chest, then whooshed out in a flare of uncontrolled panic. She scrambled to her feet and moved behind the stool, putting the only blockade available to her between them.

"What do you want?" she demanded, turning her fear into the sound of defiant anger.

Jerome's stick hit the concrete with the force of judgment as he stepped into the lantern's circle of light.

"You see what you did to me, sugar?"

She dropped her gaze from the bleary hatred in his eyes to his injured leg. His pant leg had been slit up past the knee and gaped open to reveal the purplish black swelling of skin above his wrapped ankle. The same discoloration extended to the swollen nubs of his toes.

Good, she thought, with a strengthening burst of irreverent satisfaction. Her escape attempt hadn't been all for naught. She'd taken a bit of retribution for the pain they'd caused her.

She'd also made one very dangerous enemy.

Ellie adjusted her glasses at her temples and tucked her hair behind her ears. Maybe she'd be smarter to try a less-confrontational survival strategy. Pulling her chin from its regal angle, she did what Ellie Standish did best. As loathsome as Jerome might be, she could see the man *was* in serious pain. And she was very good at taking care of people who were hurting.

"You really should have left your boot on," she suggested. "It would have helped control the swelling. As it is, you should keep that ankle elevated and pack it in ice. Do you have any ice upstairs? I could make an ice pack for you."

"I don't want any damn ice pack." He hobbled forward a step and Ellie flinched. Jerome spied the movement and laughed at her. It was a sick, slimy sound that coated her skin with a whole new set of chill bumps. "But I can think of other ways you can make it up to me."

He lurched forward, step after relentless step.

Ellie backed away. She could certainly outrun the man, but not with a cuff of stainless steel locked around her ankle.

Her gaze darted to the furnace. The tarnished brass nameplate still held fast, but she'd managed to bend up the first two letters. It'd be sharp enough to stab a man—if she could lure him close enough and shove him onto the jagged point.

"You're drunk." Her accusation drowned in the conscienceless pit of his eyes.

"It numbs the pain."

She'd walked herself to the end of the chain. Jerome hopped another step, but she dodged the clawing grasp of his fingers and edged closer to the furnace. He ran his tongue along the rim of his lips and straightened his leering smile into something grimly threatening before planting his stick and turning to follow her.

"My damn ankle could have busted. As it is, the sprain slows me down. But not so slow I can't catch you."

Instead of following her farther, he twisted the chain around the end of the stick and jerked, dragging Ellie several inches closer to him. She stumbled but stayed on her feet. He anchored the chain with the stick, keeping her within arm's reach.

Ellie put up her hands, but Jerome powered past her scratching grasp and wrapped his fingers around the loose waistband of her pants. When he yanked, she fell forward into his chest. Her nose hit a wall of smoky wool. She gasped in shock, sucking in the gagging scent of the man himself.

Caution and strategy flew out of her head as panic rushed

in. The canvas material of her pants caught and strained between her legs. He'd lifted her off her feet.

Ellie shoved hard. The instant her feet hit solid concrete again, she swung, smacking him across the face with such force that her palm went numb. As numb as the stunned expression on his puffy face.

"I swear to God, if you touch me, I'll hurt you."

While his cheeks paled, then flooded with splotchy color, Ellie realized his mask had vanished. The substitute chauffeur she'd once thought gallant wore a look of deadly intent now. She tried to scramble away when he released her, but knew she'd waited a split second too long.

His meaty hand connected with her cheek and knocked her to the floor. Ellie's yelp of pain got lost in the ringing dizziness in her skull. Her glasses sailed across the room into oblivion, and though she knew she was moving her jaw from side to side, she couldn't quite feel it. Her throbbing head echoed with the shrill sound of evil laughter.

And then he was on top of her. "Not before I hurt you. I don't want you to be easy, sugar. That's no fun." The heavy stick clattered to the floor beside her and the buttons on her shirt popped loose. Ellie screamed. She couldn't see his face, but she could feel his hands on her skin, crudely squeezing her breasts, then sliding down her stomach. "I've never done it with a princess before."

Somehow Ellie didn't think setting him straight on that score would matter right now.

Rage, pure and simple—from a woman who'd never experienced much beyond fear of failure—exploded inside her.

"You won't tonight, either."

Jerome's hands slipped inside her pants and she kicked. Savagely. Repeatedly. Until her foot connected with the swollen stump of his ankle. Jerome gave an unholy shriek and cursed her to hell. He crumpled into a ball to protect his leg, and Ellie rolled from beneath him. As she turned onto her stomach, she dove for the walking stick and came up swinging.

CADE LEFT LENNY to search for signs of Tony Costa when he heard Ellie's scream.

They didn't know the truth yet. They hadn't figured out that Ellie wasn't the real princess.

He'd been so focused on the enemy next door that he'd forgotten the one living right under his nose. "El—" He caught his mistake just in time. "Lucia!"

Flying down the stairs three at a time, Cade flashed on the image of meek and mild Ellie swinging something like a baseball bat over her head and bringing it down on the stooped form of Jerome's back. Her ripped shirt hung open. The red mark on her cheek bore the imprint of a man's open hand.

The picture was clear.

His reaction to it was not.

A primal, predatory need to defend Ellie against Jerome's vile attack surged through him, nearly overpowering his sense of reason. But Ellie herself gave him the impetus he needed to hold on to rational thought.

When she heard him behind her, she whirled around and swung at him. Cade twisted and deflected the blow with his shoulder. As he came back around, he snagged her wrist. He glimpsed the wild-eyed fury inside her that made her strong. But he was stronger. With a press and a spin, the stick was on the floor and she was wrapped tightly against him, her back to his chest. He pinned her arms to her sides and held on until the last of her adrenaline was spent.

She sagged against his forearms, her deep gasps for air

forcing him to loosen his hold. Steadying her with one arm cinched round her waist, he smoothed her hair and whispered some calming little nothings into her ear.

Jerome might be down, but he wasn't out for the count. "You bitch."

Cade jerked to attention, along with Ellie.

Jerome had managed to crawl to his feet. The lecherous bastard limped forward, his outstretched knife aimed right for Ellie's throat.

Cade shifted to the side and smashed Jerome's jaw beneath his fist, driving the brute to his knees. The satisfying crunch only whet his appetite to do more damage. But his point had been made. Jerome stayed down.

He waited for the wounded man to raise his face and meet the stark warning in Cade's eyes. "She's mine. You keep your hands off her. From here on out, until this job is done, you'll have to go through me to get to her."

Jerome slid his toadlike gaze to Ellie. Cade felt the subtle shift in her posture, moving closer. He obliged her by spreading his fingers with a possessive claim at her hip.

Jerome noted that claim, too, before lifting his beady eyes to Cade. "Don't tempt me, Sinjun."

Cade ignored the insult and the threat.

Only after Jerome had dragged himself halfway up the stairs did Cade speak directly to Ellie. "I'm sorry."

He kept Smython in his sights, but turned her to remove the ruined shirt and toss it aside. Huddled in the oversized pants and strapless, black lace bra, she made a tempting, vulnerable sight. One that was way too dangerous for his newly awakened conscience. His mind should be on business, but something else seemed to be directing his thoughts now. He saw no other injuries but the mark on her face and breathed a sigh of untold relief.

"You got the best of him, didn't you." Maybe a bit of

praise and a smile would get a response out of her. He pulled off his mask and tossed it aside. There was no need for pretense with Jerome out of sight. Cade stripped off his shirt and slipped it over her head. With a little help, he pulled her arms into the sleeves and got her covered. The cotton knit stretched and hung past the tips of her fingers. "I'm sorry it's wet. I'll find something else for you."

Still no answer.

"Ellie." He whispered her name, trying to reach her.

The shy stuff he could handle. When she didn't know what to say, wasn't sure how to say it, he could tease her along or wait her out until she opened up or her temper betrayed her. He was even getting used to that arrogant lilt in her voice when she tried to cover up her fears by faking more confidence than she felt.

But choosing to be silent. Shutting him out. How did he breach that?

And why the hell did it matter so much to him that she wouldn't even nail him with one of those holier-than-thou looks?

Finally, after hearing Jerome collapse on the sofa on the floor above them, Cade accepted the blame where he felt it was due. "I screwed up. I'm sorry I wasn't here to protect you."

He thought of Jerome. He thought of Tony Costa. He thought of their anonymous employer who was willing to sacrifice this woman to the whims of such men.

He didn't have much of a reputation to brag about himself. His one claim to fame had been his career as a soldier. But he wanted to be a better man. Better than his father. Better than the legacy his father had left him. He wanted to see respect when he looked into people's eyes.

He wanted to see it in Ellie's.

"I won't let anyone else hurt you."

The promise echoed off the concrete walls and resonated in the recesses of his empty soul. It was only half a promise, really. He could protect her physically—with his life, if necessary.

But he could sense that he'd already made inroads into destroying her trust. By signing on as her kidnapper, no matter what else happened, he'd already done damage to her innocent heart.

Ellie's shoulders rose with a quiet sigh and settled at a tougher, more defensive angle. Hugging herself, she slowly turned and lifted those big blue eyes to him. Cade could see how quickly this whole experience was dulling the dewy sparkle in those cerulean depths and making her wise to the wicked ways of the world.

He braced himself for the certain kick in the teeth his conscience was about to get.

"So who's going to protect me from you?"

"DA-DUM. DA-DUM. Da-dum, dum, dum."

Cade almost didn't hear the sound over the percussion of fading thunder and steady rain falling outside. It was a soothing kind of storm, the kind he'd liked to sleep through as a child because it quieted the world and shut out the sounds of his parents' arguments over money. As a professional soldier, he'd liked nights like this because they kept the enemy curled up in bed, too.

With any luck, the rain would keep Tony Costa tucked away in his cabin for the night. Lenny had gone over and reported seeing Costa drive up in his truck. So "Sonny" hadn't gone looking for Ellie. Yet. With any luck, he never would.

Of course, luck hadn't exactly been running Cade's way lately.

"Da-dum. Da-dum."

He paused at the top of the basement stairs and listened to the soft, melodic humming, interrupted every odd beat or so by the discordant clank of the chain.

He was quickly learning to expect the unexpected from Ellie. On first impression, she seemed quiet, docile. Mousy, even. She'd been easy enough to overlook in the outside world.

But now he didn't think he could ever *not* notice her.

His raw cheekbone reminded him that she packed a punch and had the heart of a lion. Shy didn't mean weak, he'd learned. Quiet didn't guarantee cooperation. There was always something going on in that woman's head—planning, dreaming, learning. And she could say the damnedest things when she worked up her nerve.

So who's going to protect me from you?

Hell. He was the one who was losing his whole perspective on this job. As surprising and troublesome as her efforts had been, at least Ellie understood what she needed to do. Survive. Escape. Curb her libido and tenderhearted urges and be tough. *Sheesh.* Arm her with a baseball bat and she'd be unstoppable.

Cade, on the other hand, had lost his focus. This job should have been about learning the identity of who had really hired them. It should have been about getting out of this mess of bullies and hit men and altered time frames with his skull intact.

It shouldn't be about Ellie.

But it was.

He didn't want her to be afraid of him. Not as a threat to her life or safety. Not as a man who desired her.

Yet she was smart enough to be afraid.

And it was killing him.

"Dum, dum. Da-dum, da-dum."

What was she up to?

The evening storm drowned out the sound of Cade's descent. At the bottom, he could only stop and stare.

This was a new one.

Ellie was dancing.

As much as the chain draped over her left arm would allow.

She had her eyes closed, her face tipped up toward an invisible partner. She skimmed around a small circle, three steps with each turn. His black knit shirt draped like a midnight waterfall over her rich, feminine curves, and hung down to where it kissed the tops of her thighs. She was barefoot now, and she danced the old-fashioned waltz with the grace and elegance of an era long past.

Cade's hormones stirred at the vision Ellie made. Other things stirred closer to his heart, but the only emotion he could readily identify was envy.

Heroes and happy endings. Either it was a testament to the human spirit that the threat of death, failed escape attempts and attempted rape hadn't crushed her, or the woman was a fool.

Maybe *he* was the fool to just stand there and listen to her sweet voice and watch her dreamy expression and sway with the movement of her lush body. The fool for wishing he could take pleasure in something as simple as a waltz.

When he realized he'd stepped off with his left foot to join the dance, Cade caught himself up short. His life had evolved beyond simple pleasures long ago. She wouldn't appreciate his intrusion and he couldn't afford to drop his guard and be sidetracked by her tempting innocence again.

"What are you doing?" he asked, carefully pushing the edgy agitation he felt behind an indulgent smile and teasing voice.

Ellie stopped midstride. Above the bruise on her cheek,

her lake-blue eyes shot open wide. Either he'd shocked the hell out of her, or her acting skills were improving.

"I didn't hear you." Her gaze dropped to the floor and swung to the sleeping bag.

"Obviously." He nodded toward the bag. "Hiding any sharp objects in there I should know about?"

"No."

She knelt beside the bag and unzipped it. Then she flipped it open for him to see there was nothing inside. With her head still bowed she still managed to turn and lift that wide-eyed gaze to his. Asking for what? Trust? Approval? A promise that not he nor any other man would ever touch her again?

He hated seeing that submission in her eyes. Hated that he had the power to transform the serene smile she'd worn a moment ago into that vulnerable expression that put creases beside her mouth.

Cade solved the problem by looking away. He'd brought down a seat cushion from the flowered couch upstairs to use as a pillow. He tossed it against the wall and watched it tip over before letting his gaze drift back to the sight of her ripe, round bottom bouncing up and down as she crawled across the sleeping bag, closing it up and smoothing out the wrinkles.

With any other woman he would have suspected the sexy swish was some sort of seduction, a ploy to divert him from his purpose and get him thinking about the interested heat pooling around his groin, instead. But with Ellie? None of his experience with women had prepared him for the unpredictability of Ellie Standish.

He plowed his fingers through his hair and rubbed the tense muscles at the back of his neck. It seemed that guilt was giving him a constant headache. Maybe she wasn't up to anything. Maybe she was just grateful he'd taken over all baby-sitting duties, sparing her Jerome or Lenny. And maybe he was just too tired to think straight anymore.

"What's the pillow for?" she asked, settling down into a cross-legged position on the sleeping bag and pulling the blanket over her lap.

"We're going to be roommates, so I thought I'd make myself comfortable."

"You're sleeping down here tonight? Surely you're not worried that I'm going to break this chain and disappear into the night before you can get your money's worth out of me."

The flare of sarcasm at the end of her protest eased his conscience a fraction. At least she was talking to him now. She might be subdued, but she wasn't down for the count.

With that show of spirit, he gave himself permission to look right at her. He even summoned an amused grin. "After what I've seen, I wouldn't put anything past you."

She ducked her head to hide it, but that tossed-off little compliment had made her smile, too. For a moment Cade almost felt like one of those heroes she believed in. Almost.

"It's not five-star, but I thought you'd appreciate some real food for a change." From his pockets he pulled out fruit and a bag of pretzels and set them on the stool beside her.

She made no move to accept his gifts. "Where's Jerome?"

"Upstairs. Asleep. Lenny's on patrol outside." He pulled a candy bar from the pocket of the black T-shirt he wore and held it out like a peace offering, understanding that she, too, was reluctant to drop her guard. "You're safe."

She had a long way to go from sneaking a smile at a goofy comment he'd made to trusting him enough to believe in him.

When she finally wrapped her fingers around the candy

bar, Cade held on to the other end, binding them together and forcing her to look up and read the message in his eyes. Willing her to see that, despite all that had happened—all that had yet to happen—he refused to let any more harm come to her. He couldn't tell her the words, but he could say it with his eyes.

But she didn't understand the message. When that pretty face frowned in confusion, Cade surrendered the chocolate. He should give up trying to make any kind of connection with her and just see this mess through until the end and pray that he walked away from it in one piece.

She nibbled at the chocolate and caramel, closing her eyes and savoring the flavor with an *Mmm* of approval. "Something with taste. Thank you."

When she smiled her gratitude, Cade worried he'd just made another tactical mistake. He was getting hooked on that rush of unfiltered pleasure that lightened his mood each time he made Ellie smile.

"You're welcome."

He grabbed a handful of pretzels and sat on the bottom step to enjoy the rainy-evening picnic with her. It was a ridiculous feeling, really, this sense of camaraderie he felt with her. It was almost cleansing—healing, in a way—to spend time with a woman who was completely oblivious to her charms and talents. A woman who didn't play games—who probably didn't even know what games were out there to play. When she was happy, she smiled. She called a rogue a rogue and demanded that she be treated fairly and nothing more.

She was all curves and softness, from the silky curls of her hair to the fullness of her breasts and hips. He couldn't connect the colorless wallflower he'd known her to be in the outside world with this sensuous ingenue who made the blood surge through his veins just by popping her fingers into her mouth one at a time and licking the melted goo off the tips.

When she picked up an orange and began stripping off the peel to reach the naked fruit, Cade drew in a shuddering breath. He had to keep talking before he completely forgot his reason for keeping Ellie prisoner in the first place.

"Why were you dancing earlier?" he asked.

Her cheeks blanched, then flooded with embarrassment, intriguing him with the secrets hidden inside that pretty head. "It was a silly daydream, that's all."

"A way to escape from all this?"

"It's the reason I'm here in the first place." He waited for her to explain. She lifted her shoulders in an expressive shrug. "All I wanted was one stupid dance. To dress up and go to the ball. Like some modern-day Cinderella. Only, instead of my carriage turning into a pumpkin, I ended up here. Jerome and Lenny are the evil stepsisters, and you..." How did he fit into her skewed fantasy world? She shook her head, editing his role from her story, and went back to peeling her orange. "It seems ironic that I never got that dance."

Cade popped an orange section into his mouth, but tasted nothing but his own bitterness. "Life isn't much of a fairy tale, is it."

"No. Cinderella found Prince Charming and lived happily ever after. There are no princes in my life. And by this time tomorrow, I'll be dead."

Chapter Seven

"Yeah, I'll accept the charges." He shoved the empty pizza carton off a chair and sat.

He'd been so young before that call.

"Dad? What are you doing calling in the middle of the week? Is everything all right?"

Bretford St. John's voice was deep and smooth as always. "I wanted to check how you were doing."

Should he be worried? They'd just talked on Sunday.

"I'm fine, Dad. We're up late studying for midterms." Okay, so technically he and his roommate had been playing chess, but his father had never had ESP before, and he'd certainly never been a fanatic about whether Cade stayed on task or not. "What's up?"

"I just—" His father stopped suddenly. Cade sat up at attention in his chair. His father was never at a loss for words. "I just wanted to apologize for spending your trust fund."

That was old news. The money had been gone for two years. That was why Cade was at a state-run university and not a private one. This was too weird. "Dad, what's going on?"

Cade twisted in his sleep. He hadn't had the dream for a long time. He didn't want to have it now.

The house was quiet. Too quiet.

Cade set his backpack down in the foyer and flipped on the light. He squinted against the sudden glare of the chandelier reflected in the black and white marble tiles on the floor. Without any furniture or curtains to soften the bright light, the house felt cold and unwelcoming.

"Dad?" Cade had never walked into the house before without someone there to greet him. Where was the housekeeper? He knew the other servants had been let go one by one over the past year, but Mrs. Breen should have been there. She'd always been there for his family. "Dad? Mrs. Breen?"

He'd skipped his last two midterms and boarded the train that morning after his father's chatty phone call, worried Bretford had gone on another gambling binge. The problem was there was nothing left to wager. Nothing in the bank. No land left to sell. The house itself was waiting for the new owners to settle their affairs and move in.

"Dad?"

Something like sheer panic rattled through his young, lanky frame. He needed to find his father. Now. The man needed help. And Cade was it. He was all his father had left.

The worry that had brought him home exploded into outright fear. Cade ran from room to room. A cold sweat broke out on his back and upper lip. "Dad?"

Not in the bedroom. Not in the kitchen. Not in the living room. Not in the conservatory he loved so well.

Every room was empty. Sterile. Bleak. Cold.

"Dad!"

He stopped outside the door to his father's study—the room where Bretford St. John had juggled multimillion-dollar real-estate deals and signed his divorce papers and placed stupid bets and wrestled with his little boy on the imported Persian carpet, much to his housekeeper's chagrin.

Cade took a deep, shuddering breath and opened the door.

The carpet was gone, sold long ago to pay overdue utilities or some such thing. The books were gone from the shelves, donated to a local library to help defray taxes. The only furniture in the room was the antique Chippendale desk and matching chair.

For a moment in time, Cade looked to the desk and smiled with a relief so profound he nearly fainted.

No. Cade fought the feeling in his sleep. It was all a setup. This wasn't right. He knew what was coming and he couldn't stop the pain from barreling into him and showing no mercy.

His father was asleep at his desk. Cade stepped into the room. "I'm too young for a heart attack, Dad. You really ought to..."

Cade would never be young again.

"Dad?" His lungs abruptly refused to work right. "Dad!"

He ran to the desk. He reached out to touch, but pulled back. He wanted to pick up the note. But all the blood. There was too much blood.

He sank to his knees. Shock and horror racked his nineteen-year-old body. The grief would come later. Years later. But for now he was cold. So cold. Too damn cold to ever feel warm again.

Cade wrestled his demon to the floor of his father's study and fought to wake himself from its chilling grip.

"Cade?"

In the predawn hours of the morning, after the rain had ceased and the earliest of the birds had started to chirp at the sunrise, the soft voice called to him.

The demon clawed at him, but the will to survive was stronger.

"Cade? Wake up."

He reached for the voice. He reached for salvation.

Before he awoke to the scrape of metal on concrete, before he felt the weight on his chest, he knew she was there.

He struck before Ellie could even register surprise. He snagged her by the wrist and pulled her down to the floor beneath him.

"Ow!"

"What trick do you have up your sleeve this time?"

He pried open one hand. Nothing. The other clutched a fistful of wool.

Cade froze. His body went still. His blood ran cold.

This wasn't any demon. This wasn't another sneak attack, unless covering a man with a blanket could be termed a life-threatening act.

As quickly as he had pinned her, Cade rolled off her. He sat up and pulled her into his lap. "What are you doing, Ellie?"

He massaged her wrist between both of his hands, knowing he had temporarily pinched off the feeling there.

"You looked cold. You were shaking."

He shook his head at her naive consideration of her enemy. "I've slept through a lot worse than a hard floor and no blanket."

He moved his massage to her hand, alarmed at the clammy chill he felt on her skin there. He stroked his thumbs across the silky smoothness at the back of her knuckles, then drew them along the length of her fingers.

"Like what?"

The cold was still with him. The demon still laughed in the recesses of his mind.

But what could Ellie Standish know about demons?

"Like you don't need to know." He turned her hand over and moved his attention to the supple skin of her palm, refusing to acknowledge the persistent chill inside him.

"When you were a soldier?" she asked. "Is that what you were dreaming about just now? It looked horrible."

"Yeah." That was as good a story to go with as any. Lord knew he'd seen enough hell on the battlefield and in covert ops to give most men nightmares.

Desert bunkers where rats and scorpions dropped in to spend the night would be nightmare enough for a sheltered innocent like Ellie. She didn't need to know any of the gory details of the scene that truly haunted him. "A damp basement with you feels like class-A luxury compared to a lot of the places I've been."

Cade looked up, thinking he might make her laugh and steer her away from whatever concerns had drawn her to his side in the first place.

But there was no laugh this time. No hint of a smile.

Ellie's big eyes had turned into sorrowful pools of tender pity. She looked at him as if the pain he'd endured had been broadcast across his face, as if his pain mattered to her.

"You're still shivering." The compassion in her voice cut through his carefully shielded *don't care* armor with laserlike precision.

Cade frowned and looked away, wishing that insidious need to connect with Ellie would just go away. *She* was the victim here. She had no business offering him any kind of comfort, be it a blanket or sympathy or the naive goodness in her untried heart he craved.

"Move your fingers for me," he ordered before she could say anything else to add to his guilt.

Dutifully, she waved her fingers, showing that he hadn't inflicted any permanent damage. "You didn't hurt me."

"Of course I did." He caught her hand and pressed it to his chest, holding it flush over his heart with his right hand and gently kneading and poking and prodding his way up to her elbow with his left. "Are you hurt anywhere else?"

"No."

He slid his fingertips across her cheek and traced the cool skin up to the goose egg that marred the classic line of her cheekbone. She flinched beneath his probing touch and Cade shook his head, feeling only about a half step higher on the evolutionary ladder than lowlife Jerome. "I should have brought an ice pack for that. You're damn lucky he didn't break your jaw or something worse."

"Don't you want to talk about what happened?"

He returned his attention to the inside of her wrist, ignoring her request and keeping himself in the present moment with her. If he hadn't known it was her and held back, if he'd simply reacted to the threat that had disturbed his sleep, he could have snapped her arm in two. As it was, he'd left a red mark that would eventually turn into a bruise.

Without thinking, without having a sufficient means to apologize, he bent his head and pressed a kiss to the spot.

Her pulse was warm beneath his lips. It beat an erratic tattoo as he followed the path of heat up to her palm and lingered to taste the tart sweetness of the juice from the orange that had dried on her hand.

"Cade."

When she said his name on that husky catch of breath, something awoke inside him. His good intentions fled in the wake of the bristly awareness that sensitized every pore in his body, making him hyperalert to the delectable weight of Ellie nestled on his thighs. The delicate pressure of her hand imprinting his chest. The lure of her mouth mere inches from his when he turned to face her.

"What are you doing to me, Ellie?" From the depths of those big blue eyes he saw the healing warmth that eluded him.

He'd known women who had set his body on fire. Women who could distract him from his own private hell for a few moments or maybe a few nights at a time. Women who could make him forget.

But no woman had ever made him want to remember.

No one had ever reached inside his soul, into that frozen well of jaded mistrust and guilt and forgotten dreams, and made him believe he had a purpose in this world. No one until this pure-of-heart virgin had ever tempted him to believe in much of anything again.

He had no explanation for the turmoil inside him, but Ellie did. "It's your instinct to protect. Not to hurt me. I think deep-down inside somewhere, you're a good man. Why do you fight your instincts?"

He didn't pause to interpret the meaning of her words. He only understood that in her hushed, steady tone she was granting him permission to be something more than the man she thought him to be. Something more like the man he wanted to be.

"I'll show you instincts." He breathed the words against her lips before sealing her mouth with a kiss.

At first it was nothing more than a gentle press of lips, a chance to reacquaint himself with the shape and texture of her mouth that sat heart-stutteringly still beneath his.

"Is this okay?" he asked, knowing he'd stop if she pushed him away.

The damn fool nodded, instead of saying no.

Cade tunneled his free hand into the silky fall of her hair. He bunched the toffee-brown cascade of it in his palm, then let it slide through his fingers. The curls were a rich candy that drew his lips to her temple. He nuzzled his nose there, breathing in the faint scent that was uniquely hers.

"Such pretty hair," he said. "Such soft, pretty hair."

He let go of her hand at his chest and feathered all ten fingers through her hair, cupping the elegant shape of her head and bringing her mouth back to his, seeking her heat. She kissed with her eyes open, her curious gaze darting from his lips to his eyes. She was boldly studying him, asking a silent question as she tilted her nose first one way, then the other.

But the question wasn't *why?* It was *how?* He could taste it in the nervous flutter of her orange-stained lips, feel it in the sway of her shoulders, moving in, pulling away.

Cade retreated a bit, framed her jaw between his hands. He smiled, as gently as his unshaven, weatherbeaten face would allow. He felt the puff of her nervous breath against his cheek as he stroked his thumbs along the pliant curve of her bottom lip.

"Open your mouth for me."

Her pulse quickened beneath his fingertips, keeping time with his. He dipped the pad of his thumb between her parted lips, stroked it across the softness inside, then smoothed her own taste across her lips. Her blue eyes darkened at the provocative touch. He liked how she watched him, as if she wanted to learn everything he could teach her, as if she didn't want to miss a thing. Neither did he.

Cade put his lips where his thumb had been, tracing the same path with his tongue, then slipping inside her mouth. He took a little bit for his hungry soul, gave a little more. He waited for her to touch her tongue to his, then twirled his around hers. The rhythm of his breathing got mixed up in the gaspy, guttural sounds that came from her throat. He kissed her again and again, losing himself in the slow, seductive heat of this shy-bold woman.

Finding himself in her embrace.

Ellie's response was like the sweet and tart taste of her late-night snack on her lips. She was gentle, hesitant, unsure with each new foray of his mouth and tongue. But then she'd lean into him, lift herself into his kiss, do the same delicious things back to him and insist on learning more.

"Cade?"

Her hands fisted against his chest but didn't push him away. They batted back and forth in the distance between them, looking for something to hold on to, afraid to hold on to anything. Ellie trembled in his lap, and her frustration joined the fever that burned along his thighs.

He longed to feel her body dissolve into his the way she had at the lake. He longed to know the exquisite sensation of those breasts pillowed against his chest.

"It's okay to touch me." He breathed the words at the corner of her mouth, assuring her welcome and begging her exploration at the same time. "However you want to. I won't break."

Oh, but he might just explode from the sweet heat of her curious hands. A slight brush here, a needy tug there, and he was on fire. She ran her hands across his chest, discovered a taut nipple with a flick of her thumb. At his involuntarily hiss of breath, she hesitated. With a kiss he reassured her that the zap of electricity that had pulsed through him had been pure pleasure, not pain. A quick student, she found the nipple and teased it again.

Class was in session.

Her fingers ran along his shoulders, then across the stubble on his neck and jaw. She repeated the caress, pressing harder, moaning low in her throat as she reveled in a sensation that gave her particular delight.

Cade took the cue from her and did some exploration of

his own. He slid his hands under her shirt, stroking the cool, smooth skin of her stomach, cupping the generous flare of her hips, skimming along the strong arch of her spine. She trembled beneath his fingertips at every touch, fueling his need to learn more about his willing pupil.

He spread his legs so that she slid between them. Then he scooted closer, pulling her to him until he could feel the straining peaks of her luscious breasts branding him through his shirt, making him ache to move faster, to complete her education and expand his own.

Her arms circled his neck as he lifted her, all the while teaching her with his mouth and his hands. All the while feasting on her willing lips.

He laid her gently on the floor and followed her down, lying half on top, half beside her. He unhooked the buttons on the black shirt and then reached for the hem. A drumroll of excitement pounded through his veins as he pushed the shirt up her torso, revealing her figure inch by tantalizing inch. Beneath the man-size, functional cotton, he feasted his eyes on the divinely feminine contrast of her black bra, embroidered with twisting lace vines and adorned with a tiny silk bow between her breasts.

Pulling the shirt off over her head and tossing it aside, he began the next lesson in how to drive himself mad. With just the tip of his finger, he traced each curlicue in the pattern of black lace over her left breast, working his way closer and closer to the straining peak.

Her eyes locked onto his as he watched with helpless fascination each rise and fall of her chest, as her breaths came quick and shallow. The skin above the soft globes turned pink with just a look, just a wish.

He kissed the bow nestled in the hollow between those two glorious mounds. "Beautiful," he whispered, barely able to speak. "I never knew you were so beautiful."

When he palmed a breast, she cried out. Their legs tangled together, and when she squeezed her thighs convulsively around his, he groaned against her mouth and held himself still, fighting the inferno that threatened to overtake him.

"Ellie." That croaky voice was reason trying to assert itself over instinct, compassion trying to be heard above the passion pounding in his veins.

He raised his head and looked down at her flushed skin and swollen lips. Her big blue eyes were lakes of liquid desire, untutored, uncensored—all his. If he wanted.

That was the problem.

He wanted to kiss her. Wanted to touch her. Wanted to be inside her. He desperately wanted to get Ellie Standish out of his system. But every kiss, every touch only made him want more.

And he couldn't do that to her. He was taking advantage of a very tricky situation. He was a man of the world; she was an innocent. He was her jailor; she was his prisoner. He knew exactly where this was going, and she was just learning to enjoy the ride.

He focused on his breathing, tying to slow things down. In. Out. In. Out. But the breathing only made him think of other things, things he could not, should not, would not do to this woman.

"You're so sweet, Ellie." He allowed himself one more kiss. "You make me crazy." One more touch couldn't hurt. "I want to go slow. I don't want to scare you."

He didn't want her to think this was the same kind of retribution Jerome had been after. He wanted—no, he needed—Ellie to want him. To accept him.

To forgive him.

He skimmed his hand down past her waist, seeking something besides bare, soft, tempting skin to hold on to.

She was breathing so hard her breasts kept rising and caressing him with each inhalation. He needed to move farther away or he'd be lost. He let his hand linger with possessive satisfaction on her hip.

But instead of cupping softness, he felt a sharp, hard corner. Instead of woman, he felt a cardboard rectangle in her pocket.

His innocent hostage had deceived him once again.

"Where the hell did you get this?"

She didn't realize she'd been found out until he slipped his fingers into her pocket and pulled out a slim black notebook. She must have picked his pocket sometime before covering him with the blanket. Maybe right before. Maybe this whole teach-me-to-make-love schtick was just an elaborate distraction to keep him from noticing that Lenny's book was missing.

Cade shook his head and swore. He'd fallen for the oldest decoy in the book—a sexy, irresistible woman.

Ellie snatched at his wrist when he pulled the book out, but she was no match for his strength. Anger gave him a quick shot of adrenaline, clearing his head.

"I'll never learn a damn thing with you, will I?" he accused, blaming her for far more than a stolen notebook. He still hovered over her supine figure, pinning her in place before she could summon the strength to struggle.

Their passion cooled like unfinished dessert. But as Cade swelled with his anger, Ellie retreated into herself. She hugged her arms over her chest in a defensive shield and shook her head slowly from side to side. "I can't believe I let you kiss me."

"You kissed me back, Princess."

"You started it!"

"You said yes!" His lips curled into a tight-lipped smile that felt as raw as the rest of his sensitized, unsatisfied body. "I can't believe I bought that whole tenderhearted-virgin routine."

She shoved at his chest and Cade gladly moved away from her and this condemning conversation. She rolled onto her side and sat up, facing away from him, snatching up the shirt to cover herself and rubbing her mouth with the back of her hand as if she wanted to wipe away the touch and taste of him from her body. "I don't do things like that. I've never let a man touch me like that before."

Cade stood and plowed his fingers through his hair. He could still feel the pull of her body, feel the wrench of her innocence inside his jaded heart. "I could tell."

"You...?" Her cheeks flushed crimson, then faded to cold, pale porcelain. She pulled her knees to her chest and hugged her arms around her legs. "I was that awful?"

Even Cade wasn't that cruel. "No, Ellie. That's the problem." He flashed the notebook in front of her face. Nightmares and salvation were forgotten in the face of their present reality. "Remember where you are, and who I am, and what's going to happen if you don't start cooperating."

Instead of showing fear, she tilted her chin at an indignant angle and rose to challenge him. "I didn't know stealing from a thief was a crime. Does Lenny know you have that?"

"Don't you get it?" Cade wrapped his fingers around her upper arm and gave her a warning shake. "You keep pulling crap like this, and I can't give you any privileges. No chocolate. No outhouse—"

"There's only one privilege I'm interested in."

Freedom. It was there, written on her face as clearly as the promise to deny that request was etched on his.

Ellie pushed up her glasses on her nose and turned away. She buttoned the shirt up to the neck, as if that prim defense would keep him from remembering the tempting treasures that lay underneath. "I thought the book might be something important I could use to barter for my freedom. I don't know why you're so worked up over a bunch of shorthand and symbols, anyway."

The petulant defeat in her flat voice and downturned face made him reach out. He lingered above the crown of her head, longing to touch those silky locks just one more time. She must have sensed his presence. Ellie jerked away, crossed to the far side of the stool and curled into another touch-me-not posture.

Cade sucked in a lungful of damp, dusty air and knew he'd need a lot more than fresh oxygen to work Ellie out of his system. He walked a fine line with his conscience already. Tonight, feeling her in his arms, tasting her, erasing Jerome's foul imprint from her body and claiming it for his own, he knew he'd crossed that line.

Nothing like complicating an already impossible mission.

He jammed the notebook back into his pocket and crossed the room. Thank God she hadn't gone for his gun or knife, or he'd be a dead man. Or more likely, with his instinctive reflexes, he'd be without a hostage.

The chain rattled on the concrete behind him as Ellie crawled into the sleeping bag. His stomach knotted at the desolate sound. If he was in Ellie's place, he'd have done the very same thing.

His anger seeped out on a resigned sigh. He had to admire the hell out of a woman who had the guts to do whatever it took to survive. "You can blame me for taking advantage if it'll soothe that virginal outrage of yours."

Ellie said nothing. Agreed to nothing. Forgave nothing.

It would have been easier on his ego if she'd admit she'd really wanted his kiss. That she hadn't simply endured his touch in order to hide an ulterior motive. Or worse, because she pitied the grown man who couldn't shake the nightmares of his past.

But then, he already carried a truckload of guilt on his conscience. Why not pile on a few bricks more?

"THE NECKLACE WAS most persuasive. Easton's agreed to the ransom. I'll call him later to make arrangements for the exchange tonight." Winston Rademacher glanced into the side-view mirror of his rented SUV and adjusted his Italian-silk tie. "I'll set up something in one of the towns nearby. Goshen or Milton, perhaps."

Cade tossed another log into the fire pit where he was heating water for a shave and a bath. He needed to clean Ellie's scent off his skin and regain some objectivity to focus on this job. Rademacher hadn't even wanted to venture into the ratty house today, preferring to stay near the more luxurious appointments of the vehicle. Cade brushed the dirt off his hands and walked over to where Jerome and Lenny were talking to him.

"I thought we were driving back into the city for the exchange." Cade challenged the latest alteration in their original plan.

"I remind you, Your Grace..." The snide mockery Winston gave the title screeched along Cade's nerve-endings like nails against a chalkboard. But because he still needed information from Winston, he let the dig slide, unchallenged, into that unmarked pit where his soul had once resided. "You're merely the hired muscle in this endeavor. I'll do the thinking and you'll do the following of the orders. Otherwise, that money your father owes me will have to come out of your pocket."

Jerome snickered at the insult from his perch on a stump, not realizing he was nothing more than hired help to Rademacher, either. "He's got your number, Sinjun."

Cade let Jerome wallow in his own ignorance for now. He fisted his hands at his sides, conquering the urge to ram one of them down Rademacher's throat. Not because he minded paying a rightful debt, but because the man never let the old news die.

Rademacher laughed out loud. "We all know the measly sort of income a soldier-turned-public-servant like you makes, don't we? Believe me, your special skills are more valuable than your earnings or your title. A smart man capitalizes on his assets. He doesn't play up his weaknesses. Of course, your father never learned that lesson, either, did he?"

"Enjoy your potshots while you can, Rademacher. If this job goes any further south on us, I'm bailing. Then I'll come after you personally and put my *special skills* to work on you."

"Hey, for once I agree with the pretty boy," Jerome chimed in, puffing a cloud of smoke. He injected his incessant whine into the conversation. "That princess has been nothing but trouble. I say we cut our losses, cut her and get the hell out of the country."

Winston's long nose wrinkled in distaste, whether at Jerome's stench or his opinion was impossible to discern. He flashed those dark, enigmatic eyes at the crippled team leader. "Cutting people seems to be your answer for everything, Mr. Smython. I trust Princess Lucia hasn't been harmed at the expense of your temper?"

Jerome's beady little eyes darted to Cade. He still wasn't thrilled with his possessive claim of their prisoner. Fireman wanted old-fashioned justice, inflicting pain to pay for his pain. Cade crossed his arms over his chest and braced his feet apart, readying for a fight, reminding Jerome he was ready to inflict a little pain of his own if he should get out of line with Ellie again.

Jerome might not like it, but he got the message. He ground his cigarette beneath the boot of his good foot and looked at Rademacher. "She has a full-time bodyguard now."

"I see." Winston's disgust lightened to curiosity as he glanced back at Cade. "So you've taken a personal interest in this job. Is that why you're so eager to bail before you've seen the rest of your money? Put your noble aspirations aside, Sinjun. I promise you, a woman of the princess's stature won't have a thing to do with a man like you. No money. No honor. A worthless title. You're fooling yourself if you think otherwise."

Cade had no false notions about being good enough for a woman like Ellie, either. She didn't need a royal title to stand above him in both class and reputation.

"I don't plan to marry the woman," he answered honestly. And despite her eagerness to learn more about having a relationship with a man, he didn't think she'd settle for anything less than a ring on her finger. He didn't want her to.

He could teach her a thing or two about sex, if she was willing. Yeah. He'd enjoy doing that. But someone else would have to teach her about love and happy endings. He'd never believed in them himself.

Though somehow, the idea of another man teaching Ellie anything was about as appealing as the idea of Jerome putting his hands on her again. Dismissing that faintly unsettled feeling as a couple of territorial hormones still running their course, Cade turned his attention back to attacking Winston's snobbish amusement.

"I thought the goal was to return Princess Lucia in one piece. The way things are going, I didn't think we could guarantee that unless I kept her away from Romeo there."

Rademacher's nostrils flared with a deep breath. His thin

lips parted to release the air, looking for all the world as if this conversation over the hostage's welfare suddenly bored him.

He swung his gaze to Lenny, who stood quietly back from their meeting, leaning against the trunk of an equally indomitable oak tree. "Mr. Gratfield, you're in agreement with the idea of abandoning this project?"

Lenny rubbed his hand along his jaw, giving the question consideration before speaking. "Things haven't gone as smoothly as I would have liked. The girl got away from us yesterday morning."

"Got away?"

Lenny nodded. "Sinjun ran her down. I brought Jerome back here to fix his leg. Did you know we have a neighbor about a mile and a half up the road?"

Winston's squinty eyes narrowed an impossible fraction without closing. "What are you talking about?"

"She ran to the neighbor's. An old fisherman was there."

"Did she talk to him?"

Cade answered that one. "No. Nothing that made any sense, at least."

Winston adjusted a cuff link on the crisp French cuff of his sleeve. Was that a sign of nervous energy? Cade wondered. Did this man who claimed to be an expert at "connecting" the right people have connections with a hit man? Or was the sudden, subtle activity an indication that he, too, was worried about the unexpected development? "Did this fisherman recognize her?"

"Why don't you tell us?" Cade challenged.

"I beg your pardon?"

"The fisherman said his name is Tony Costa. But we're more familiar with his code name. Sonny. He served as a sniper in the Korosolan Army."

"You're joking. Just down the road?"

"I don't buy coincidence," said Lenny. His matter-of-fact intonation echoed Cade's suspicions.

Winston played with the other cuff link, his forehead creasing in a thoughtful frown. "I'll look into it. I don't think Easton's on to us. He's still busy interviewing possible suspects."

"Any of them your client?" asked Cade. The opportunity was too good to pass up.

But then, Rademacher was no fool. He was incredibly loyal to their mysterious boss. Instead of an automatic response, he took his time to think before speaking.

It was easy for Cade to see how his father had been duped by the man's cold expression. Across a European gaming table or across an abandoned clearing in northwest Connecticut, Winston Rademacher revealed nothing.

"Your fascination with an employer who chooses to remain anonymous borders on insubordination." Winston smoothed his lapels and slipped his hand inside the front of his jacket. Cade dropped his hand to his holster and unsnapped it, reacting instinctively to the threat of whatever weapon Rademacher might be hiding, rather than the imperious Napoleonic image he created. "What do they do to soldiers who disobey orders?"

"You can get court-martialed or demoted."

Winston withdrew his empty hand and buttoned the front of his coat. He ran his tongue along his lips, as if he was savoring the idea. "Interesting."

Cade snapped up his chin into the military bearing he had once worn with such pride. "You want to kick me off the team?"

Winston remained unimpressed with the challenge. "No, Sinjun. I want to keep you right where I can see you."

Dismissing Cade's challenge, dismissing Cade himself,

Winston opened the door and climbed into the SUV. He started the engine and rolled down the window to give one final command.

"Have the princess cleaned up and ready to go. I'll be here tonight at nine." His imperious gaze slid over Cade, Lenny and Jerome. "In the meantime, make yourselves presentable, as well."

He drove off without even kicking up mud onto the vehicle's undercarriage. The man liked things too damn neat for Cade's taste. Once he turned onto the asphalt road and headed south, Cade nodded to Lenny. The big man picked up a pack and a rifle from inside the kitchen and jogged out to the trees.

"What's going on?" Jerome planted his walking stick into the ground and vaulted onto his good foot. "Lenny, where you going?"

But the big man disappeared without answering. Cade didn't waste any time listening to Jerome's arguments. He snapped his holster shut and set about stoking the fire. "I don't know about you, but Lenny and I aren't real comfortable with the idea of Sonny next door. I sent Lenny to keep an eye on him."

Jerome limped after him. "Who's giving the orders around here?"

"I am." Cade whirled around and faced him, using Jerome's startled flinch to make his point about the little man's combat readiness. "Unless you want to deal with Sonny on your own. I need our vehicle running without a hitch. Can you get the gear packed?"

Jerome weighed the chances of his bum leg against a legendary, albeit retired, hit man. "Yeah. I'll take care of the car."

Cursing and grumbling every uneven step of the way, Jerome hobbled over to the car. He lit a cigarette, then opened the hood to check inside. *Idiot,* thought Cade. Fireman's own excesses would kill him if nobody else got the job done first.

Time was running out.

He filled two buckets with water and put them on the fire to heat up. Lenny would be setting up a hidden watch post to keep an eye on Tony Costa by now.

Cade would stay behind and protect Ellie from Jerome and any other threat, and prep her for what threatened to be the final night of her short, sweet life.

Chapter Eight

Ellie paced the concrete floor in the morning light. It filtered in through the dirty windows, illuminating the pictures she'd drawn in the dust.

Since she couldn't identify the tires of the vehicle that had driven up to the house that morning and parked outside the windows, nor make out any specific words from the discussion of the group of men that followed, she'd busied herself recalling the images she'd seen in Lenny's notebook. She'd thumbed through the pages by lantern light last night while Cade slept. With the last few hours of her life ticking away, there didn't seem to be much point in getting a good night's rest.

She wondered if he'd figured out yet that she hadn't picked his pocket when she'd gone to cover him with the blanket, but had done so earlier. He'd fallen into a deep, troubled sleep that made it possible for her to crawl over and reach into his hip pocket without him noticing.

But an hour or so later, his troubled sleep seemed to worsen. That restless, shivering sound he'd made while he slept had frightened her as much as a nightmare of her own would have. Despite her best efforts not to care, she hadn't been able to resist his pain. She didn't know how she could help him, but she had to do something. Maybe he'd been on the verge of waking himself up when she'd pulled the blanket over his legs and chest.

And then he'd…they'd…

Ellie made a shivering sound herself. She hugged her arms around her middle and lifted her fingertips to her lips. She could still taste Cade on her mouth, still feel his urgent touch on her skin.

What Ellie knew about men, she could pour into a thimble and still have room left over to fill with foolish dreams.

But even she knew Cade had done more than kiss her. He'd consumed her.

Without her knowing when or how, he'd turned comfort into desire, and desire into need. They'd needed each other. And for a few, blazing, unforgettable minutes, everything she'd ever longed for in her lonely life had been right there in the palm of her hand.

Three days ago she'd thought a dance would be enough to sustain her through her lonely life. One grand, glorious waltz would provide enough adventure to nourish her until she found the man of her dreams—and worked up the nerve to talk to him. But now that Cade had kissed her—twice— had kissed her and held her and shown her how wildly responsive her body could be to a man's touch, she wanted more.

Cade seemed to have known from the beginning that she had no experience with men. But the crazy thing was, he didn't seem to mind. His touches had been encouraging, enjoyable, erotic. Not punishing or mocking like Jerome's. Cade had shown her that a man *could* find her attractive. That her shyness hadn't sentenced her to a solitary life.

Maybe she'd been wrong to think in terms of potential spinsterhood. Maybe there was a future out there for her beyond devoting herself to her king or her parents. Maybe she could find a man who would be devoted to her.

If he was perceptive enough to find some beauty behind her thick glasses and plain features. *If* he was persistent enough to get beyond her shyness. *If* he was patient enough to help her understand how to please him and, ultimately, to please herself.

Three days ago, all she'd wanted was one dance.

Now? She wanted Cade St. John.

He was perceptive, persistent and patient.

And handsome and sexy and more aggressively male than any man she'd ever met. He needed her in a way that her limited experience couldn't define. Needed her in a way that made her feel alive and important and absolutely necessary.

He was also ready to kill her.

Ellie shook all the way from her head to her bare toes as a corresponding chill worked its way through her system. No wonder she'd never drawn the attention of men before. She was crazy. Common sense told her to fight, to run. But some insane intuition kept bringing her back to Cade time and again, telling her to talk to him, to trust him, to put herself in his hands and believe that everything would be all right somehow.

Ellie had always relied on common sense.

And so she planned to fight and run, and bury those burgeoning feelings and crazy intuitions deep inside where they couldn't get her killed.

With that debate settled for the third time that morning, she walked around the stylized symbol she'd drawn in the dust and studied it. Breaking the code in Lenny's notebook might or might not help her gain her freedom. But it beat going stir-crazy. And the book was important to Cade. Important enough to steal and then blow his top over when he found out she had it. Solving the riddles inside would surely give her some kind of advantage to work with.

Ellie squatted down and traced the lines with her finger. It looked like a winged arrow shooting into the middle of a semicircle. She'd found this symbol in at least three different places in Lenny's notebook. A doodle of some kind amongst the bits of words and numbers.

She ran her finger down the line in the middle, then circled around the outer curve. It felt as if she'd just written the letter *D*.

Ellie's eyes opened wide, and a similar recognition unfurled inside her. "They're letters. *D*." She followed the arrow lines backward. "*K* and *F*."

She'd seen those same three letters numerous times in letters she'd transcribed for King Easton. "KDF. Korosolan Democratic Front."

Was Lenny a member of the extremist political party that had only recently joined the Parliament and retired from its militant ways? Had they hired Lenny to carry out one of their purported bombings or shootings? Was kidnapping Princess Lucia part of some new revolution?

She leaned back on her haunches. "They can't do that." King Easton had worked tirelessly to integrate the KDF into the Korosolan government. Was the KDF using her—or rather, Lucia Carradigne—to destroy her peaceful homeland? "They can't do that," she repeated, a surge of patriotism firing her temper.

"Who are you talking to?" Cade's velvet voice skittered along nerves that had already flashed on alert.

Ellie stood, smearing her toes across the dust and erasing the symbol she'd drawn. "No one."

A bell in her head and some kind of drum in her chest pounded out a rapid, unexpected response. But the surprise of being caught off guard faded as a new rhythm took over inside her.

He'd shaved.

She'd expected to discover that pure danger lay camou-flaged beneath his scruffy beard. Instead, she saw two boy-ish dimples softening the sharp, aristocratic lines of his handsome face. When she realized she was standing there gawking at him as if she'd never seen a man before, she looked away. Her cheeks flushed with heat and she had to open her mouth and take a deep breath to cool herself off and think straight.

She couldn't afford to notice that his bottom lip jutted out in an amused smirk right now. That his whole mouth sat slightly crooked on his face thanks to a small scar at the left corner of his top lip. She needed to make herself an opportunity to escape.

She finally managed to get some words past her feverish confusion. "I don't mind talking to myself. I'm the best company I've had all weekend."

"Ouch." He picked up the blanket and folded it loosely in his arms.

When he headed for the stairs without another word, El-lie lunged after him, touching his arm only long enough to ask him to stop before stepping away from him. "I'm sorry. I didn't really mean that. I don't want to be alone." She eyed the gray wool bundle. "What are you doing?"

"I'm setting up a blind so that you can take a bath. I can keep Jerome in the house, but I don't want him looking out the window and getting an eyeful."

"A bath?" Thoughts of escape, thoughts of Cade and company crashed to a sudden halt. Had she heard him cor-rectly?

"It's nothing fancy. I scrounged an extra toothbrush for you, but I couldn't find a washcloth. I'm ready to pour in the hot water as soon as I get the blanket set up."

She tried not to salivate with anticipation. "Is there soap?"

Cade grinned, his dark eyes dancing with devilry. "You interested?"

Ellie felt the grit under her nails, the bruises and scrapes on her arms and legs. She thought of the chain coming off her ankle and the chance to breathe fresh air. "Yes."

But when she assumed he'd unlock her chain and she'd precede him up the stairs, he didn't move. Instead, he tucked the blanket underneath one arm and nodded at the place where she'd scuffed the floor. "What were you making over there?"

A dozen different lies ran through her head, but she knew he'd see through each and every one. "I drew a picture that was in Lenny's notebook. Are you a member of the Korosolan Democratic Front?"

His smile vanished. "No."

"I think he might be."

"Really?"

She ignored the skepticism in his voice. "What else would KDF stand for? It's in there several times. I can show you."

He looked down at her outstretched hand, then back to her eyes. "I don't think so."

But Ellie wasn't ready to give up on her idea yet. That notebook had to be the key to something. If she understood the key, then maybe she could buy her own freedom by helping Cade decipher the information. "I think some of the other symbols are map coordinates. Latitude, longitude. The rest is written in shorthand."

"When did you read all this?"

"I wasn't taking the book when you woke up last night." She paused to let the full impact of what she was saying sink in. "I really was just covering you up."

A flash of disbelief, then anger blazed in his eyes. "I can't trust you for a minute, can I?"

"No more than I can trust you."

He drilled her with one of those enigmatic indigo glares that spoke such volumes—if she could only understand the message.

But when he turned to go, she understood she was being abandoned.

Ellie dashed after him. Her chain made a pitiful racket on the floor. When she reached the end, she shouted after him, "You really did look cold."

He stopped halfway up the stairs. She watched the muscles in his back expand and contract with a weary sigh. Then he turned around and marched down the stairs with such purpose that Ellie backed away. But she had nowhere to go. He was so much bigger and quicker that she finally just stopped and let him advance and have his say.

Only, she saw no anger in his frown, and the long fingers that stroked her cheek, then tunneled into her hair, were warm and gentle. "Ellie."

When he said her name like that, as though he just didn't know what to make of her, didn't know what to do with her—as though *he* was the one who didn't understand much about the opposite sex—she went all soft and tender inside. His confusion humanized him, took this larger-than-life man and made him real to her.

Ellie's heart went out to that vulnerable man beneath the too-tough-to-care outer shell. She leaned her cheek into the callused warmth of his hand. "You were suffering in your sleep. Maybe it was a nightmare, instead of the cold, but I wanted to help."

"You don't have to take care of me." His fingers massaged the base of her scalp, but she thought he might be taking comfort, not offering it. "I've been looking after myself since I was nineteen. Nightmares and all."

Ellie tried to picture Cade as a young man, but couldn't

quite make an image of this hardened, cynical man of the world as an innocent youth who still had ideals he believed in.

Tears welled in her eyes, but she blinked them back. She doubted if he'd appreciate her sympathy. "That must have been hard, losing your father like that and then seeing reports of his death splashed in all the papers. Do you miss him?"

Cade's hand went still in her hair. His expressive eyes shuttered and he withdrew completely. "Don't you want to ask about the scandal? Find out how a wealthy duke could blow an entire fortune and end his life in disgrace? How a man could devote his life to trying to find that one big deal, that one perfect game that would turn his world around and make him a winner so his wife would come back to him? Isn't that what you really want to know?"

"No." Ellie frowned, fighting back against the bitterness he slung her way. "I was worried—"

"That's what everyone else wants to know."

A sharp bite of sarcasm colored his voice. But Ellie recognized the defensive mechanism for what it was. She'd heard that same tone in her father's voice whenever he'd talked about her brother, Nicky. She heard the same heartbreak and anger and guilt. She saw the pain denied in the angry swipe of his hand across his eyes, taking any trace of telltale moisture with it.

But Ellie felt no such need to hide the pain she felt for him. She pulled her glasses from her face, transformed Cade into a blur and let the tears come—huge, slow tears that burned her eyes and scorched her cheeks as they trickled down her face.

"I'm sorry," she said. "I didn't realize talking about your father was so painful for you. I didn't mean to bring up a bad memory. But when you said you were on your own...I thought I could help.... I thought... I know how much I miss my family—'' She caught her breath on a sob.

"Ellie." Suddenly Cade was right there. In full focus. Close enough to see without her glasses. "You're doing it again."

"Doing what?" She sniffed loudly and tilted her face up to drown in a pool of perplexed indigo blue.

"Giving a damn about things you shouldn't." He closed the short distance between them and kissed her. It was hard, healing and over before she could either protest or respond. "Thank you for caring, but don't waste your time. Don't try to fix me or help me or do any other damn thing for me. I said I take care of myself." He pulled a blue bandanna from one of those endless pockets and dabbed at her eyes and cheeks. "Here."

Ellie sniffled and dutifully dried her tears. His gentle touch and indulgent grin made her feel all of nine years old.

But it was a woman's heart that ached for him, that understood his lonely battle, that despaired over ever hearing him admit to any emotion besides lust or greed. "I'm sorry. I didn't mean to cry. I'm sure it's just the stress of everything."

There he was again, swimming into focus. He smoothed her bangs off her face and studied the movement with his eyes. "Don't apologize. My family is a topic I just don't discuss."

Ellie nodded. She had one more stuttered sniff to take before she could curb the tears. But when she inhaled, she absorbed the clean, soapy scent of his shaving cream. It was a normal, healthy scent that seemed at odds with the dangerous man of mystery who wore it.

Cade St. John was more than just a mercenary. He had to be. A man couldn't be gentle and funny and fiercely protective without caring about something. He couldn't show her tenderness without having known it himself first. He couldn't sympathize with her pain without having suffered himself.

And yet he denied all that. He denied that he hurt. He denied that he wanted to help her. He denied that he was a good man.

Why?

Ellie had no answers. She had no experience to fall back on, no instincts she trusted. She only knew that she couldn't give up. There had to be a way to reach Cade's conscience. And the way she knew best was to give something of herself. Her time, her intelligence, her perseverance.

"Maybe if you did talk about it," she suggested, putting her glasses back on and getting down to business, "you wouldn't have the nightmares."

"Nice try." He pushed the bandanna back into her hands when she tried to give it to him. "Keep it. C'mon. Let's get you into that bath."

He pulled a set of keys from his pocket and knelt down to unlock the ankle cuff. Since he didn't want her to care, she went back to offering her expertise in exchange for her freedom. "Don't you want to know about Lenny's notebook? I can translate the shorthand for you."

"Why would you want to do that for me?" He handed her the oversize running shoes.

"Because if I help you, then maybe you'll—"

"I can't let you go, Ellie."

She wasn't above begging. "Do you need the money that badly? Maybe there's another way. I know you don't want to hurt me."

"No, I don't want to hurt you. But there's more than money at stake here. A hell of a lot more." The cut-and-dried timbre of his voice brimmed with hidden meaning.

But he didn't elaborate. "I need you to be Princess Lucia for a little while longer."

And that meant she needed to find another way to escape.

Not only was her life on the line, but over the next few hours, if she wasn't very careful, she could lose her heart to this hard, hurting man who didn't want to be her hero.

And of all that she'd endured thus far, that would be the worst humiliation of all.

AT SOME POINT during this mission, Cade thought, he must have made the conscious decision to be an idiot. He was certainly behaving like one!

Jumping down poor Ellie's throat over his dad. He *had* been reliving a nightmare when she woke him last night. He'd seen men die in battle, had lost comrades he called friends on a dozen different missions around the world.

But no image had ever stuck in his head like the one of his father slumped over in his office chair, with half his brain and a ton of blood pooling on the desktop beside him. He'd been the first to read the tearstained suicide note. The one to call the police. The one who opened the door when the press and their cameras showed up the next day. The one who answered the phone when the creditors started calling.

He was just a kid in college. Just a kid!

He'd known his father was sick, that his gambling was an addiction that couldn't be cured by love or reason. Once his mother had left them, Cade knew he was the only one there for his father. But he couldn't help him. There hadn't been a damn thing he could do to help.

These past few days with Ellie had dredged up all those buried feelings. He couldn't really help her, either. His hands were tied. And as much as he wanted to give her the safety and freedom that she wanted—that she deserved—

he knew his first priority was the job. He had promised to do this thing. Given his word. And like any good soldier, when he signed on to a mission, he saw it through to the end.

Even if an innocent victim got in the way.

And now she wanted to help *him?* Oh, God. He needed to see a shrink to understand that one.

With a towel wrapped around each handle, he carried two buckets of boiling hot water from the fire and poured them into the old iron tub to heat the water from the pump he'd filled it with earlier. It was a lot of trouble to go to, considering he'd have to take Ellie right back down to that filthy basement once she had washed. But Rademacher had insisted on turning over a clean hostage.

More importantly, Ellie had gotten all excited over the prospect of taking a bath. And after dealing with those big, sorrowful tears that had turned him inside out with guilt— that made him feel as if he himself was crying—he wanted to do something that would make her smile again.

Not that she couldn't take care of herself. He had to admire the moxie of a woman who could pick his pocket and beat Jerome off with a stick, all in the name of survival. She was smart, too, piecing together the puzzle of Lenny's notebook and offering it up in trade. He hadn't ruled out the KDF as his secretive employer, but he wasn't quite ready to take his hostage's word on that fact.

Cade tossed the buckets aside and hung the towels over the line he'd strung up to give Ellie some privacy. "All right, Your Highness. It's good to go."

Though he hated keeping up the pretense of calling her by another woman's name, Cade used it to distance himself from that inexplicable pull he felt toward Ellie. Jerome might be within earshot, anyway.

Ellie rose from the stump where he'd instructed her to

sit and tiptoed over the tufts of grass to the tub. She'd already removed all her clothes except for the oversize shirt, which covered her down to her thighs, but clung to all the best spots—her flared hips, her round bottom, those incredible breasts.

She held the shirt together with one hand and dipped the other into the water. "Mmm." She smiled a small Mona Lisa smile while she traced circles in the water with her finger. "Delicious."

Cade tried not to notice the fluctuations in his body's temperature as he watched her, despite the overcast dampness of the day. "Get in before it gets cold, Princess."

The low-pitched command sounded harsh even to his own ears. He'd moved beyond detached and unemotional on this job a long time ago. Maybe about the time he saw Ellie's bare breast for the first time. Or was it after the dreamy-eyed waltz in the basement? Or maybe that unexpected clip to the jaw that had unmasked him the first night was what forced him to walk a fine line between doing his job and doing what he thought was right.

Ellie pushed her glasses up her nose, a habit he noticed that cropped up whenever she got nervous. But she wasn't reacting to his order. This was something more personal. She clutched at the neckline of the shirt and made no move to climb in. "Turn around."

Cade's heart flip-flopped in a crazy rhythm that felt foreign in his chest. Part of him wanted to wrap her in his arms and shield her from any prying eyes, reassure her that her body was a treasure worth admiring—as long as he was the only one doing the looking. But a smarter part of him remembered the cut on his face, the long run through the woods, the stolen notebook. It was the part of him that had survived on these crazy jobs for so many years.

"Uh-uh." He shook his head, refusing to be fooled into

honoring her demure shyness. "I don't trust you out of my sight. Get in, or I'll put you in there myself."

Yep, he was an idiot.

Now she was blushing. A delightful shade of pink that went from cheekbones to thighs. Cade's pulse quickened in response. Oh, yeah. Like he ever should have conjured the image of putting his hands on Ellie's naked body.

Definitely an idiot.

"Would you hold these for me, please?"

Cade snapped out of his fevered trance and took hold of Ellie's glasses as she handed them to him. He wondered if it was any easier for her to be less self-conscious if she couldn't see what others saw.

He stuck her glasses in a pocket and waited in dry-mouthed expectation as she turned around and started pulling the shirt off over her head. Damn. Her blush seemed to follow every bit of skin that was revealed. Her buttocks. The graceful arch of her spine. The long column of her neck.

Like a gawking teenager, Cade waited for her to turn around. Hoped she would turn around. Prayed. The anticipation alone had him adjusting his stance to ease the responding tightness in his pants.

Idiot. Idiot. Idiot.

Cade wasn't aware of breathing again until Ellie sank into the water and removed all that untouched bounty from his sight. He tried to ignore the gentle sound of the water lapping her bare skin and the little coos of contentment she emitted.

He walked the perimeter of the makeshift blind he had built, scanning the tree line for any signs of unwanted guests, while keeping Ellie in his peripheral vision. When she tipped her head back to rinse her hair and exposed about ninety miles of milky white throat that he hadn't yet kissed, Cade finally turned his back on her.

This was ridiculous. Ellie Standish was a prim, near-sighted secretary who had no fashion sense and no self-confidence.

She was a means to an end. A necessary ally because the others still believed she was Princess Lucia.

And he was fooling himself by trying to maintain those misconceptions about her.

He'd long since given up on the idea of remaining un-attached to Ellie and her innocently alluring charms. But he had to conquer those urges that made him want to strip down and join her in the tub. He needed to put his mind to work on the job at hand and ignore the painful awareness of his body and the guilt that plagued his conscience.

What would really kill those urges would be to have a heart-to-heart with Winston Rademacher—see if he could find out what made that cold bastard tick.

He'd said he connected people. Thus far he'd connected one fake princess, a wealthy king, three mercenaries for hire and... And who else? Who was behind the kidnapping?

And how did the hit man next door figure into it all?

The frustrating lack of answers ate away at Cade's focus. He raked all ten fingers through his hair, then curled his hands into useless fists. If he knew what was going on, he could formulate a plan, go on the offensive, instead of re-acting to unfolding events.

He had allowed his reputation as a loyal Korosolan to get trashed so he could do this job. He'd traded in war-hero status to become the traitor Ellie accused him of being. And for what? The chance to get turned in or blown away by an unknown boss?

Just who was Rademacher working for?

The KDF might have been having second thoughts about their alliance with King Easton and had decided that taking his granddaughter was the best way to renegotiate their settlement. They could have hired Rademacher to do their dirty work so that the kidnapping wouldn't get blamed on them if things didn't go according to plan. Winston wouldn't gain much from either the success or failure of the job, but he'd have a hell of a time playing the game.

But as much as Rademacher enjoyed playing games—and people—Cade thought a more likely scenario was that Rademacher was working for his protégé, Prince Markus. Under Winston's advice and tutelage, Markus had been raised to be the perfect prince. With Rademacher's thoroughness for details, he'd want to see Markus become the perfect king. *Royal advisor* had a much more powerful ring when it was attached to a man who ran his own country.

So was Cade working for an idealistic political group? Or serving the needs of a greedy man? And was either option one he could survive?

"Cade?"

He had almost switched himself back to soldier mode when Ellie called his name.

For a man who desperately wanted to focus on the job and not the woman, he had assigned himself the worst possible task on the planet.

He had to watch her bathe.

And watch, he did. Awestruck.

Ellie rose like Venus from the waves. With one arm folded across her chest hiding next to nothing, and the other crossed lower, hiding little more, she stepped from the tub. The water ran in rivulets from her hair across her shoulders and gathered in the cup formed by her arm and breasts. As Cade boldly stared, tracing the path of long, golden-brown hair and water, he saw the goose bumps rise on her skin. His body temperature rose in pore-popping counterpoint.

"Could I have a towel?"

Was it a trick of his aroused body, or was there more seduction than shyness in her voice?

"A towel." He repeated the words, doubting the innocence of her request.

She had the good grace to duck her head and blush. Cade leaned forward, his body helplessly drawn to the discovery of exposed pink skin from the ruddy dots on her cheeks all the way down to...

Cade swallowed hard. He tried to be a gentleman and look away. But then, he'd never been much of a gentleman. "Do you have any idea how sexy you are?"

Her body-wide blush darkened and she laughed off the compliment. "The towel, please?"

Although reluctant to hide such a work of art, he pulled one of the white towels off the line and held it out to her. He grinned in indulgent delight, watching her debate which hand to move in order to take the towel.

"Allow me."

He spread his arms wide, holding the towel like a thin cotton wall between them. Ellie raised her bright blue eyes to him and squinted. "I wish you were the nearsighted one."

Cade grinned, glad she couldn't see the evidence of the power she had over him bulging in the front of his pants. "Twenty-twenty vision does have its advantages. Come here."

It was a gentle request, one that Ellie responded to by taking a hesitant step toward him. Cade met her halfway, wrapping her up in the towel, looking down and catching a glimpse of her delectably round backside.

She took over tucking the ends of the towel around her

breasts in a makeshift sarong. Cade let his hands slide to her waist, not quite having the strength to move away from temptation.

"Do you really think I'm pretty?" she asked.

It bothered him that she still saw herself the way he used to—the wrong way. True, she wasn't a conventional beauty. But she was a mind-boggling delight to the senses. Her luscious figure, soft skin and softer hair made her irresistible to the touch. He never tired of looking into those eyes, which reminded him of the clear mountain lakes of Korosol.

And warmth. Ellie produced an enchanted, incandescent heat. But she warmed more than his body. She fired up his mind. Her shy vulnerability, blended with a backbone of steel, opened fissures around his jaded heart. She was melting his icy detachment from the world and making him care about things that normally sent him running toward safety and freedom—and loneliness—in the past.

"Definitely pretty." He couldn't see these self-doubts as false modesty or a feminine ploy for attention. She already had his attention. All of it.

He cared that she was embarrassed. He hurt because she was scared. He stewed in guilt because he couldn't help her escape.

But there was one thing he could feel good about doing for her. He could straighten out a few misconceptions.

Cade stood a little taller, suddenly feeling a bit more like that good man Ellie insisted he could be.

He tightened his grip on her waist and pulled her forward. He brought her closer and closer until the light of focus clicked on in her eyes. "What I'm thinking right now goes way beyond pretty."

With one hand Ellie clutched the towel in a death grip at the deep, shadowy cleft between her breasts. She flattened the other hand against his chest. The tentative touch seared him with some of that magical heat she possessed.

Cade sighed with a lightning-charged shimmer of awareness that was grounded in an unfamiliar contentment. The normal wary tension eased out of his muscles, and a different sort of tension took its place. There were definite benefits to having the hots for a nearsighted woman. She had to get incredibly close to be able to see into his eyes. He liked her close like this. Inside and out, he liked it a lot.

He braced his legs apart and pulled her an impossible inch closer. The dampness of the towel worked like friction, sticking to her skin as he slid his palms across the thin terry cloth and found the spot where his cupped hands fit perfectly around the curve of her bottom.

He dipped his face to her temple and buried his nose in the rich, clean scent of her damp hair. "I don't know how you manage to come across as a classy lady and an irresistible seductress at the same time."

"So you think I'm pretty enough to..." Her awkward blush warmed her cheek against his. "Do you think a man would...?" Her breathy sigh tickled the hair beside his ear and made him shiver from his scalp to his toes. "Sorry. This is so awkward for me."

"What is?" Cade lifted his head and lost himself in the embarrassed confusion of those lake-blue eyes. But he thought he already knew.

"I don't want to die without...I've never known a man... Would you...?"

"Ellie." He caught her lips in the gentlest of kisses, thanking her for her sweet, sweet request. The virgin pretend princess was talking about sex. "I want to do that, too."

"With me?"

Her startled response kicked him right in the heart. He'd told a lot of lies these past few days. But this time—even though it scared the hell out of him—he told the truth.

"Yeah." He zeroed in on her mouth. "Definitely with you."

He claimed her mouth in a possessive kiss, pretending for the moment that making love to Ellie wouldn't be the biggest mistake of his life. She slipped her hand around his waist and he found a way to lift her onto her toes and bring her closer still.

As her mouth opened beneath his, he swelled with the humbling awe of how quickly she could break through his once-impregnable emotional barriers and breathe heat and life into the chilly recesses of his mind. There was no practiced finesse in the stroke of her fingers or the press of her lips or the dance of her tongue. Just a pure, unrestrained passion that drove him wild.

He was hot and he was hard, and he wanted to strip that flimsy towel off her, lay her down on the ground and show her just exactly what kind of wonderful things that a man— that *he*—would want to do with her.

But Ellie was a shy woman who demanded patience, whose unexpected smiles and pithy responses were worth the wait. She was the kind of woman he'd heard about as a teenager—before he'd understood the complexity of his father's addiction or had to deal with the destruction it caused in the lives around him. Ellie was a good girl. The kind of woman a man was supposed to marry and have kids with. He was supposed to learn his lessons from women who knew the score. But ultimately, he was supposed to come home to someone like Ellie.

His attraction to her was a completely new experience for him, because he knew he could never really go home. He knew there was no woman like Ellie in his future. No marriage, no children to taint with the St. John name. Maybe that was all this craziness was about—wanting what he knew he couldn't have. Dabbling with what he knew would never be his. So it was safe to be attracted to Ellie. Safe to teach her a few of those life lessons she had yet to learn.

"I wish I could tell you what you want to hear." He nibbled a path down her throat. Down to the shadowy softness between her breasts. "But I can't promise—"

"You don't have to promise anything."

Cade froze. His warm, wonderful fantasy world crashed to a bleak, blinding halt.

He didn't know what stunned him more—the rigid determination in Ellie's shaky voice.

Or his own 9-mm Browning sidearm jabbed in the middle of his gut.

Chapter Nine

Ellie held the gun tightly, surprised by its weight. Tucking her elbow to her side to support her hand and keep the gun leveled at Cade, she backed beyond arm's reach, squinting to keep him in her sights.

"Stay away from me."

He obeyed her order by splaying his arms out wide to either side in reluctant surrender, showing himself to be an unarmed man. His eyes narrowed, transforming his gaze from a lover's visual caress into a killer's cold glare.

She was giddy with the success of her trick, unhooking his holster while his mind and lips and hands were occupied elsewhere. Her body was still quaking from the raw force of his touch on her skin, the demanding need of his mouth on hers. In another time and place, she'd have surrendered to his strength, believed his praises. If he was a prince and she his princess, she'd have made love with him. She would have willingly given herself to this man and discovered the wonder of loving and being loved for the first time in her life.

But Cade St. John was no prince.

And she was no princess.

At the last moment, before losing herself in the illusion of a dream come true, Ellie dredged up thoughts of home and freedom and living to see the next day. She resisted her body's blind desire to open up and give herself to him. It was easier to focus on Cade's threats to keep her prisoner than to believe the sincerity of his kind words about being pretty.

That was what she had to focus on now—not the cold-hearted betrayal that dulled the luster in his indigo eyes. Distrust loomed like shadows in the blue darkness there, tugging at some corresponding emotion deep inside her. It wasn't guilt. She was rational enough to know she was the victim here. It was more a sense of loss that made her insides quiver and feel empty—a feeling as if she, too, had been cheated of something important almost within her grasp.

But whether it was guilt or emptiness that made her pause, she forced herself to harden her compassionate heart and move on. This wasn't the time to stop and help the man. She wanted her freedom.

Because the alternative was death.

"Don't move or I'll shoot. I don't want to, but I swear I will. Since you won't help me, I'll have to save myself. I'm sorry." She clutched the towel around her chest and pointed her head toward the beat-up black sedan. "You're going to stay right there and I'm going to get into that car and drive away from here."

"How? The keys are in my pocket." There was no velvet in his voice to soften the sarcasm in his words. "Do you know how to hot-wire it?"

Drat! She clenched her jaw to stifle the unladylike urge to say something worse. Would it really hurt the forces of nature to allow one thing to go her way? "Give me the keys."

"No."

Ellie wrapped both hands around the butt of the gun,

squeezing her elbows beside her breasts to hold the towel in place. She squinted to bring the big target of his chest into focus and pointed the gun right at the middle of it. She articulated each word with exact, commanding precision. "Give me the keys."

"You'll have to take them from me." Cade shrugged his massive shoulders with an annoying lack of concern. He splayed his fingers at his hips, settling into a stance that was a bit too relaxed to be trusted. "And if you get close enough to reach them, one of two things is going to happen. I'm either going to snap your wrist—or I'm going to kiss you senseless in retaliation for that damn seduction you just pulled on me."

"Kiss me...?" Ellie sputtered with indignation. But all of a sudden she couldn't seem to catch a deep breath. She had no doubt Cade could carry out either threat without breaking a sweat. Even though she held the gun in her hands, she had a feeling the power between them had just shifted.

"*Do you think I'm pretty? Would a man really want me?*" He threw her bone-deep doubts back in her face, mocking her. "I thought you were an innocent. That you really were shy. But I see you can play games like any other woman."

"I *am* innocent. I haven't done anything to deserve this. I just want to stay alive. I want to go home."

Cade stayed as cool as the clouds gathering in the sky above them. "Then you're going to have to shoot me."

Ellie looked hard into those dark-blue eyes, searching for any sign that he was bluffing. She stared until the pain of a headache stabbed behind her right eye. She looked away before he ever even blinked. "I'm running, then. I'm going up to the main road and I'll find someone to help me."

"You're running into the woods dressed in a towel? People will think you're crazy."

She saw her mistake, but it was too late to reclaim the upper hand. His words had struck home. She had no plan. She had no clue. She wasn't even sure if the gun had some kind of safety thing she needed to release before she could fire it.

But she tilted her chin and refocused the weapon and tried to make good on her escape. She took a step back. Then another. And another. "Don't follow me."

"I have your glasses."

Thunder rumbled in the distance like an ominous death knell punctuating a last chance slipping through her fingers.

She looked to the right and then to the left. She couldn't even see the trees.

Her breath stuttered in a painful wheeze inside her chest. She'd failed. Her courage faltered and tears stung her eyes. A few salty drops gathered in front of her pupils and refracted her vision for a moment of crystal-clear perception. It lasted long enough for her to see Cade's stone-cold expression. She blinked, squeezing out the tears and turning Cade into a big, black-clad blur.

She could have pulled the trigger. But when the monstrous blur moved toward her, she backed away, dropping her hands and surrendering to her vulnerability. She couldn't shoot Cade. She couldn't run and she couldn't strong-arm her way out of this.

"A piece of advice." She didn't want to hear it. He stepped into focus and pried the gun from her unresisting hand. "Never point a gun at someone unless you're prepared to use it."

He put the pistol in his holster and locked it down with one hand. The other cinched around her upper arm. His touch was warm and heavy and embarrassingly impersonal as he guided her back to the house. He stopped just long enough to pick up her discarded clothes and toss them her way.

Ellie caught them and hugged them close, fighting tears of frustration and fatigue, and crazy feelings she didn't understand.

He opened the basement door and took her down the stairs. He told her to dress, then stood there—a silent, voyeuristic sentinel—while she complied. When he knelt at her feet to lock the chain around her ankle, Ellie finally spoke. "I hate you."

He stood up, towered over her, ate up the extra space in the room with his broad shoulders and dark-eyed glare. Ellie tipped up her chin and held her ground. There was something cold and lonely in his solitary stance. Something that touched her gentle woman's heart and made her ache for him. When he handed her her glasses, the gesture of kindness eroded what was left of her rebellion.

"I'm sorry. I didn't really mean—"

"Hate me, Ellie," he commanded in a voice that resonated low in his chest like the thunder outside. "It'll be easier for me to walk away from all this if I know you hate me."

CADE CROSSED his booted feet at the ankle and sipped his beer. The images in the notebook he was studying swam together into an endless series of squiggly lines. He'd cracked a number of codes in his time, but the basics of old-fashioned shorthand eluded him.

I can translate the shorthand for you.

Ellie's pleading voice echoed in his head, staying with him the same way his body still sparked with the imprint of her in his arms, the same way the fresh, clean taste of her lingered on his tongue.

He took a swallow of beer and swished it around in his mouth, trying to lose the taste of her in its bitter flavor.

She'd bargained for her freedom with compassion, with intelligence and, finally, with herself.

And he'd been tempted. Oh, God, had he been tempted to take her up on her offer and give her whatever she wanted. But when Ellie pulled his gun on him, he realized how screwed up his focus had become. He'd lost sight of his original purpose for signing on for this job.

But with the gun at his stomach and the deception in her eyes, he'd been able to remember just who Cade St. John was supposed to be. A washed-up war hero who'd sold out his king in order to make some money. A lot of money.

Somewhere along the way, he'd lost sight of what he needed to do. He'd forgotten who he was.

All he had was a title and some special training. And his word. He'd given his word to a friend—one of the few people in this world he'd ever cared about disappointing.

He'd stayed true to his word thus far. He'd done what was necessary to ensure the success of this job.

And what did he have to show for it?

A warm beer, an achy body, a frustrated heart and Jerome—passed out and snoring on the plaid couch across from him.

Cade lifted his bottle and toasted the worthless bastard.

Jerome, at least, kept his goals straight. He wanted money and women. He wanted retribution for the pain and trouble Ellie had caused him.

Simple. Worthless, but simple.

Cade's goals were considerably more complicated.

How the hell had he ever gotten the notion that Ellie Standish could save his sorry hide? Rescue him from outcast status and help him find a way home?

She wasn't just sweet and innocent and tempting and full of a hope he had long since lost.

She was strong.

Her giving spirit hadn't been broken, couldn't be broken—even by the likes of him and his deceitful plan.

But at the same time he acknowledged the discovery, he mourned the loss.

Because Ellie would never be his. Not after all he'd put her through. Not with what he had left to ask of her.

She should hate him. It would be healthy to hate him.

So much for salvation.

Jerome's cell phone chirped in his pocket, startling him without fully rousing him. His bruised, puffy eye opened a tiny slit and glanced about the room. When the phone rang a second time, Cade got up and reached inside the front of Jerome's jacket. He pulled out the cell phone, checked the number and punched the talk button.

"St. John," he identified himself.

"Where's Smython?" Winston Rademacher's crisp, accented voice sounded like an accusation.

Jerome's battered eye drifted shut. Cade shook his head and turned away, striding to the far end of the room near the fireplace. "He's indisposed at the moment. What do you need?"

Winston considered the question for a moment before answering. "I'll bet you're a gambling man, aren't you, Sinjun?"

The clear reference to his father goaded him. But Cade resisted the taunt. "Not really."

"You should be. King Easton has decided to play the part of an American cowboy and turn our standoff into a showdown. His right-hand man, General Montcalm, is apparently quite taken with Princess Lucia." Cade knew Harrison Montcalm. The man had been a good soldier and an even better leader for many years in the Korosolan Army. He also knew the general was more than "taken" with Princess Lucia. The two had married in a private ceremony only days ago. "He wants her back. At the king's direction, Montcalm has contacted the American authorities to help with their search. I'm afraid our time has been cut short. Have the princess ready in an hour. I want to finish this deal."

Uh-oh. Cade pushed his fingers through his hair and rubbed at the tension gathering at the base of his scalp. "Every time you change the plan, that puts us at a disadvantage. We've got the drop-off set up for tonight. We can't put backup into place on such short notice."

He couldn't find out the truth in an hour, either.

Cade went on the offensive. "That's been your intention all along, hasn't it, Rademacher? You're going to hang the three of us out to dry, then walk off with the money—and your man as the next king."

"Who's hanging us out to dry?"

Cade glanced over his shoulder. Great. Sleeping Ugly had finally decided to rouse himself. "Who are you talking to? Is that my phone?"

Cade figured he had about thirty seconds before Jerome fully oriented himself to the idea of being awake. He turned his mouth back to the phone. He had to work fast. "What does Prince Markus think about your change in plans? If we're captured, we might talk. I, for one, would love to drop some names."

"You wouldn't dare—" Winston retreated a verbal step, catching himself before revealing anything incriminating regarding the identity of their employer. Cade could almost envision a thin, smug smile creasing Rademacher's angular features. "Good show, Sinjun."

His praise marked the acknowledgment of a worthy adversary. But he quickly turned the compliment around and put Cade in his place. "I find your obsession with my client tedious. One reason I've kept the identity secret is for just such a contingency. My client doesn't know you and Smython and Gratfield are working for me, either. You should be grateful for the precautions I've taken."

"What's to keep us from turning you in?"

An image of the snowy-haired hit man living next door popped into his head. Of course. Plan B. Eliminate the hired help.

"I know you have a hard time thinking beyond the moment, Sinjun, but I'm a man of vision. I expect this project to be a success. You'll have your money, your father's debt will be paid, and I'll have what I want."

"Which is what?"

But Winston was too cool a player to be rattled. "Understand that what we're doing isn't just for personal profit, but for the good of our country."

Sounded like the KDF party line. But Cade still couldn't reconcile the man who looked down on commoners who had to work for a living with the man whose interest in politics was altruistic. He could also interpret "good" as meaning a younger monarch would make a stronger king. Prince Markus had to be the motivation behind the kidnapping.

"So you'll be there with us when we deliver the princess and pick up the ransom?" Cade challenged him to back up his pretty speech with actions.

"Of course not." The man was too good to dirty his hands with something as mundane as actually handling the transaction. "I did promise my client I'd keep an eye on this project until the very end, though. So keep looking over your shoulder, Sinjun. I'll be watching you."

"Give me the damn phone!"

Jerome had finally shaken off his mixture of beer and painkillers. He jerked to his feet and limped across the room, smacking his walking stick on the floor with each step, making no effort to hide the message that each smack was an imaginary blow aimed at Cade. Though the man was bracing for a fight, Cade had no intention of wasting his time giving him one.

"You're welcome to it." He slapped the phone into Jerome's outstretched hand and stalked from the room.

He had an hour to prove Winston Rademacher was carrying out Prince Markus's orders. One hour to prove that another royal was behind this plot to unseat King Easton. One hour to get the hell out of this mess before Winston called on Tony Costa to clean things up.

And somewhere in the midst of those seemingly impossible tasks, he had to figure out what to do with the impostor princess, who lay chained and waiting to die down in the basement.

SHE WAS GOING to die.

Like their first meeting in the basement three short days ago, Cade worked in swift, efficient silence. He unlocked her chain and packed a small duffel bag. He pulled her glasses off her nose and tucked them into her pocket. While she stood at his silent bidding, he draped the blanket over her shoulders and gave her his stocking cap. He pulled the black wool down over her face and hair and tucked her braid inside the collar of the black knit shirt she wore.

A shiver of fear and longing cascaded down her spine as his fingertips brushed the nape of her neck. He must have seen the clench of muscles, because he stopped moving. She could feel the wall of heat he created behind her and almost leaned into it.

She was hopeless, completely hopeless, seeking comfort

from the man who was about to become her executioner. Instead, she huddled inside the blanket, finding no comfort in the cold, scratchy wool.

He was going to do it. He was really going to do it. He was going to march her up those stairs and kill her.

Because she was the wrong woman. In the wrong place. With the wrong dream. She felt a bit like Dorothy in *The Wizard of Oz*. She should have been content in her own backyard. In her own quiet, unassuming world, instead of wishing for grand adventures. There, she'd have been safe. She'd give anything to feel safe again.

"How could I have been so wrong about you?" Her words fell into the dead air of the basement. She turned to look over her shoulder, but without her glasses to bring him into focus, he was just a big shadow amongst the other shadows. As big a mystery to her inexperience and shy sensibilities as ever. "You kept giving me hope, Cade. You shouldn't have done that. It was cruel."

He folded his hands around her shoulders and gently squeezed. Ellie jumped at the unexpected reassurance. "You're the one with the hope, Ellie." He bent his head to her ear and whispered through the wool. "Hold on to that."

"I'll need it, right?"

His chest contracted in a weary sigh and he released her. "C'mon. Let's go." With his hand at the small of her back, he guided her to the stairs. "And whatever you do out there, keep your mouth shut."

The air outside chilled her skin, despite Cade's ski mask and the blanket. Or maybe the shivery sensation came from the icy countenance Cade wore as he walked her out to the black sedan.

He held her by the arm and opened the trunk. "No."

Ellie gasped in remembered horror and backed up a step. She slammed into the wall of Cade's chest and was trapped.

"Get in." His whisper was as commanding as a shouted order.

She shook her head in violent protest. In her stunted vision all she could see was a gaping black hole. What if there was another dead body in there? What if it was an empty hole waiting for *her* dead body?

Her sinuses plugged with tears she was too frightened to let fall. Adrenaline poured pure fight into her veins, and despite Cade's warning, she refused to cooperate.

His hands closed around her shoulders and half-pushed, half-carried her forward. She managed to get her foot up on the bumper and push back, but she was no match for his strength. He simply lifted her up and set her inside.

An instant later she smelled Jerome's smoky stench and braced for his skin-crawling touch. "Here. This ought to quiet her."

"Get away from her."

A loaded syringe dropped into her line of vision and she screamed. But the tranquilizing liquid never touched her. A large hand snagged Jerome's wrist and smacked it against the side of the trunk.

Jerome cursed. The syringe flew out of sight. Cade released her to deal with Jerome's predictable, ineffectual rage. Their scuffle was enough of a distraction for her to scramble up onto her haunches. But the blanket had tangled around her legs. She twisted and worked herself free, intending to jump out and hit the ground running.

"Is there a problem?" Ellie froze the same time Cade and Jerome did. She knew that voice. European accent. Proper. Refined.

She squinted hard, but try as she might she couldn't make the man's face come into focus. Automatically she reached for her glasses in her pocket, but Cade's hand was there to stop her.

And while she couldn't make out much of the world around her, she could tell by the shifting of shadows that Cade had moved in front of her. But he wasn't preventing her escape from the trunk. She frowned beneath the mask. He stood shielding her, blocking her view of everything except the broad plane of his back.

Blocking her from someone else's view.

Jerome massaged his sore wrist and moved away from the car. But she heard him blame her for his pain, tattling like a child scolded for fighting. "The two of them have gotten pretty chummy," he said. "But I don't trust her."

"Is that right?" Ellie tilted her ear toward the man's voice. He'd had business with King Easton. Or was it the Carradignes? She knew the owner of that voice. Hovering in the background of royal comings and goings, she overheard a lot of things. "Imagine. Our own lowly Sinjun setting his cap for a princess."

His haughty remark was meant to tease, but Ellie heard little humor there. The unmoving expanse of Cade's back told her he found the joke lacking, as well.

Was there a fourth kidnapper? Or did this man play some other role in her abduction?

"Smython," the smooth voice ordered, "contact Gratfield. I'll have him drive. I don't believe either one of you is worthy of escorting Her Majesty to the rendezvous."

"He can't," Jerome whined.

"Why not?"

"Lenny's not here." Cade was speaking now, tossing off the order. "I sent him on a wide reconnaissance of the area."

"Expecting trouble?"

"Always."

Like right now. Right here.

Ellie felt bombarded by all kinds of nonverbal messages. Cade's battle-ready posture. His do-or-die tone of voice. Faint memories of the fourth man in a conversation with... with... The scene hovered in the fringes of her mind. The man, was talking to...the butler!

The Carradignes' household butler. A nice, older man. A bit of a character. Quincy Vanderling. Quincy and this man were discussing...what? Oh, why couldn't she remember?

"You have an instinct for survival that your father lacked." The scene vanished from Ellie's mind as she began to absorb events much closer at hand. The familiar voice blended praise with an unforgivable taunt. "If Bretford had had your strength, maybe he wouldn't have seen the need to kill himself."

Cade's shoulders lifted slightly as he shifted on his feet, the only outward signs that the other man's words had struck a nerve. "If people like you hadn't taken advantage of his addiction, maybe he'd still be alive today."

Ellie's view of the standoff might have been limited, but she didn't need eyes to hear the other man's throaty laughter and his heartless amusement over the St. John family tragedy.

"Touching. Loyal to your father even though he gambled away everything that was rightfully yours."

"Loyalty makes people do funny things."

Cade propped his hands on his hips—a sure sign of the fight to come. It didn't immediately register with her that she was siding with one enemy against another, but Ellie found herself secretly rooting for Cade.

The cultured man's laughter stopped. "If this is another half-witted attempt to determine where my loyalties lie, save your breath. Now lock her up and let's move out."

Ellie's struggle was automatic as Cade turned and seized her by the shoulders. Sympathy aside, she was not dying without a fight. "No! Let me go."

Cade hushed her, but it came too late to avoid her mistake.

"Wait." The man who had given the order moved into her peripheral vision, little more than a brown blur framed in the peepholes of the mask she wore. Cade froze. Ellie froze. The man came closer still. "Get her out of there."

Cade shifted slightly. Shielding her from view? He pushed her down into the trunk. "I thought we had a tight time frame."

"Get her out of the trunk," the man repeated impatiently.

Ellie held her breath, not yet understanding the full implication of his suspicions. Cade lifted her out of the trunk and stood her on the ground in front of him. His fingers snaked around her upper arms, pinning her from behind.

The brown blur moved closer. Ellie went still. Cade's hands clenched, then loosened their grip while the other man studied her. Then, in a move too swift to react to with anything more than a surprised gasp, he snatched the stocking cap off her head.

Ellie's squint matched his, bringing his startled expression into momentary focus. "Winston Rademacher," she said.

Shock was too mild a word to describe her reaction to the royal advisor, who seemed to be giving the orders here. Prince Markus's right-hand man laughed. The joke was on him, but Ellie felt the sting of his laughter. It labeled her as a nobody who had done something quite unexpected for someone of her station.

"*Enchanté, mademoiselle.*" His nostrils flared as he inhaled deeply and looked skyward toward the gunmetal-gray clouds that promised as much temper as he was concealing. "This is rich."

Jerome misinterpreted Rademacher's displeasure. He managed to sound accusatory and apologetic all at the same time. "I just hit her once. Only 'cause she came after my busted leg."

"Cease your prattle, man." Ellie turned her face from Rademacher's unblinking scrutiny. "This woman is not Lucia Carradigne."

"What?" Jerome sputtered in shock. "She was wearing the red dress from the picture you gave us."

"Playing dress-up, were we?" Winston Rademacher stroked his smooth-tipped finger across her jaw, then angled her chin so that she was forced to look at him. Though most of him remained out of focus, his dark, slanted eyes sent a clear message. Ellie was history. "You're Easton's secretary. A commoner. And you had these fools believing you're a princess?"

His disbelief bordered on insult, though a bruised ego was the least of her worries at the moment. She pushed at her left temple, wishing she had her small, round lenses to hide behind. "Yes."

"Brava." He released her with a smile that had her backing up until her hips butted the fender of the car and she could retreat no farther. "This is damnably inconvenient. Nothing personal, mind you. But I simply can't have you around to repeat my name." He turned. "Sinjun."

Cade's big, rangy body drifted up beside her. "Yeah?"

"Shoot her." Rademacher gave the order and headed for the SUV.

Ellie's lungs emptied on one big whoosh of air and she grasped the fender, feeling light-headed and so far beyond fear that she could barely stand, much less think of a protest.

But Cade stopped him. "We already have a dead body in the lake. You sure your boss wants to leave a trail?"

Winston spun around, the rise in pitch of his voice the only outward sign of his patience unraveling. "My boss has given me carte blanche to do whatever I see fit to achieve our goals. Right now I question whether or not you knew she was a fake."

Cade looked him in the eye and lied. "I didn't."

"Prove it."

"Prove what?"

Winston took a step toward Cade. "Your loyalty. To me. To this entire project." He pulled a white handkerchief from his pocket, and even Ellie's eyes could see him wiping his hands as if he had dirtied them. "Unless you've gone weak like your father. Don't forget—you owe me."

"I haven't forgotten."

Jerome snagged Ellie by the elbow and dragged her into the middle of the battle of wills. "I'll shoot the lying bi—"

Winston cut him off. "Is there anything you do that isn't coarse and self-serving?"

"I deserve it. I'm the one who's paid the price here." Jerome's grip tightened in a painful pinch. Ellie grunted and tried to twist free. "She's giving it away for free to Sinjun. Isn't that right, sugar?"

His crude endearment ended in a gurgle as Cade's iron-hard forearm tightened like a noose around the short man's neck. Cade lifted him right off the ground. Ellie backed away from Jerome's flailing good leg. His cheeks and lips turned purple, then pale.

"Release him," Rademacher commanded. He'd pulled a small, snub-nosed revolver from inside his coat. He cradled the weapon with the handkerchief in his hands and pointed the business end at Cade's temple. A matter of inches and a steady hand were all that stood between Cade and instant death. Ellie's heart lurched in her throat. "Release him," he said again.

"Sure." The moment Jerome's eyes rolled up and his eyelids rolled down, Cade released his unconscious body and tossed him to the ground. He turned so that his eye replaced his temple as Rademacher's target. He didn't flinch. "He doesn't know how to treat a lady."

Oh, God, he was still defending her. With his life. Right up to the moment he had to kill her. Tears stung her eyes. Were all men this impossible to understand? Or just the ones she fell in love with?

Ellie gasped, as shocked by the revelation as she was by the violence unfolding around her.

Had she fallen in love with Cade? How? When? Why?

Captor and protector. Her tutor in both kissing and cunning. Equally adept at rousing her temper and breaking her heart. How could the fates be so cruel, to let a man like Cade shatter her sheltered world? A man who lived by his own set of rules and whose hard heart had no place for a shy, rebellious virgin like herself.

It wasn't love, it was infatuation. Fascination. Fantasy.

The Cade St. John of her dreams needed her, desired her, cherished her.

The real man was pulling that big black gun from his holster.

"I'll do it." Cade never looked away from the gun pointed at his face until Rademacher lowered his weapon. "She's been my responsibility. My mistake. I'll take care of it."

Ellie held her breath in the dead air that followed his callous, toneless vow. So much for last-minute heroics on her behalf. There had never been a man in Ellie's life before Cade St. John. There would never be another.

After Rademacher put his gun away, Cade slipped the

clip of bullets from his own gun. He slammed them back into place and Ellie jumped. He meant to do this. Now.

Rademacher reached into his jacket again.

He answered Cade's questioning frown with a dismissive wave and pulled out a palm-size cell phone. "I'm calling an associate to mobilize an alternate plan."

"Plan B?" Cade asked.

Huh? Ellie looked from one man to the other. Maybe none of them ever made sense.

"Yes." Rademacher punched a programmed number and lifted the cell phone to his ear. "Now kill her."

Cade parted his legs into a balanced stance and pointed his gun at her.

Oh, no. No, no, no, no, no.

Should she run? He'd shoot her in the back. Should she attack him? As if she had a chance.

"Wait." Ellie put up her hand. If death was inevitable, she'd face it head-on. She pulled her glasses from her pocket and put them on so that she could look fate straight in the eye. There'd be no shy retreat for her this time. She was Eleanor Standish, goddaughter of the late Queen Cassandra. Trusted employee. Sister. Daughter. Friend.

"Forgive me, Ellie." Cade took aim.

She shrugged and offered him a serene half smile. "I guess I'll never get that dance."

The look in his indigo eyes intensified fiercely. Ellie blinked and adjusted her glasses. Was he telling her something more than goodbye? Why didn't the man come with subtitles? She squinted, trying to decipher his...apology? No. His eyes were warning her. Ellie frowned. Warning her about what?

She stared into the black chasm of the gun barrel, then followed the steel barrel up to Cade's midnight gaze again.

His finger squeezed the trigger. Ellie squared her shoulders and tilted her chin, standing tall and proud despite her fear.

Cade spun around. She jumped at the crack of repetitive gunfire. Ellie clutched at her chest. But it was Winston Rademacher who flew back as if he'd been jerked on a string, then crumpled to the ground. Ellie leaned forward, too shocked to do more than stare at the circle of bright red pooling at the front of the man's starched white shirt.

Before Ellie could process what had happened, Cade was moving. He shot out two tires on the SUV. "What are you—"

"Get in!"

Cade grabbed Ellie and pushed her toward the beat-up sedan. He opened the driver's-side door and shoved her in ahead of him. She scrambled across the seat to avoid being crushed as Cade slid in right behind her.

Clutching the gun and the wheel in one hand, he pulled out his keys, jammed them into the ignition and revved the engine. He threw the car into gear and stomped on the accelerator. The tires spun on the gravel roadway, spitting up rocks until they found traction in the mud underneath. When the car lurched forward, Ellie buckled up.

Cade slammed his door. In a miraculous feat of steering with his knees, he palmed the back of her neck and pushed her head down beside his thigh. "Stay out of sight!"

Ellie squirmed against his rough grasp. "Stop it! What's going on? Where are you taking me?" Her cheek pressed into his rock-hard thigh at an awkward angle, but he had her locked down as securely as that steel chain in the basement had. "Cade—"

The rear window exploded behind them, spraying the back seat with broken glass. Ellie grabbed his leg and huddled closer, forgetting her desperation to be free a moment ago.

Next she heard the rapid *pop-pop-pop* of gunfire. Some-one was shooting at them! With a gun a lot more powerful than Winston Rademacher's small pistol.

Jerome had regained consciousness, she thought, or Lenny had come back to camp. For surely a man with a bullet in him couldn't pin them down with such an attack.

Cade returned fire. Something exploded beneath them and the car swerved to the right. Cade swore, Ellie prayed.

In the distance she heard Rademacher shout, his voice hoarse with pain, "Kill them! Kill them both!"

"Hold on!" Cade ordered.

He released her and grabbed the steering wheel with both hands. His gun clattered to the floor. He fought each wrenching turn.

"Cade?"

She stretched her arms across his lap and found his seat belt. The wheels hit paved road and bounced into the air. When they landed again, Cade gunned the engine and Ellie buckled him in.

The smacking sound of shredded rubber on asphalt gave way to the earsplitting whine of a metal rim sparking against the concrete.

"We're losing it!"

"Cade!"

Ellie sat up in time to see the world spin around her. The ruined wheel slid off the shoulder and hit the mud from last night's rain. With one wheel sucked in like an anchor, the car fishtailed and plunged into the ditch.

Chapter Ten

"Come on, honey. We gotta move. We gotta move now."

Cade's voice cut through the hazy fog in Ellie's head. She shook her head and groaned, shutting her eyes to orient herself in the spinning darkness. She felt Cade's hands on her, rough and quick. Cupping her head and neck, sliding down her arms. Ellie understood the inspection for what it was, felt the urgency in his touch that told her time was precious. She opened her eyes and latched on to his wrists, stopping his search. "I'm okay. Just shaken up, I think."

"Good girl."

Then strong arms were lifting her, holding her close, setting her feet on the ground.

By some miracle, her glasses had stayed in place. The first thing she saw was the slash of red across Cade's cheek. With the warmth of Cade's sheltering hug still working its way down to her wobbly legs, Ellie reached up and touched the spot with two fingers. They came away sticky and moist with blood. She frowned, studying the wound more closely. "You're hurt."

"It's not bad," he said, pulling her hand down. "It's the cut you made with the lantern handle. I hit the side of the car when we bounced and it opened up again." He tucked her hand into his and pulled her along behind him, climbing up the far side of the ditch toward the lake. "Let's go."

Ellie's too-big shoes slipped on the muddy embankment and she fell to her knees. As her pant legs soaked up the dirty moisture, she thought of infection and blood loss and nasty cuts that *she* was responsible for. "We need to clean that out before it scars."

"Not right now, we don't."

Cade hauled her up onto her feet and darted into the woods, forcing her into a steady jog behind him. Ellie grit her teeth against the jolts of pain that jarred through her rattled skull and back with every footfall. The roiling line of clouds and rain blocked what was left of the setting sun, transforming the ancient oak and pine forest into a maze of spindly-armed giants and ghostly shadows.

Cade shortened his stride and Ellie kept pace, running farther into the woods, running farther away from the road and that tangible link to civilization. Where was he taking her? Why was she blithely following him?

The guilt she felt for inflicting pain and damaging that handsome face gave way to a need to justify her actions. She'd been his prisoner, after all. With all the odds stacked against her, she'd been desperate to use whatever means she could to beg, bully or buy her way to freedom.

And now he wanted her to run with him through the woods of Someplace, U.S.A., without so much as a *why* or *where* or *sorry about almost having to shoot you.*

Ellie dug in her heels and stopped, nearly toppling over, while Cade kept running. But poised and alert as always, he stopped, turned and caught her. He shifted so that he faced her, cupping her elbows in his palms. Like that, he backed her into a stand of young oaks.

"I'm sorry." His dark eyes scanned her from head to toe. "You holding up okay?"

Ellie's chest rose and fell in deep, quick breaths as her body screamed for oxygen after their continued exertion. He was barely breathing hard. The cur.

But that wasn't the frustration that made her grab two fistfuls of the front of his black T-shirt and pull herself right up into that brilliant indigo gaze. She searched the shadows and secrets and darkness there for some sign of the truth.

"You *are* a good guy, right?"

"When I can be." He spared a moment to glance over his shoulder to secure their position before sliding his hands from her elbows to her back and pulling her body into heated, dangerous contact with his. His eyes danced with a hidden message she tried to understand. "Commander Cadence St. John, Special Operations, at your service. I'm working undercover for King Easton. You'll just have to take my word for it, since I don't carry ID with me, for obvious reasons. Sorry to have to introduce myself this way."

Ellie's clutch on his shirt tightened. "You're still in the army? You're not a deserter or traitor?"

The corner of his mouth crooked into a rueful smile, and he laid a gentle hand on her cheek. "I'll tell you everything later, I promise. Right now we need to put some distance between us and Rademacher."

"Why?"

"Mostly because he wants us dead. I don't think that he appreciates being shot, that you're not Princess Lucia and that we can implicate him in criminal activities." He hunched his shoulders down to her level and looked her in the eye. His impatient glare warred with the indulgent care of his hands. "Can we continue this conversation later?"

Ellie adjusted her glasses and looked beyond Cade's shoulders. The wide-open space of her childhood home in Korosol seemed a long way away. Here, she saw little but wind-whipped trees and hills and the sun disappearing beyond the horizon. It was hard to keep her hopes from sinking with it.

"If our object is escape, why are we running back south?" Doubt lingered in her voice. "You're heading toward the house."

"It's not the way they'd expect us to go. Besides, I have a different destination in mind. Trust me?"

His question hung between them in the expectant silence, broken only by the patter of raindrops on the canopy of leaves above.

He'd asked her that once before, running through the woods, and she'd told him no. Her brain, her logic, her life experience told her she shouldn't trust this man.

But her heart told her something different.

The cold rain came in the silence between them. It splattered her cheeks and nose, and ran in rivulets down her glasses, smearing her perception of Cade and the world around her. He hadn't killed her when he could have, should have. Instead, he'd shot the man who'd ordered her death. He'd shielded her body from bullets, pulled her from a wrecked car.

Asked her to trust him.

Army commander. Duke. Hard-edged man who held her as if she mattered. Who suppressed his impatience within his tensed muscles while he waited for her answer.

Ellie slugged her way through a lifetime of doubting her instincts and nodded before finding her way back to those indigo eyes. "Yes."

He planted a swift kiss on her lips that was grateful and full of promise.

"Thank you." When he pulled away, he swept his thumbs across her cheeks, wiping away the raindrops, leaving behind a trail of warmth. She could see a faint light smoldering in the depths of his eyes that hadn't been there a moment ago. He wrapped his hand around hers, turned and scanned their surroundings, then led her off on a loping run again, getting back to business as usual.

Ellie inhaled deeply and kept pace beside his shortened stride. She wasn't sure why a simple agreement seemed to give him such calming pleasure. Why *her* profession of trust had been worth a kiss.

But she did understand one thing. By leading with her heart instead of her head, she might very well have sentenced herself to death.

"I HATE RUNNING."

Ellie lay on her stomach in the mud, dutifully staying low while Cade crept up to the crest of the hill and peered down into the clearing where Tony Costa's cabin stood. Though what he hoped to see through the rain and cloud cover that blocked the moon, she couldn't tell.

Cade was finally beginning to show signs of the physical strain that left her panting for air. Her legs ached. Her lungs burned with the need for oxygen. Her wet clothes stuck to her like a cold second skin and made her teeth chatter. When he slid back down beside her, he plowed his fingers into his rain-soaked hair and combed the water out of it.

"How's your leg holding up?" He reached down and squeezed the calf of her leg, remembering the cramp she'd developed on her first sprint through the woods.

Remembering a detail about her. Ellie was touched and a bit flustered by his concern. She rolled onto her back and sat up, pushing her glasses up her nose, then wringing the excess water from her braid.

"Everything's tired. But I'm fine." She had to raise her voice slightly to be heard above the sound of rain. "I thought he said he didn't have a phone. Are we just going to go in and ask if he'll drive us into town?"

Cade shook his head. "His truck's gone." He paused as if weighing the decision to add something more.

That worried her.

"What?" Ellie smoothed the loose strands of hair around her face and tried to tuck them behind her ears. But the heavy weight of wet knit had stretched the sleeves of the shirt well beyond her fingertips, leaving her arms flapping like useless fins as she worked to free her hands.

Cade reached for her hair and completed the task for her. Then he tunneled his fingers into her hair and cradled the back of her head, turning her to face him. She could tell from the forced smile on his mouth that he wasn't going to share his concerns. Not completely. "I have a phone," he told her. "I'll call my contact once we're holed up for the night. What we really need are supplies."

Could she still trust him when he only gave her half-truths?

Tugging her hand from her sleeve, she wrapped her fingers around his wrist, finding a reassuring warmth beneath the surface chill of his skin. "You're going to steal from Mr. Costa?"

"It's called survival, honey."

He massaged his fingers into her scalp, seemingly savoring the soothing touch as much as she did. Not for the first time, she wondered at his use of that endearment. Did it mean anything? Or was it just an easy nickname to toss off? Countless dowagers and old men and store clerks had called her *honey* over the years when they didn't know her or couldn't remember her name.

Did Cade see her the same way? Or rather, not see her? He was handsome enough to have any woman on the planet. She was plain as a bucket. A muddy, water-logged, four-eyed bucket. If Cade truly was an army commander, that would explain the innate sense of honor she recognized in him. It would also explain his determination to keep her safe. Could there be anything more to his dangerous kisses and hungry looks and gentle touches than forced proximity and a sense of duty? Did he pay her this tender attention because she was the only woman—the only person— around?

Cade misinterpreted her extended silence. He flicked the raindrops from her glasses and crooked his mouth into a boyish grin. "Hey, I'll leave some money on the kitchen counter, if that'll make you feel better."

She stared at him a moment in blank confusion. Then she remembered her comment about stealing from Tony Costa and laughed at his silly effort to ease her concern. It was a tiny giggle that started in her throat and worked its way up into laughter.

At the sound, his cocky grin softened into a wide, natural smile. His chest swelled and relaxed with a soulful sigh. Drawn to the movement, Ellie placed her hand over his heart and felt the strong, sure beat quicken its pace. He covered her hand with his own and held it there. "That's better."

Okay. So she definitely felt noticed. Cared for. At that moment, it didn't matter what Cade's motivation might be. He made her feel important. All kinds of sweet, drizzly feelings warmed her from the inside out, strengthening her in body and spirit.

Her rush of gratitude was so intense that Ellie had the strangest urge to throw her arms around his neck, hold him close and kiss him senseless. But then, that had never been her way. Of course, she'd never spent any time with a man she wanted to kiss senseless. And she wasn't sure how to go about doing that, anyway. Besides, she was loath to spoil this deep, safe, connected feeling they shared right now.

"Ellie." Hearing her name in that dark, helpless fog of a voice thrilled her more than any *honey* could.

A flash of lightning illuminated the sky and left her blinded for an instant. The crack of thunder that followed on its heels was enough to shake her from this schoolgirl stupor. She was stranded in the woods with a virtual stranger to whom she'd given her trust, while a supposedly faithful royal confidant and a few hired goons pursued them with guns and knives and nasty tempers.

Those sobering thoughts were all she needed for the sensible Ellie to come shining through. "What do you need me to do?"

He pulled her hand away and gave it a squeeze. "Stay down. Stay put until I come for you."

And then he was gone.

Ellie crawled up just far enough so she could watch Cade descend over the rocks on the other side and run in a zigzag pattern toward the white clapboard cabin. He glided over the ground like a wraith, and it amazed her how a man so brawny could be so light and quick on his feet. Despite the danger, the beauty of his form kindled a heat inside her that made the darkness and the moisture and the sense of malevolent eyes watching her from the shadows a little less noticeable.

After he'd darted up onto the back porch and disappeared inside, Ellie crouched and waited on the hilltop behind a stand of tall grass and weeds. She made herself blink and look away from the cabin. She didn't know what kind of supplies he was after, but apparently he wasn't finding them. The seconds ticked into minutes and Ellie found herself clenching and unclenching her fingers in the mud beneath her, digging a miniature trough.

Disgusted that the goop collected under her fingernails was all she had to show for what could be the last few minutes of her life, she sat up and wiped her nails on her pant leg. Now she knew why she always jumped in to help get things done. She hated waiting.

Four days ago she'd been transcribing dictation and making phone calls and moving, unseen, through the background of the affairs of court and the king. Now, instead of being rewarded for her dedication and reliability with one perfect waltz at a grand ball, she was huddling in the mud wearing man-size clothes and praying she could just go home.

But she'd settle for Cade reappearing. Her watch had long since been confiscated with the rest of the items in her purse. And though it was probably only a matter of minutes, it felt like hours had passed since she saw him jimmy the door with his knife and go inside.

"Be patient," she warned herself out loud. But when her fingers began their nervous digging a second time, Ellie shook herself free of this feeling of abandonment. She couldn't just sit here. There must be something she could do to help.

She could scout around. Keep watch while Cade was in the cabin. Her eyes were working just fine with her glasses, despite the dampness on her skin that kept them sliding down her nose. That was it. Do something.

Even that simple, self-assigned task made her feel less antsy about sitting alone out here. She crinkled her nose as she tried to assess her surroundings. The first line of rain had been heavy enough to soak everything around her and fill the air with the dank scent of compost and rot.

Not ten feet away, there was a pile of old moss-covered tree trunks that had run out of soil for their growing roots and toppled over. The real storm was yet to come and she had better be looking for some kind of shelter. The nature-made overhang could at least offer her a break from the wind, if not keep her warm and dry. Ellie climbed up on her hands and feet like a bear and sidled over to the dead trees, minding Cade's request to stay out of sight.

The galloping hoofbeats of continuous thunder pursued her across the distance, drawing her attention to the skies in the west, where lightning and wind stirred the clouds like a witch's cauldron. Ellie shivered from within, thinking of the violence heading their way, of the violence they'd left behind.

She climbed over the top of the highest trunk and dropped down on the other side. She rubbed her hands together, grateful for the reprieve from the weather—and froze.

The air temperature had dropped a good twenty degrees since nightfall had arrived. But that wasn't what let whatever body heat she had left seep out into the ground at her feet.

"Lenny." She inched back a step, slipped, caught herself on the slimy bark of the tree she'd just scaled. "I, uh… You startled me. Cade's here. With me." She tried to defend herself with words.

He stared at her through the darkness, unblinking, unsmiling. He held a small gun in his hand, pointed right at her. He'd always been so quiet, so big, so immovable.

A bolt of lightning exploded across the sky and Ellie screamed. She slapped her hand over her mouth to stifle a second scream as a trailing edge of electricity in the clouds dappled the sky like fireworks.

It provided enough light to see what she needed to. More than she ever wanted to.

Lenny was dead.

Sitting on a rock with a thick pen clutched in his fist,

not the gun she'd imagined in the shadows. His forehead bore a dime-size hole.

"Oh, Lenny." Tears stung her eyes and burned in her throat. He sat there, his gray, puffy cheeks forever frozen in a look of surprise. He looked for all the world as if he'd been sitting there, writing a note, when someone discovered his hiding place just as she had. She'd screamed at the discovery, but someone else had shot him.

She'd screamed.

The realization ripped through her with the electrifying charge of one of those lightning bolts. "Stupid move, Ellie."

This hill was only a mile or so from the cabin where they'd left Jerome and Winston Rademacher and the other man Cade had mentioned. She didn't know if the rain would muffle the sound or not, but she wasn't waiting to find out if she'd given away her location. *Their* location.

She'd endangered them both.

"Cade?" She whispered his name on a panicked plea, then kick-started her body past the shock of finding Lenny and scrambled up the stack of fallen tree trunks. "Cade?" Would they go to the cabin first if they'd heard her? To the dock? "Cade?" She had to warn him.

The boats she wore on her feet gave her little traction. She slipped on the moss and tumbled backward, rolling into Lenny's body and knocking him off his perch. His big, stiff body fell like a mighty oak onto her legs. This time she stopped the scream in her throat.

She pushed and tugged and scooted out from beneath him in the slippery mud. As she backed away from the mercenary's lifeless body, her hand hit something solid. She looked down before rolling onto her hands and knees and picking it up.

Another notebook. Small and black. Just like the one

she'd stolen from Cade. Was Lenny writing his memoirs? Confessing his crimes? Had he been working undercover, too?

Whatever the reason, the other notebook had been important to Cade. Using nothing more than that piece of knowledge to make her decision, she stuffed the notebook into a pocket and scrambled out of the shelter.

She didn't stop at the crest of the hill this time. She sat on her bottom and half-slid, half-fell down the other side into the clearing. When her feet hit level ground, she took off running. "Cade?"

A bright flash distracted her from her run toward the cabin. But it wasn't lightning this time.

It was help.

The sweep of headlights cut through the curtain of rain as a pickup truck pulled into the gravel driveway beside the house. Like a moth drawn to the flame of promised safety, Ellie ran straight for the vehicle.

Fat drops pelted the uneven ground, splashing mud onto her legs and filling her shoes with water. "Help us! Please." She waved her arms in the air to get the driver's attention.

When she heard the gears grinding into park, she slowed her aching legs to a walk and let her mouth drop open, breathing in huge gulps of air and spitting out the water running down her face. A bolt of lightning burst across the sky, standing the hairs on the back of her neck on end. She ducked and covered her ears as an explosion of thunder hammered the air at nearly the same instant.

"Ellie…!" Cade called to her, but whatever else he said was muffled by rain and distance.

The cab light of the truck came on as the driver opened the door. A shock of snowy hair gleamed white and bright. The fisherman!

What was his name? She squinted into the spotlighting glare of the headlights. "Mr. Costa?" She remembered his reaction when she'd run to him the other day and collapsed at his feet. She hurried her step when she saw him climb back into the cab and close the door. "I'm not crazy. Please. We're in trouble. We need your help."

A different door slammed off to her right. "Ellie!" Cade shot out the back of the cabin and came toward her at a dead run. Because he was dressed in black and lost in the shadows, she couldn't make out the contortions of his upper body.

"We can get that ride into town." She shielded her eyes from the headlights and turned his way. He was putting something into his pocket. No. Taking something out. "I found Lenny on the other side of the hill. He's dead."

"Get out of the light!" His hoarse shout made no sense.

"Did you hear me?" She pointed to Tony Costa. "He'll help us—"

Ellie turned to show him their white-haired neighbor. Her eyes rounded in shock. Her mouth opened in a silent scream.

Tony Costa had pulled a rifle from his truck and was taking aim.

At her.

"No!" Perfectly targeted in the headlights, Ellie instinctively backed away. Suddenly it seemed as if her vision had taken on super powers. With her senses translating everything in slow motion, she spotted the black line of the rifle barrel and followed it up to the cold, unblinking eye that had her in its sights. Costa's long, tanned finger curled around the trigger and squeezed.

Fortunately Cade moved in real time.

For the briefest of moments, he was airborne in the light. She heard the rifle report as loud as the thunderstorm itself.

Cade slammed into her, knocking her to the ground. They slid in the mud and disappeared into the darkness beyond the headlights.

"Are you hit?" he rasped in her ear.

Crushed between man and earth, Ellie could only shake her head.

He rolled off her. Air rushed into her lungs and Ellie sat up. "Are you?"

Instead of answering, Cade rose on his knees and steadied his gun with both hands. He shot twice, taking out both headlights.

"Move," he said. Ellie had already scrambled to her feet by the time he cupped her elbow and urged her into a stooping run toward the lake. "Get in the boat."

A string of curses in fluid French and botched English chased them down to the dock. A rain of unseen bullets smacked into the ground at their feet with such force that Ellie could no longer distinguish between gunshots and thunder.

"Cade?" Mud and gravel gave way to wood beneath their feet.

"Get in." Ellie jumped down into the boat a step ahead of Cade. "Get the ropes."

She crawled over the seats and lifted the first rope from its mooring post while Cade started the engine. Tony Costa slammed the door of his truck and gunned the engine, spinning out gravel and mud until he found traction.

Ellie moved to the back rope. But soaked with water, it had expanded into a tight ring around its post. She fought to untie the knot, but the swollen hemp wouldn't budge.

The boat's motor roared to life. It danced in the water, waiting to be thrown into gear. Costa's truck barreled across the clearing. Cade fired blindly into the darkness.

"Ellie!"

Lightning flashed. Costa careened to a screeching stop. "It's stuck!"

Ellie jumped back as a small projectile dinged off the side of the boat. Cade hit a switch on his gun and an empty magazine popped out. He loaded a second round of bullets and kept shooting. The next heavenly illumination revealed Costa braced behind the cover of his truck, taking sure aim at the boat.

"Today, Ellie!"

She spied what she needed in the same flash of light that temporarily blinded Costa. She lunged across the seats and pulled Cade's knife from his boot. The steel blade was thick and shiny and made a satisfying thunk against the aluminum bulkwark as she chopped through the rope.

"Go!"

Cade backed the boat away from the dock. "Stay down," he warned, turning the exposed stern toward Costa and throttling the engine up to full. Ellie rocked between the seats, hunkering down into a ball while the old boat skipped out toward open water beyond the range of Costa's rifle.

The storm churned rough whitecaps along the surface of the lake, but Ellie's stomach gladly endured the lurching ride. After several minutes Cade slowed the boat to a cruising speed and snapped his gun back in the holster.

"My knife?" As he breathed easier, so did she. She scooted across the seats and handed him his knife, handle first. In one, seemingly fluid movement, he slipped the knife into his boot and reached for her.

Ellie willingly walked into the snug circle of his arm. She wrapped her arms around his waist and cuddled close, burying her nose in the wet-heat smell of Cade's chest. "Why was he shooting at us?"

"The usual reason."

She didn't have the strength to muster a smile. "Does everyone want us dead?"

He pressed a kiss to the crown of her head and tightened his grip around her shoulders. "No. Not everyone. I like you in one piece."

She hugged him tightly, silently sending him the same message.

"Tony Costa's a hit man. I imagine Rademacher hired him to get rid of Lenny and Jerome and me when the job was done. You got added to the list when—"

"—it turned out I wasn't a princess."

Cade released the wheel to tip up her chin. Lightning rippled through the clouds above him, silhouetting him like a dark champion against the backdrop of the roiling sky in the instant before he kissed her.

A giddy sense of relief rushed through Ellie, making her legs weak, making her heart strong. She was finally in a place without dead bodies, without men who harbored greed and murder in their eyes. She was with Cade. Her hero. Her brave, outcast hero.

She stretched up on tiptoe, trying to offer him solace in return for saving her life. The friction of their wet clothes and searching mouths bound them together in a healing, calming heat. He explored her lips leisurely, tenderly, thoroughly, before lifting his head and tucking her under his chin.

He returned his attention to the wheel. "You're a princess in my book. They don't come with any more class and grace under pressure than you do. Hang tough a while longer, okay? I'll call in for backup, but I imagine we'll have to find a safe spot to hole up for the night."

Like Ellie, the storm had spent most of its energy. But she wanted to live up to the gruff compliment in Cade's words. Despite the reassurance of his solid strength, she was keenly aware of the danger of being out on the open water while lightning still sparked in the clouds above them.

She rested her cheek over his heart, imagining she could somehow protect his most vulnerable spot there. "Your hide may be tough, but you're not impervious to lightning bolts. Find someplace to stop. Soon."

The laughter in his chest rumbled like a soothing caress in her ear. "Yes, Your Highness."

He shifted their positions so that she could take the wheel and steer while he pulled out his cell phone and punched in a number. Though he worked with his typical machine-like precision, he moved up behind her and wrapped his arm around her waist, pulling her back against his chest as if he took as much comfort in their physical contact as she did.

She could hear his heartbeat and the distant ringing of a phone somewhere across his cellular connection. Ellie found herself listening as intently as Cade when the line clicked, indicating his call had gone through.

But he waited for the other party to speak first. "Allo?"

Cade's heartbeat stuttered at the man's foreign greeting. Then his heart resumed its steady rhythm at a faster pace.

"What's wrong?" Ellie whispered.

He clamped his hand over her mouth, shushing her. His whole body stiffened with an alert readiness that knocked the supports right out from under the false sense of contentment his embrace had given her just moments ago.

He said five words in their native language. "Any news about the scandal?"

"Excuse me?" The other man sounded as confused as Ellie.

Cade continued in English. "If the king's around, tell him his travel plans have changed."

Was he speaking in code? Or babbling gibberish? The Easton she knew wasn't going anywhere until he'd found the right grandchild to name as his successor to the throne.

Ellie held her breath, waiting for the other man's reply.

"I'll give him the message."

Cade released her and turned off his phone.

Ellie had a bad feeling about whatever had just transpired. "I hate to make the association, but does *scandal* have something to do with you?"

"Not now, Ellie."

He guided her down to a seat and hooked a life jacket around her neck before opening up the throttle again and steering the boat toward an unknown shore.

A very bad feeling, indeed.

Chapter Eleven

Easton Carradigne, King of Korosol, walked into the study he'd commandeered at his daughter-in-law's penthouse and found his grandson, Markus, setting the phone down on the desk.

The phone.

He stepped into the room undetected, leaving the door slightly ajar. There were servants down the hall, clearing the dining room table after dinner. He felt reassured, knowing someone could hear him if… He didn't enjoy being alone with Prince Markus. Not if he could help it.

Easton stood at the edge of the carpet, watching while his grandson opened the humidor on the desk and helped himself to one of the Carradignes' imported cigars. "Good evening, Markus."

He noted the subtle jerk of Markus's shoulders. He'd startled him. Good. He didn't like it when that boy was up to something. But when he turned around, he wore one of those charming smiles that showed off his teeth, instead of his character. He dipped his head in an informal bow. "Grandfather."

The king walked into the room and crossed to the desk. He sat in the leather chair, asserting that this was *his* space—for the moment, at least—on which Markus was trespassing. "Does Charlotte know you're here?" Though they'd had their differences in the past, his son's widow was a consummate hostess. "She'd have invited you to join us for dinner, I'm sure." Enough hinting that Markus's visit seemed suspicious, if not unwelcome. "Did you have someone on the phone before I came in?"

Markus took the time to trim and light his cigar, puffing several times before answering. "I was expecting a business call, so I picked it up. It was a wrong number."

Easton's antennae revved up to full alert. Only one person had the number to that particular phone. It was impossible for anyone else to dial into it.

Markus unbuttoned his charcoal blazer and sat. "Where's that mousy little frump who runs around answering the phone for you, anyway? I want to tell her to patch my calls through to here."

Easton gripped the arms of his chair and squeezed until his bony knuckles turned white. If there was any way he could ram that cigar down Markus's throat and still maintain his controlled kingly status, he'd do it. "Ellie is vacationing with friends. She wanted to see some of the country before she returns to Korosol with me."

"And Cousin Lucia? I haven't seen her the past few days, either."

"I imagine she's with her new husband." He couldn't resist one fatherly dig. The boy was thirty-five years old. He needed to learn values sometime. Easton cringed as he listened to his own thought processes. Markus was spoiled enough that he still thought of him as *the boy*. "There are a few Carradignes who make the effort to spend time with their families."

The message missed its mark. "Of course." Or maybe it hadn't. "Just like you were always there for us growing up." Markus stood, ignoring the etiquette of asking for permission or allowing his king to stand first. "Well, I'd better be going. I have a friend holding a box for me at the Metropolitan Opera."

"I thought you were expecting a call."

Markus smiled. It reeked of insincerity. "Maybe I just stopped by to see how my aging grandfather was feeling. You haven't looked well lately." He leaned forward, bracing his hands on the opposite side of the desk. Looking down on him. "How are you? Really?"

The sniveling weasel! Easton rose, countering his grandson's position. He would not let this *boy* see his weakness. He would not allow Markus to consider the notion that his grandfather's deteriorating health meant he was one step closer to becoming king. "Your concern is touching, Markus. Now unless you have some real business to conduct here, I suggest you go play with your friends and leave a man to run the affairs of state."

Something willful and hurt and angry flashed in Markus's eyes. Easton almost considered apologizing for the insult. But Markus blew out a puff of smoke, and by the time it dissipated, his expression had blanked into that mask of false charm once more.

He pulled away from the desk and buttoned his jacket. "Grandfather."

There were no more pleasantries. No attempts to mend fences or reestablish trust. After Markus departed, Easton sank into his chair. The stress of the past few days was telling on him. That encounter with his grandson left him feeling light-headed and weak.

If Ellie was here, she'd fix him tea and make him lie down. But Ellie wasn't here. And if that call meant what he thought it did, she might never come back. His late wife Cassandra would never have forgiven him for what he'd allowed to happen to her goddaughter.

Despite the selfish twist of his remarks, Markus was right. Just as he had so many times in the past, as king, he'd put his country before his family.

And Ellie *was* family. She was every bit as dear and necessary to his life as his own granddaughters.

God, he was an old fool.

A sentimental, guilt-ridden old fool.

But he was a good king.

The game was over. He had subjects to protect.

Responsibility weighed heavily on his shoulders, but determination lightened the load.

Easton sat up straight and reached for the secure cell phone that Markus had picked up. He punched a button and verified that the call had come through.

Suspicious of Markus and what he might have figured out from that call, Easton picked up the Carradigne phone and contacted the captain of the Royal Guard, Devon Montcalm.

He issued an order that was calm and succinct. "Something's gone wrong. Tell your men to move out."

"I DON'T THINK I'll ever be dry or warm again."

Ellie held out her hands toward the iffy source of heat, then hugged herself and rubbed her arms as the chills shivered through her body.

Cade had ditched the boat in a shallow stand of reeds and trees along the shore, then led her through the darkness to this elegant abode. An old roadside motel whose road had deteriorated into an overgrown concrete path offered them shelter for the night. Using his knife to jimmy the lock, he'd broken into a room.

While he'd gone outside to check the propane tank and fire up the generator, Ellie explored. The small room, with its one double bed and adjoining bathroom, looked as if the owners had simply walked away—months ago—leaving everything in its place. Though a coat of dust covered everything, she'd found soap and towels and a spare lightbulb in a drawer to fix the single lamp and give them light.

Unfortunately there was no running water.

Still, they'd stripped off most of their wet, mud-caked clothes and hung them in the bathroom to dry. Now she huddled in her underwear in front of the rattling, built-in space heater that smelled of burned metal and oily fumes. She'd wrapped a towel around her like a skirt and hung one over her shoulders to try to conserve body heat.

It wasn't working.

"Here."

Cade came up behind her and draped a blanket over her shoulders. He wrapped his arms around her, blanket and all, and pulled her into his bare, solid chest. He pressed his cheek to the hair at her temple and folded himself around her, generating a furnace of warmth both inside and out. Ellie closed her eyes and sank into his embrace, willingly trapped between walls of heat.

Cade breathed in Ellie's sweet scent and held her until he felt her shivers subside. As the chill of her cheek warmed beneath his, he adjusted his stance so that he could feel the ripe curve of her bottom pushing against his loins. It was a decadent indulgence, he knew, but with Ellie he'd discovered that he couldn't quite get enough of just holding a woman in his arms.

His mother had never been a touchy-feely person. Her brand of contact had been little air kisses blown on either side of his cheeks. His father had been the hugger. The wrestler. The parent who ruffled hair and jabbed him playfully in the arm. Once Bretford was gone, he'd denied himself the unique closeness that came when two people cared enough and trusted enough to connect with simple physical contact.

Even the women he'd known had been a series of one- or two-night stands. Good sex with little cuddling in between.

But Ellie was different. Sure, the woman was a sexual revolution waiting to happen. But along with the smoldering sensuality of her figure and fiery spirit and soft, soft hair, there was a quietness about her. A gentle acceptance and wide-eyed faith in the world around her. That gentleness soothed his ravaged soul and gave him a sense of calm that he'd forgotten in his adult life.

Not to say that all his thoughts centered around the serenity this woman provided in the face of hit men and kidnappers and traitors.

He smiled against her velvet-soft cheek as she reached up and adjusted her glasses on her nose in that sweetly self-conscious way of hers. But she didn't pull away. If anything, she snuggled closer, and Cade adjusted his arms to oblige her.

He'd pared down to just his briefs and cargo pants, leaving the top button unfastened at his waist. While they'd worked to prepare the room, he'd seen her attention wander to that unhooked buttonhole again and again. His body hummed with awareness at her shy curiosity. For propriety's sake he should button his pants, instead of letting them sit loosely on his hips to dry out. But he didn't feel like following propriety's rules right now. He felt like holding Ellie.

But like all good things in his life, this quiet intimacy couldn't last. She was thinking now. He could tell it in the restless shifting of her body, the way her fingertips went up to her glasses a second time.

"If you really are on the right side of the law and you're

working for King Easton, why didn't you help me escape sooner?'' He knew he wasn't going to like where she was going with this. ''Three days you kept me chained up in that dungeon like an animal. You hunted me down. You let Jerome—''

''No. I never let—'' He took a deep, steadying breath, tamping down the possessive, protective, guilty anger that flashed in his veins at the memory of Jerome Smython attacking her. ''I never wanted him to touch you. But if I'd intervened at the beginning...'' Oh hell. How could he really justify her suffering?

She turned in his arms, and by necessity, so she could look up into his face, she put some unwanted distance between them. ''You would have blown your cover?''

Cade dropped his arms to his sides. That rare feeling of contentment oozed out of his body. As badly as he had needed it, and as carefully as she had given it, he didn't deserve her trust.

''Yeah. I needed you to stay undercover, too.''

''Why?'' Those big blue eyes expected him to give her an answer that would make everything okay.

He didn't have one. He crossed to the nightstand and picked up two of the granola bars he'd stolen from Tony Costa's stockade of supplies. Food, water and ammo had been the goal of that raid. With his pockets full, he would have chalked it up as a success...if it hadn't been for the blood-freezing sound of Ellie's scream and the sight of her spotlighted for target practice by Korosol's most notorious killer for hire. She was moving once she saw the danger, but he didn't think he'd get to her in time. He couldn't stand the thought of anyone hurting her. He couldn't let Eleanor Standish wind up dead.

She was too important to him.

''I'm not going to like this answer, am I,'' she prompted

him. But regret and discovery left him too raw to deal with this kind of conversation right now.

"Later, please?"

She came up beside him and snatched one of the granola bars out of his hands. "Now."

Cade blinked and looked down at the determination stamped onto her lovely features that he'd once mistakenly thought plain.

What the hell? Endangering an innocent woman wasn't the most shameful thing he'd ever done in his life. It hurt like hell right now, but he'd lived through worse.

He'd just give it to her hard and fast. "I needed you to be bait."

He saw her reaction to the unflattering word in the sudden pallor on her cheeks. But instead of telling him off or backing away, she unwrapped her snack and took a bite.

"To trap Winston Rademacher?" she asked, munching through her words.

"To keep the kidnapping ruse going long enough for me to find out who was behind it."

She swallowed. "It wasn't a ruse to me."

"I know." Cade was the one who finally had to move away. He took off half the granola bar in a single bite and put the length of the room between them.

Ellie climbed onto the bed and sat pretzel-style near the edge. She ate with one hand and clutched the blanket around herself with the other. "Do you think the person who wanted to kidnap Lucia will try to hurt King Easton again?"

He opened a bottle of water and took a long drink before answering. "Yeah."

"He's seventy-eight years old, Cade. His health is deteriorating. And though his mind is as sharp and spry as ever, his body's failing him. He may look like a sixty-year-old, but he gets run down easily now.''

Her concern for the old guy touched his heart and made him turn around. He had a soft spot for his king, too. "He *is* almost eighty.''

"It's more than that. He's sick. I think he's dying.''

A sudden emptiness opened inside him at the pending loss. "I didn't realize." He tried to make sense of his body's breathless reaction to the news. "He's always been accepting of me. He's treated me with respect, like I have a right to be a member of the court, even after…'' He couldn't bring himself to say the words.

Ellie rose to her feet and crossed to him. The gentle hand she nestled in the curling chest hair over his heart sizzled as much as it healed. "Even after your father killed himself?''

"Yeah.'' This wasn't his best topic. But the hint of moisture that glistened in the corners of her lake-blue eyes kept him talking. "You'd be surprised how important money and land and reputation can be to people.''

She pressed her lips together in a frown. They quivered at the intensity of the emotion she was suppressing. Anger? "They matter a lot to someone. Enough to hurt that sweet old man.''

Okay. Business like this he could handle. His mood brightened with amusement at her ladylike display of temper. He covered her hand with his and cherished the warmth of it against his beating heart. "Not if I can help it,'' he promised.

She was equally resolute. "Not if *we* can help it.''

"Ellie—''

"No.'' She pulled away, and Cade realized the mistake he'd made in underestimating her temper. "You're not the only patriot in this room, Commander. Even if all you'll let me do is watch your back, I'm going to help.''

Pride surged through his veins along with his body's vivid awareness of this shy woman's fire. He tossed aside his snack and pulled her into his arms and kissed her. Kissed her hard. Kissed her fiercely. Kissed her with tender thanks and wolfish pride. Kissed her until she made that purring sound in her throat that made him painfully aware he was a man and she was a woman.

An innocent woman.

A virgin.

A virgin who clung to him, and melted into him, and kissed him back with unabashed passion.

But a virgin, all the same.

As the supposed voice of rational experience in this embrace, Cade pulled back. He rubbed his hands up and down the delightfully smooth skin of her shoulders and back, trying to ease the primed tension out of her, wishing he could ease that same tension out of his own body.

He looked beyond her to the table at the far side of the room. The black notebook. Shorthand. That was it. Keep her busy. Keep him busy. Get the job done.

He'd find his satisfaction in getting the job done.

He had to try, at any rate. He had to be a gentleman about this. It might not be his true nature, but Ellie deserved something better than a man who walked the line between peace and violence, whose most famous claims to fame were a worthless title and a father who had put a bullet in his own head.

Leaving her behind, Cade crossed the room and picked up Lenny's notebook. He tossed it to her from a distance, needing to avoid personal contact with her right now if he wanted her to stay a virgin. "Here, Sherlock." He summoned a smile for her. "You can do more than watch my back. Translate."

His abrupt mood swing and shift in topic probably confused the hell out of her. Taking everything she offered one minute, pushing her away the next. But it was a matter of survival. For both of them.

But Ellie proved to be a trooper, as always. She pulled loose a strand of hair that had tangled in her glasses and tucked it behind her ear. And then something perked up in her eyes.

"Wait. I found another notebook with Lenny's body." She managed to hold the blanket and towels in place while she dashed into the bathroom and came back waving a second black book triumphantly. Just as quickly as it had appeared, her smile faded. "Will somebody go back and take care of him?"

She meant Lenny's body. No telling what horrific condition the body had been in when she'd seen it, and she still had the heart to worry about the man's dignity. "Yeah. I'll see to it."

"You've done a lot of hard, horrible things in your life, haven't you?"

He didn't answer that one for her. Once you'd cleaned up a room after a messy suicide, there weren't a whole lot of things left in the world a man couldn't handle if he had to.

"You do them so people like me can be safe." She walked across the room with such purpose that Cade pulled himself up to wary attention. She paused for a moment, doing nothing more profound than look up into his eyes. Then she braced her hand against his shoulder, stretched up on tiptoe and kissed his cheek. "Thank you."

He was sunk. His willpower was totaled.

He had fallen for this virginal temptress with the unbreakable spirit and forgiving heart.

The very idea terrified him.

And he wasn't a man who scared easily.

"Ellie..." What should he say? What should he do?

She dropped back on her heels and gave him the sort of smile that made his insides quake. "You say 'You're welcome,' and I get to work."

He'd better do the same.

She curled up on the bed again, near the lamp, opened up a notebook and began to read. Cade wondered why he wasn't running as far away from her as he could get. He wondered why he wasn't running to her.

He wondered why a man who knew so much about the world was learning his most important lessons from a woman who knew so little about it.

Three-quarters of an hour later, he'd learned that Lenny had spent most of his post-army career working for the Korosolan Democratic Front. What had first started as jobs for hire—bodyguard, intelligence gathering, even overseeing some of their more violent protests against the monarchy system of government—had become a calling for him. The party's democratic movement had appealed to something in the quiet giant, and he had fought tirelessly to preserve the party's ideals after their leader had signed an agreement with King Easton to begin a peaceful inclusion into Korosolan government and society.

The first notebook he'd picked up revealed that Lenny had joined the kidnapping plot as an inside man for the KDF. He perceived such manipulation of power as typical of a corrupt political system.

Cade had taken his gun apart and cleaned it, then reloaded two fifteen-round magazine clips by the time Ellie finished reading Lenny's second notebook.

"'W.R.'—that has to be Winston Rademacher—" she reasoned out loud, "'entered Sonny's house, 4:00 p.m.'"

Cade wrapped up his weapon and laid it on the table beside the lamp. "He must have been at Sonny's cabin when he called to change your delivery time." Rademacher had certainly been thorough in covering up his client's identity. "He planned to off us all along—whether you could identify any of us or not."

"The last thing Lenny wrote is 'Unify with king's man.'" She looked up and met his gaze beyond the lamplight. "Do you think he knew you were working under-cover?"

"I don't know. He was smart enough to realize that Easton wouldn't just let his granddaughter go for a ransom." In his head, he tried to play back any clues he might have dropped that would have given his identity away to Lenny. "Easton appointed me as acting ambassador to America because he'd been receiving anonymous threats about naming a successor to the throne. He wanted somebody in place with a little bit of power, but..." He had known all along why Easton had picked him for this job. "He wanted somebody believable in place who could be persuaded to join any treasonous plans."

Instead of agreeing to the idea that his infamous reputation preceded him, she did a typical Ellie thing—the unexpected. "That shows how much Easton trusts you."

He ignored the kind words that battered at his long-held understanding of himself and his talents. "To my knowledge he told no one else. Not even his advisor, General Montcalm, the captain of the Royal Guard."

"Okay." She reasoned things out along with him. "So Lenny was basically spying for the KDF. Do you think he found out who hired Rademacher to kidnap me—I mean, Princess Lucia?"

"Lenny's notebook clears the KDF. That leaves me with one other suspect."

"Who?"

"Markus Carradigne."

Ellie snapped her fingers and jumped off the bed. "That's it!"

"What?"

"I was trying to remember a conversation I'd overheard. Lucia had brought the red dress to the Carradignes' penthouse to show us before she donated it to charity. That was before she and her sisters decided to help with my Cinderella fantasy." Cade followed her movements as she paced. "Winston and Quincy Vanderling, their butler, were arguing about something in the hall. I stopped because I didn't want to interrupt. I guess word got out that she was rejecting the gift, because I heard Winston specifically say that Lucia was to keep that dress, compliments of Prince Markus. She was to wear it and have a wonderful time at the ball."

Cade stood. Adrenaline coursed through his veins. "He set up Princess Lucia."

Ellie faced him. "You were told to kidnap the woman in the red dress."

"Lucia gave you that dress."

"Prince Markus had Lucia kidnapped."

"Prince Markus." Cade loved it when he was right.

"But how do we prove it?" she asked. "Hearsay won't stand up in court."

We? Ellie paced again. Cade was learning how her personality worked. The way she showed she cared was by helping others. Her parents. Easton. Lenny. Even himself. He decided it was time someone did something for her.

And he knew exactly what it should be for his Cinderella.

He picked up the old transistor radio Ellie had found. It

played mostly static, but it worked. "I'll get a confession from Rademacher."

"You shot him."

"I hit him in the shoulder. I hurt him enough to make him bleed, not to kill him."

"You can't go back. He has Tony Costa with him. And Jerome. Any one of them could kill you."

He didn't downplay her legitimate concern. But he was pretty good with a gun himself. And he had something more than money motivating him to complete this mission in one piece. "I can't do anything about it tonight, anyway. Rademacher has had to regroup to tend his wound. And the rain with no moon makes it virtually impossible to track us—or them."

"But in the morning?"

The pallor on her cheeks tugged at his heartstrings. She definitely needed to stop worrying about other people's problems for a change. "We'll worry about the morning when it comes."

He took the notebook from her hand and set it on the table. He turned on the radio and scrolled through several different versions of static until he found one station playing American country music. It was a little twangy for his tastes, but the song was perfect. The woman singing even mentioned the word that had popped into his head a moment ago.

"What are you doing?" she asked.

Cade took a deep breath. He didn't have to gear up for this task. He wanted to do it. More than anything, he wanted to do this for Ellie.

He turned around and treated himself to her wide-eyed look of wonder. Remembering one of the few things his mother had taught him, Cade clicked his heels together and bowed at the waist.

When he straightened, he extended his left hand. "May I have this dance?"

The expression on her face transformed from shock to hope to frowning doubt as her shyness kicked in. "Are you sure?" She tried to use the radio as an excuse. "That's not really a waltz."

"You can't be too picky about your fantasy. It's either that or me singing. You haven't heard me sing, have you?"

She laughed. A rich, warm chuckle that filled his soul with joy.

Yeah. She was smiling now. Everything felt perfect.

Then her voice softened to a whisper that wound its way right into his heart. "I'd love to dance with you."

The blanket fell away as she placed her right hand within his and reached up to wrap her left hand around his neck. He shivered at the electric contact, though she was the one who might be cold. When he folded his hand around her waist, he thought he might drown in those big blue eyes.

He stepped into the fantasy with her as he spun her around the small room. He might be wearing camo pants, instead of tails, she might be wearing towels, instead of jewels and a gown, but all he saw was Ellie. Smiling. If he never did another good deed in his life, he knew he could die a happy man because he'd made Ellie Standish smile.

The towel at her shoulders got lost in a turn. But it gave him the chance to move a step closer. He splayed his fingers across the warm silk of her back and pulled her in so that their hips were touching. Each brush of her curves against his harder frame, each accidental touch as they continued to move in sync, stirred notions in his veins of a different kind of dance.

The music on the radio changed and Cade altered the dance. He pulled the hand he clasped into his chest and held it over his heart. Ellie must have heard the same sensual tune. She slid the hand behind his neck up into his hair and pulled herself closer. Together they slowed their waltz to a simple back and forth sway in time with the music.

And then the music didn't matter anymore. Cade lifted her right hand to the back of his neck and encouraged her to hold on to him that way. To his mind and body's delight, she took the suggestion and ran with it, sending all ten fingers dancing into the hair at his nape.

It gave him the freedom to wrap both hands around her waist and pull her hips into the hardness below his belly. He squeezed his eyes shut and rested his forehead against hers, too overcome for the moment to continue the dance. He slid his hands down to her bottom and squeezed. He dragged them up to the strip of silk and elastic that criss-crossed her back, then repeated the process, plucking fine little tremors from her skin as if she were a priceless instrument.

He stopped moving entirely and opened his eyes. He gazed down into hers and silently asked for permission to take this dance to its ultimate conclusion.

In answer, she reached behind her back and unhooked her bra. His whole body contracted on one low, keening moan as the peach-tipped globes spilled out against his chest.

"You're beautiful, Ellie," he said in a raspy voice, his straining body nearly reaching the climax of this seductive waltz. "So beautiful."

He angled his mouth to her lips and kissed her, played her. And then Ellie herself changed the pattern of the dance. She wrapped her arms around his neck and lifted herself into his kiss, rubbing those pebbled peaks into his chest.

And then there was nothing to do but to see this feverish new étude through to the end. Cade scraped his beard along her cheek, then kissed and tongued his way along the sensitized skin down the column of her neck until he could feast on the purring hum in her throat.

Ellie's hands explored him at will, touching, testing, pressing, grasping. His shoulders, his back, his arms, his chest, his buttocks. Every needy, healing touch triggered a new sensation until his blood was pounding an erratic drumbeat in his ears.

Ellie arched like a bowstring in his hands and he moved the dance lower. He palmed one breast. Squeezed it. Lifted it with his hand. He touched the tip with his tongue and then blew across it.

"Cade!" Her fingers dug into his shoulders, seeking purchase as she rocked with a part of the dance she had never experienced before. He tormented the other breast with the same lusty attention, delighting in how quickly she learned the steps of mutual pleasure.

Her skin flushed. Her chest rose and fell in an erratic rhythm. She ground her hips into his. She was ready. He was past ready. It was time.

Strengthened by the power of her trust, humbled by the gift of her surrender, Cade swept her off her feet and carried her to the bed. He stripped what was left of their clothes and lay down beside her, pulling her back into his arms and resuming the dance of hands and tongues and lips and hearts.

He slipped his fingers into her sweet, feminine folds and found her primed and tight and ready. When he rose above her and guided the tip of his shaft along the same path, he felt her arms stiffen slightly, holding him at a distance. He propped himself up on his elbows and tried to give her the pace she asked for.

Her lips were red and swollen with his kisses, her eyes

the deepest blue he'd ever seen them. Her fingertips danced across his chest and doubt danced in her eyes.

He stroked her hair. It had fallen loose from its braid long ago, thanks to his busy hands. Now he carried tendrils of it across her shoulders, offering her as much modesty as a woman with an aroused man lying on top of her could be afforded.

"Am I too heavy for you?"

She shook her head. She'd gone quiet on him again. But he wouldn't do another thing if he wasn't sure this was right for her, too.

"I know I'm your first. If this scares you, if you want to change your mind…" It would kill him to leave her now. But the rain had left the air nice and cold outside. He could survive. If that was what she wanted, he could survive. He would always do the right thing by Ellie. "If you want to wait for someone else—"

"No." Her firm denial vibrated through her body. Those blue eyes flashed with anger. She framed his face in her hands and made sure he was looking her straight in the eye. "The reason you're my first is because you're the first man I ever wanted to be with. You're the *only* man I've ever trusted enough to be myself with."

Her accepting him in such an intimate way was helping him to heal. In Ellie's fierce, tender care, he could move beyond the hurts of the past. He could learn to trust again.

But she still hadn't relaxed, still hadn't told him what was wrong. They were safe for the night. If she wanted this and he wanted this, then what was the problem?

"Ellie, honey, talk to me."

When she pushed at her glasses in that nervous gesture, he pulled them off and set them on the nightstand. They were close enough for her to see every nuance of his ex

ression, and there was nothing she needed to hide from
im.

"I don't know what to do."

"Oh, honey." His relief was a tangible thing, shaking
hrough his body, stirring himself against her. "You are
oing everything right."

"But—"

"No." He kissed her mouth. "Listen to me." He kissed
er breasts. Her fingers dug into his shoulders as she tried
o hide her reaction to his touch. "The best thing about
naking love with you is that…it's with you."

He kissed her full on the mouth and entered her in one
ure stroke. He felt her barrier, broke past it, swallowed her
asp of pain. "I'm sorry," he said, holding himself still,
iving her time to get used to the size and sensation of
eing joined like this.

"I'm not."

Then she smiled. And Cade knew everything was going
o be all right. She wrapped her arms around him, wrapped
er legs around him, too. Together, they resumed the in-
vitable dance.

When she cried out his name and convulsed around him,
'ade emptied himself into her and let the love he felt for
er fill his empty heart.

Sometime later, with Ellie nestled against his chest in a
ound, secure sleep, and the steady patter of the ever-
resent spring rain to keep him company, Cade thought
bout all the reasons he and Ellie could never be together.
. good woman like her could do better than an outcast like
im. *Should* do better. She might accept him despite his
eputation, despite having nothing to offer her beyond a
illied name and days and nights of worrying whether he'd
ome home to her in one piece—or not at all. She accepted
im.

But the rest of the world wouldn't accept *them*.

He wouldn't put her through the kind of scorn and abandonment he'd endured. She'd given him the precious gifts of her body and her faith in him. He wouldn't reward her by destroying that gentle soul of hers the way his had been destroyed.

But for now, tonight, he fell asleep dreaming that she was his.

Chapter Twelve

Ellie never thought she'd be looking at the cabin where she'd been held hostage for three days. But here she was, lying on her belly in her stiff, muddy clothes behind an arch of exposed tree roots, keeping watch over the ramshackle structure, the ancient outdoor bathtub and the empty fire pit.

Connecticut, Cade had finally told her as they hiked around the body of water called Tyler Lake. She'd been kidnapped in Manhattan and transported to the rolling hills and tree-studded slopes of northwest Connecticut. Beautiful, she thought.

She never wanted to see this place again.

Ellie had insisted that time was critical, and when Cade would have taken her back to Manhattan first, she'd assured him that completing his mission was more important. And this time he wouldn't be working alone. She could help. Torn between duty to her or his country, Cade had been reluctantly swayed by her arguments.

Her assignment now was simple. Watch the house while Cade snuck his way inside and scouted around. If anyone showed up while he was in there, she was supposed to scream.

But what if the danger was already inside with him?

The SUV with the front tires that Cade had shot out yesterday was still parked in the gravel driveway. Had Tony Costa driven Winston Rademacher to a hospital before returning to his cabin and trying to gun them down? Or was Rademacher inside? He'd had a gun, too. Was Costa tracking them? And where was Jerome?

Ellie sank to the ground with a silent groan and offered a silent prayer for the umpteenth time that morning. *Keep Cade safe.*

She'd waited twenty-six years to fall in love with a man. Yesterday morning she'd worried that she'd given her heart to a traitor. This morning she knew her heart belonged to a hero.

Did he know that? Did he understand that she had waited to give herself to the man she loved? Or was she supposed to say the words? And did Cade even want to hear them?

She knew he'd been around women before. Maybe all he wanted was a fling. Could she be sophisticated enough to give him her heart and her body and then let him walk away when he needed to? Maybe he wouldn't even notice her, once she got lost in a crowd of beautiful, accomplished women.

She didn't understand men. She didn't understand love. The only thing she understood right now was how frightened she was. Not for herself. Not anymore. For Cade. He'd been hurt so much already in his life—losing a father he'd truly loved to suicide. Facing off against self-serving snobs like Winston Rademacher who enjoyed throwing the St. Johns' tragic history in Cade's face—even using it as a means of extortion.

Despite all that, Cade still protected her. He was true to

his word and loyal to his king. He made her body ache
with sweet passion and filled her heart with pride and love.

"Come on, Cade," she whispered urgently. She steadied
her glasses on the bridge of her nose and surveyed the area
around the cabin again. Where was he? Shouldn't she be
hearing voices? Or, heaven forbid, gunshots?

They'd come back to capture their enemy and learn the
truth.

So where was the enemy?

As if she had the power to summon, the back door
banged open. Jerome's filthy-mouthed curses filled the air
as he limped out ahead of Cade. "I tell you, I don't know
where he is."

He didn't need his walking stick to support his sprained
ankle because Cade had him by the scruff of the neck, half-
dragging, half-carrying him over to the fire pit.

Cade pushed him down on the nearby stump. "You do
know why Sonny's on the team, don't you?"

"Backup," Jerome replied with a taunting sneer, as if
he thought he had some kind of advantage. "In case somebody like you screws up."

It wasn't her finest moment, but Ellie had to press a hand
to her mouth to stifle her giggle as Cade grabbed Jerome
by his shirtfront and shoved him up against the cabin wall.
She felt justified in seeing the bully roughed up a bit.

"Have you seen your partner Lenny lately?"

Cade had snagged Jerome by the throat. "Not since last
night."

"I sent him out to keep an eye on Sonny," Cade said.
"Sonny found him first. Lenny's dead." That sober reminder of what she'd seen knocked the laughter out of Ellie
and the fight out of Jerome. "Sonny's here to clean up

Rademacher's mess. With Lenny gone, that means you and me.''

Jerome paused to consider the threat. He even scanned the woods surrounding the cabin. When his darting gaze came her way, she hunkered down so she wouldn't be spotted.

Cade shook him by the throat again. ''Now I will tie you up and leave you out here for target practice if you don't tell me where Rademacher is.''

Jerome nodded, caving beneath the threat of an unseen hit man gunning for him. ''They took Sonny's truck into Goshen. He said he was going to find a guy to patch him up and get some clean clothes.''

Cade was the one glancing over his shoulder now. ''I just saw Sonny's truck at his cabin. Nobody was home.''

She saw the panic flush Jerome's face. Felt it inside herself, catching her breath and speeding up her heart. That meant Winston and Sonny were around here somewhere. Hiding. Watching.

Cade knew it, too. ''Ellie?''

She hadn't expected him to call to her. He'd made her promise to stay hidden. Should she go to him? Or stay put?

The hair on her neck beneath her braid prickled, as if some unseen watcher's gaze had just lit on that spot. She rubbed her nape and turned around, silently cursing her vivid imagination. No one. Just miles of oaks and pines and maples.

Breathing deeply to force her pulse rate to a more moderate level, Ellie turned back around to resume her watch.

And looked right into the barrel of Winston Rademacher's gun.

The scream that erupted from her lungs died in her throat as he brushed the gun against her temple.

"I need your help, Miss Standish." He urged her out of her hiding place with the clear directions of his gun. "If you'll be so kind as to come with me."

He still wore the same brown suit from yesterday, but had rigged up a sling from the sleeve of his once-crisp white shirt. Bloodstains and wounded shoulders didn't matter. He still had the gun. And he had the cold, heartless eyes of a man who wasn't averse to using it.

Ellie obeyed his command and headed for the cabin. The sleeves of the shirt she wore had stretched to comical lengths. Earlier she had rolled them up. Now she pushed them up past her elbows, out of the way.

Rademacher poked the gun into her ribs. "Keep your hands where I can see them."

She lifted both hands into the air, walking ahead of him in the universal posture of surrender. Cade released Jerome, who collapsed on his weak ankle, but for once didn't whine about his pain. Instead, he started crawling, amazingly fast for a short, stocky man who smoked too much. He was more afraid of Sonny showing up than of Winston's actual presence.

Cade, on the other hand, turned and braced for a fight, showing no fear. His indigo gaze swept over her, fiery and full of promise. When it landed on Rademacher, Ellie looked away, unable to stand the cruel intensity of those eyes.

Rademacher didn't seem to understand the deadly intent of Cade's expression. He laughed as Jerome disappeared around the front of the cabin. His laughter was a cold, mirthless sound that matched his eyes. When he looked at Cade, the laughter stopped. "Drop your weapon."

Cade refused. "Let her go."

A trigger was cocked beside her ear. Ellie jumped at the

sound, but remained deceptively calm. "Your weapon, or her life," Rademacher said.

"No!" Ellie begged. That would leave Cade completely unprotected. "Sonny's here somewhere."

"Shut up." She clamped her mouth shut at the impatient order.

But she couldn't stifle the protest in her throat as Cade bent his knees and set his gun on the ground. With the toe of his black boot, he kicked it into the mud puddle at Rademacher's feet.

Winston's mouth thinned into a grim line as dirty water splashed onto his polished leather loafers. He picked up each foot and flicked the mess off each toe. By the time he stood squarely on both feet again, Ellie had an idea.

"I had planned to use Mr. Smython as a scapegoat," Winston was saying, "but you've foiled that plan, as well, for me, haven't you. But I'm sure you'll do nicely in that role, Sinjun. After all, your family's used to scandal. Mr. Costa will find Smython.

"I want you to call King Easton and confess to the kidnapping plot. Your involvement has been well documented. I'm sure you can convince him that your loyalties changed when presented with a large sum of money. Like father, like son, you might say." He nudged Ellie with the gun. "If you're not convincing, I'll kill her."

"Don't listen to him." Ellie begged Cade to be a patriot, not a traitor. Not even for her. "Easton believes in you. So do I."

"That's so touching I might spit up." Winston sighed impatiently and inclined his head toward the SUV. "Now, Sinjun, there's a phone on the front seat. Go call Easton. Make your confession convincing or I'll put a bullet through her head."

"You hurt her and you're a dead man." The power be-hind Cade's vow chilled her to the bone.

Winston didn't flinch. "As are you. The only way Costa will release the hit on you is if I give him the word. I made the same arrangement for Miss Standish's contract. If I'm dead, there will be no one who can save her."

Cade looked at her then. Really looked at her. That intense indigo gaze softened with something like tenderness. It was an apology.

"No."

But he ignored her protest and opened the door to the SUV. He pulled out the phone and punched in a number, all the while keeping Ellie in his protective sight.

That was it! If he could communicate with her with just his eyes, she could do the same. She shifted her eyes to the left, toward Rademacher, twice. Three times.

He turned the phone toward his mouth as someone had picked up. "Cadence St. John here. I need to speak with King Easton."

Winston's focus shifted slightly as he listened for the appropriate confession in Cade's words. Ellie stepped on one of her shoestrings and pulled it loose.

"Do you mind if I bend down and tie my shoe?" she asked. Winston's eyes narrowed to tiny squints, as if her interruption irritated him. "You wouldn't want me to trip, would you?"

He considered her request for a moment. Maybe he thought he'd found some kind of soul mate who couldn't tolerate having anything out of place. "Do it."

Ellie knelt and tightened the laces on her right shoe. But that wasn't her real goal. Blood, cobwebs, grass stains, mud—bring it on. After the past three days, a little grime meant nothing to her.

But it made a world of difference to Winston Rademacher.

Faster than he could eke out the question, Ellie had scooped up a handful of mud and water.

"What are you do—?"

She tossed the slimy mess right in his face and dove for the ground. Cade lunged forward, leaping like a jaguar upon its prey. Winston's gun fired. Ellie screamed.

The struggle was brutal and brief. Apparently Cade's knife was quicker than Winston's gun.

"Cade!"

Cade snatched up Ellie in his arms and squeezed her tightly. "You damn fool," he reprimanded her, thanked her, praised her, loved her. He rolled into the mud, carrying her with him, running his hands along every inch of her he could reach, checking for any sign of injury. "He would have shot you. You took a foolish chance."

She folded her arms around his neck and kissed him into silence. "I knew you'd save me."

The gurgling sound of a dying man intruded. "Touching."

Instinctively Cade shoved Ellie behind him and crawled over to Winston's supine body. Cade knew his knife had hit home, severing a vital artery in the man's thoracic cavity. Too damn stubborn to be dead already, the bastard would die of blood loss in a matter of seconds.

Cade watched the blood trickling from the corner of Winston's mouth. The stain it made on his collar must be driving him nuts. Good. Cade leaned in closer. "Prince Markus hired you to kidnap the princess, didn't he."

Winston's squinty eyes fluttered closed.

Cade pushed. "Prince Markus is behind this, isn't he? You're going to die, dammit. Tell me the truth."

Winston's eyes popped open one last time. His bloody lips curled into a gruesome smile. "Go to hell."

"I'll see you there."

Winston Rademacher's eyes closed for the last time.

Cade felt Ellie's face buried in the center of his back, hiding herself from the grim conversation he'd just shared.

"Is he dead?" she whispered.

Cade nodded. So were his chances of proving that Markus Carradigne was guilty.

He turned and gathered Ellie into his arms, pressing a chaste kiss to her forehead. There was one part of the mission he hadn't failed yet. "Costa's out there somewhere. Let's get you home."

He rose to his feet and reached for Ellie's hand.

A bullet slammed into his left shoulder and knocked him to the ground.

"Cade!"

He heard Ellie scream and knew he'd been hit. His shoulder was on fire. He saw her crawling toward him. "No! Get back!" He desperately searched to get his bearings, to find his gun. To find any kind of weapon. "It's Costa."

His legs tangled with Rademacher's as he rolled over to find cover. Rademacher had a gun. Cade folded his body to change direction without sitting up and exposing himself to more gunfire. "Stay down, Ellie," he warned her, hoping she had sense enough to stayed covered behind the SUV.

He spotted Rademacher's gun beside the front tire. He reached for it. A black boot stepped on his hand and crushed his knuckles into the gravel.

Cade swore in frustration, ignoring the pain. He couldn't help Ellie. He had to save Ellie.

He looked up into the tanned face framed by snowy-white hair.

Tony Costa smiled. "I hate the ones that get away," he said, slurring his words.

With his sniper's rifle hung over his shoulder, Costa pulled the pistol from his belt and pointed it at Cade's heart.

Two loud reports of a gun fired at close range rang in his ears. Cade lurched at each explosion, but to his astonishment, he hadn't been hit.

Two bright-red circles expanded on the front of Tony Costa's shirt and he crumpled to the ground. Dead.

Cade looked up and saw the shooter.

Pride in this woman's unwavering determination warred with the sorrow crying in his heart. Ellie still stood, feet braced wide, both hands on his gun, ready to fire again. Tears streamed down her cheeks.

"Ellie?"

"Costa should have helped me when he had the chance."

Cade went to her. He pried the gun from her unresisting fingers and curled his good arm around her shoulders. He didn't know what else to do but hold her as she buried her nose against his chest and cried. He offered his strength to her shaking figure and prayed that God would forgive him for ever getting her involved in this. Forgive him for forcing his job on her. Forgive him for loving her when he had no right to.

Cade heard the footsteps. He sheltered Ellie with his body and raised his gun to protect her with his life.

Then he recognized the brown-haired man with the military haircut and piercing hazel eyes. Devon Montcalm. Captain of the Royal Guard.

Four men who wore the same black suits and armament secured the area. Devon holstered his sidearm and walked over to them. "I see we missed most of the action."

A fifth man rounded the corner of the cabin with Jerome, who was handcuffed and uncharacteristically quiet. Uncharacteristic, but not unexpected, given the size of the rifle trained on him.

It was over.

Cade knew he'd failed his mission. He couldn't prove that Prince Markus had put Rademacher up to planning the kidnapping. He knew it in his gut, but he couldn't prove it. He'd failed.

But he'd kept Ellie alive.

For that one thing, he should be grateful.

Still, as Devon's men swarmed around them, checking dead bodies, tending his wound, treating Ellie for shock, Cade knew a sense of loss, every bit as profound as the night he'd walked into his father's study and found him dead.

He was going to lose Ellie.

In the outside world he had no place in her life. And she had no need to be a part of his. Not when this was his world.

He had to do the right thing here. He'd sworn to always do right by Ellie.

Several minutes later Cade was sitting in the back seat of Devon's SUV, holding Ellie in his arms. Holding her for the last time.

Devon climbed behind the wheel and started the engine. He looked at Cade in the rearview mirror. "Anything we need to know?" he asked.

"I need to talk to King Easton." He squeezed Ellie tightly, almost unable to speak when she snuggled against his chest. *Do the right thing.* "But I need to get Ellie home first."

KING EASTON watched Nick Standish swallow his little sister up in a bear-size hug. "Thank God you're home. Thank God you're safe."

Nick's children, Josie and Jakob, hugged their aunt. Amelia—Nick's wife and Easton's granddaughter—hugged her. Then the rest of the family—his eldest granddaughter, CeCe, and her husband, Shane; the newlyweds, Lucia and Harrison; and even Lady Charlotte Carradigne—swarmed around his personal secretary, hugging and talking and crying and hugging some more.

Easton's gaze drifted past the welcoming crowd to the man standing alone in the archway leading from his office. Cade St. John has always looked a bit rough around the edges. But this evening he needed a shave. His shirt was torn, his face was scratched, his left shoulder was packed in gauze and adhesive tape.

There was a heavy weight on the young man's broad shoulders tonight, Easton thought. And a heavier sadness dulled his dark-blue eyes. His eyes had always reminded him of Bretford St. John, laughing, full of life. Cade was a bit of a rogue like his father. His heart was just as big, his emotions ran just as deep. He'd borne the brunt of his father's shame, the grief of his father's loss for too long. He'd like to see Cade happy for a change. Maybe he needed to quit volunteering for hazardous-duty missions. He needed to quit risking death and start living his life.

Cade's eyes sparked with a sudden, intense light. A wise old observer of people, Easton followed the young man's hungry gaze and lit upon Ellie. Nick had tucked her beneath his arm in a gesture of love and protection. But while the circle of conversation buzzed around her, her gaze was on Cade. From the midst of her family and friends, she sought out the one person who stood all alone.

Easton grinned. He might lose his ever-efficient secretary, after all.

Easton frowned. Commander St. John turned and walked out of the Carradigne home—alone—while Ellie watched him leave with glistening eyes.

Had he demanded too much from his loyal commander and faithful secretary?

He'd listened to Cade's debriefing and accepted the young man's claim that Prince Markus was behind the kidnapping plot. Unfortunately the proof had died under Cade's knife when Winston Rademacher had refused to implicate his protégé.

They couldn't file criminal charges against anyone but Jerome Smython. But Cade's word was good enough for Easton to pen a formal announcement.

He would never name Markus as his heir.

And somehow he vowed to find a way to bring that boy to justice and finally make him accountable for his actions.

With that unpleasant business decided, Easton decided to assert his prerogative as king and take care of something more personal. "If you'll forgive me, I'd like to borrow Ellie for a few minutes."

"Your Highness," Nick protested, "she's just come home."

Easton waved aside his concern. "Don't worry, I'm not putting her to work so soon. This is something personal."

He held out his hand and waited for Ellie to link her arm through his. Though she shied away from the personal contact with her employer, Easton would have none of it. He patted her hand and held it in place. "Walk with me out on the terrace."

On the terrace overlooking Central Park, Ellie breathed in the surprisingly fresh air and turned to face him. Concern creased her forehead. "Are you all right?" She inspected Easton closely. "You look tired. I could fix you some tea."

"Tea…" He'd started to say that tea would be lovely, but he caught himself before giving in to his own selfish wants. Tonight, he owed *her*. "Tea is unnecessary. If I look tired, it's because I've been so worried about you."

"I'm sorry." She reached up and stroked his cheek. It was a welcome, intimate gesture she wouldn't have had the courage to try four days ago. Bully for Cade St. John, Easton thought.

He'd had an idea last week, but hadn't really fleshed it out. So he made up a plan as he went along. He was this young lady's ruler, after all. She had to listen to him.

"As you know, I planned to meet with some of my other grandchildren here in America. My second son's children, specifically. I was about to depart for Wyoming before you were kidnapped. Now we can make the trip together." He leaned against the railing and looked at the lights of the park, trying to sound as uncalculating as possible for a conniving old control freak like him. "Of course, that means packing up the entourage and traveling again. I think it's about time I get to know James's boys."

"We're leaving New York?" There was something like outright panic behind that soft-spoken question. Ellie had planned to go with King Easton on his trip, but that was before the events of the past few days…before Cade.

"Yes. Day after tomorrow, I think."

His second son, James, had been a delightful child, but Easton had never quite understood his wandering ways as he'd gotten older. He'd married three times. All for love. Certainly for the adventure. He'd moved to the American West and become something called a wildcatter. Though there was no big game involved in the profession, he'd heard there was oil and money and the thrill of instant success or sudden failure.

James was the least royal of all his children, but he had always seemed the happiest. He fathered four children, two by each of his last two wives. "Tate and Tucker are the older pair of James's sons," he explained now, taking note of Ellie's nervous pacing. "Dillon and Wyatt are the younger ones. Maybe they've adopted some of that brash American spirit and can infuse the monarchy with some of that modern energy."

Ellie stopped pacing when she realized he'd stopped talking. She tried to appear interested in his news. "I hear Wyoming is a wide-open state. The mountains and plains there sound like my home in western Korosol."

Easton shook his head at the wistful longing in her voice. Love was wasted on the young. If wise old men didn't step in from time to time, there'd be no more wise old men. And Ellie was naive enough that he couldn't rely on subtleties.

He clasped her by the shoulders and looked down into her dirt-streaked face. "Ellie, I love you like one of my own granddaughters. I'm sorry for what you mistakenly had to endure. But I'm grateful to you. Your country is grateful."

"I'd do it again for you, sir."

"I won't ask you to. If you like, I'll send you home to your family in Korosol. It hasn't been easy, but I can manage without you for a while." When that offer didn't earn a smile, he knew what he had to do. "Of course, if there's something else you'd rather do…at the embassy, perhaps?"

At last some life sparked in her pretty blue eyes. "Could I go there now? After I clean up? Tonight?"

He nodded. "I'll have the car brought around for you."

''Thank you.'' What the devil? She stretched up on tip-toe and kissed his cheek. ''Thank you.''

After she danced out the door, Easton pulled that special cell phone from his pocket and placed a call.

A king's work was never done.

ELLIE RODE IMPATIENTLY up the elevator at the Korosolan Embassy to the top floor, where the acting ambassador's apartments were located.

A shower and shampoo made her feel presentable again, but then she'd dressed so quickly in her hurry to get over here that she hadn't taken the time to put in a new pair of contacts or think about what she should wear.

Cade had seen her in a gown that didn't fit, men's clothes that didn't fit and two small towels that didn't fit anybody. She wasn't sure what one wore to a seduction, anyway. The plain cotton nightgown beneath her trench coat would just have to do.

When the elevator announced her arrival at the eighth floor, the old shy Ellie knew a moment of doubt. She was nervous. What if she messed this up? She was excited. She'd always longed for adventure, and this was the most impulsive thing she had ever done. She was afraid. What if Cade didn't want her? What if she'd misread that longing in his eyes that touched the same longing in her?

The door started to close again, startling Ellie from her thoughts. She punched the door open button, her decision made.

She wanted this night with Cade.

In the real world. Just the two of them. Without watching their backs or worrying about king and country.

She wanted to kiss Cade senseless.

And she wanted to tell him she loved him.

Then it would be up to Cade how her adventure played out.

He answered the door on her first knock.

He stood there, staring at her as if she was some kind of apparition. He, too, had showered. His black hair glistened like polished coal. He was barefoot, shirtless, bandaged and clean-shaven, revealing the boyish dimples that softened the harsh cynicism lining his face.

He wore a loose-fitting pair of jeans. Unsnapped at the waist.

Ellie's gaze slid to that spot, and a remembered heat pulsed in her veins and raised the temperature in her breasts and belly.

She should profess her love. She should say something. But all she could do was stare. And remember. And wish.

"Ellie."

He said her name in that helpless way that reminded her why she loved him in the first place.

Then he gathered her in his arms and kissed her. She combed her fingers into his still-damp hair and held on as he picked her up and carried her—into his office. Not the romantic boudoir she had imagined. An office. Big walnut desk. Bookshelves.

He set her down.

She clutched her coat around her waist and tried not to show her disappointment when he circled the room and put the width of his desk between them. It was as if he needed some kind of shield to protect himself from her. As if physically distancing himself would allow him emotional distance, as well. He raked his fingers through his hair, standing it up in a spiky disarray that she longed to fix for him.

"Um…" He swallowed hard. She watched his Adam's apple bob up and down his throat and wondered what it would be like to kiss him there. "What are you doing here? Can I get you something?"

He was nervous.

Cadence St. John, Duke of Raleigh, decorated war hero and all-round tough guy, was nervous.

Good. She didn't want to be the only one in the room who wasn't sure what to do.

She declined his offer of refreshments. "I came to see you." *I want to seduce you, see if making love—if loving you—is just as good out here in the real world as it was in the backwoods of Connecticut.* "I just want to talk."

"Talk?"

"I want to thank you for saving my life. And for being there when I needed you. I don't usually rely on anyone else." She had to smile at the irony of it. "I'm usually the one other people rely on."

The tension in the room eased a notch. "I want to thank you, too," he said. That velvet fog in his voice seeped into her brain and intensified his words. "You saved my life. And I don't mean shooting Tony Costa. In here." He pressed a fist over his heart. "You saved me in here. I'll always be grateful to you for that."

Grateful?

A frisson of anger sparked along the nerve relays he had lulled with his soothing voice.

Did he not believe that he deserved to feel something more than gratitude? Had the Winston Rademachers of the world convinced this brave, handsome, caring man that he was nothing more than muscle for hire? A gun? A rank? A name?

"Damn you, Cadence St. John."

"Ellie!"

She'd just cursed. For the first time since her father had

cared the urge out of her as an adolescent, Eleanor Standish cursed.

She was mad. She was more than mad. She was enraged that the world had hurt this man so much that he didn't believe he deserved to be loved.

She untied her coat and let it fall to the floor.

"Ellie!"

She had no idea what kind of picture she made in that translucent cotton gown with the soft glow of lamplight picking up the golden highlights in her hair and the peachy perfection of her skin. But it must have been a good picture.

Cade's eyes locked on her breasts and lit with hunger.

It was all the encouragement Ellie needed. She walked around the desk, looped her arms around Cade's neck—and kissed him senseless.

Several minutes later, with her glasses on a bookshelf, her nightgown hiked up around her hips, perspiration beading between her damp breasts and Cade's jeans jutting out with proof of his desire for her, Ellie came up for a breath of air.

She was unsteady on her feet, but Cade's big hands straightened her clothes, then settled at the flat of her back, supporting her. His chest expanded on an uneven breath, and his voice was hoarse from deep within his throat. "What was that for?"

She touched the bandage over the mark she had made on his cheek and wished she could take back the pain he had suffered at her expense.

"You need to be kissed daily by someone who loves you, and I want that someone to be me."

She dropped her gaze to the center of his chest and clutched her fingers into fists between them. That profession of love had sounded about as goofy and naive as a country girl whose experience with men was limited to her books and fantasies and one very long, very dangerous weekend.

Maybe she should try a more sophisticated approach. "I kissed you like that because I want you in bed. I want to show you—"

He pressed a finger over her lips and shushed her. He tipped her chin and replaced his finger with a calming, healing, soul-shattering kiss.

"I like the first answer better. That's my Ellie talking."

Dear heaven. It sounded very much as if he'd said something wonderfully possessive. "Your Ellie?"

Now Cade hesitated. He pulled away from her and Ellie leaned her hips against his desk, feeling too unsure to stand on her own. In a series of rapid, machinelike motions, he handed her her glasses and lifted different stacks of paper from his desk to show her.

"Look." He put a legal-looking document in her hands. "There may be a way I can regain at least part of my father's estate. I had our legal department fax over information about forgiving the debts of military personnel."

"That's great."

Just as she reached the second paragraph of the document, he set it aside and placed a certificate in her hand. "It's an investment of my mother's, given to me one time ages ago when she was feeling guilty. I dug it out of an old trunk in the spare bedroom. I can cash it in and use it to buy a tract of land. It's not enough to start building, but I could take out a loan for that."

"Shouldn't you save it?"

Cade took that paper away, too, and replaced it with a small square of pink paper. A phone message. His mouth dimpled with boyish excitement. "Read it."

She read the note out loud. "'Easton's job offer. Take it.'"

She looked up, confused.

"I talked to Easton a couple of hours ago," Cade said. "He's grateful for my military service, but he asked if I'd serve my country in another way."

"You're not going on another mission, are you?"

Not a dangerous one. Not so soon.

The paper fell to the floor as he captured her hands with his. "He just named me official ambassador to the United States."

"That's wonderful, Cade!" Given time, she knew everyone would see his worth the way she and Easton did. "Congratulations."

But he wasn't celebrating. He looked down at their hands, twining their fingers together, testing the fit of her hands in his. "If you give me time, I promise to show you I'm worthy of my title and the responsibility Easton is entrusting me with. I'm thirty-three years old. It's time for me to come in out of the field before I slow down and start making mistakes, anyway." His fingers tightened in an almost painful grasp. "If you're patient with me, Ellie, I'll show you I can be that good man you keep talking about.

"Once I'm on my feet and I've made the St. John name respectable again, I want to ask you to marry me. If you'll wait."

He held his breath and locked her in the depths of those beautiful indigo eyes. Ellie wanted to cry. She wanted to throw something. She wanted to set him straight.

"And I thought I was the one who didn't know how a relationship worked." She pulled his hands to the back of her waist and walked into his embrace. "I don't want to wait."

His welcoming smile vanished. His hands loosened their grip on her. "I understand."

"I don't think you do. I love you. This man." She splayed her fingers over his heart and willed it to beat with steady self-assurance beneath her hand. "The man I made love to in that motel. The man who saved my life time and again. The man who brought me my glasses so I could see and who turned me over to my brother tonight because he thought that's what would make me happy. *You* make me happy.

"That other stuff doesn't matter to me." How could she make him believe her? And then she knew.

She leaned over and swept all the papers and blotters off the top of his desk. "It's after midnight. It's time for your next kiss."

"I love you, Ellie Standish."

"I love you."

He followed her down and made quick, sweet, frantic love to her right there on the desk. The wood at her back was hard. The man above her even harder. Ellie loved his needy grasping hands. She pushed down his jeans. He pulled up her gown.

Later they tested the leather couch. And much later, Cade took her to his bed.

By the time the morning sun came through the bedroom window, Ellie believed he finally understood how she felt.

She was finishing up a phone conversation with her old school chum and best friend, Jillian Grace. "You'll love it, Jilly. King Easton is kind and sweet and needs to be pampered a bit. I worry about his health, but beyond that, working for the Carradignes is a wonderful job. You've always wanted to travel. So coming to America would be perfect for you."

"Recruiting your job replacement?" Cade walked up behind her, fresh and clean and naked from his shower. He wrapped his arms around her waist and nuzzled her neck. Ellie scrunched her shoulders against the tickle of sensation his wicked tongue created on her bare skin. "Remember to invite her to the wedding."

He was doing it to her all over again, and she loved it.

"And Jilly?" She stopped to catch her breath as his fingers found her breast. "Maybe you'll find love, too."

She hung up and turned into Cade's arms, turned herself into his kiss. When he left her lips to nuzzle the vibrations in her throat, he asked her about the phone call. "Are you really willing to leave a king behind and settle for a lowly duke?"

Ellie cupped his face between her hands and held it close enough to see his eyes. "I'm not settling for anybody. To me, you're not a commander or an ambassador or even a duke." She moved her lips closer to his. "You'll always be my Prince Charming."

He sealed the kiss and gave her his heart.

And she would always be his very own princess.

*   *   *   *   *

Will King Easton ever find an heir?
Rejoin his quest in November 2002
with the next installment of
THE CARRADIGNES: AMERICAN ROYALTY
THE INCONVENIENTLY ENGAGED PRINCE
by Mindy Neff
Available from Harlequin American Romance.

HARLEQUIN®
INTRIGUE®

What do a sexy Texas cowboy, a brooding Chicago lawyer and a mysterious Arabian sheikh have in common?

CHICAGO CONFIDENTIAL

By day, these agents pursue lives of city professionals; by night they are specialized government operatives. Men bound by love, loyalty and the law—they've vowed to keep their missions and identities confidential....

You loved the Texas and Montana series. Now head to Chicago where the assignments are top secret, the city nights, dangerous and the passion is just heating up!

NOT ON HIS WATCH
by CASSIE MILES
July 2002

LAYING DOWN THE LAW
by ANN VOSS PETERSON
August 2002

PRINCE UNDER COVER
by ADRIANNE LEE
September 2002

Available at your favorite retail outlet.

HARLEQUIN®
Makes any time special ®